THE DIVIDED MAN

Book Two
by
John Sauer

unwritten.

TABLE OF CONTENTS

ENEMIES AND ALLIES

They found trouble in the rolling prairies of the Sand Hill country of Nebraska, on the narrow two-lane strip of pavement between what had been the towns of Hyannis and Ogallala. The highways they had traveled were desolate and lonely, the land uncluttered and rolling like gentle waves to the horizon, empty save for the occasional ranch house or windmill.

Getting here had been a strange journey that began with a nuclear war and went through the wheel of fire in the sky that some could see and some could not: the Spirit World. Luke Kimball had opened a door between worlds, and the gods had returned—all of them, from Native American to Inca and Aztec to Norse gods of legend ... and more he could not yet conceive of. A god had taken his soul, leaving him a human-machine, able to think and reason, but not feel. Other gods had sent him on a quest to bring seven people together in a place where the balance between men and gods could be restored —or broken forever.

It was not a job he had wanted, but it was also a mission he could not refuse. In a short time, it had taken him from the Boundary Waters of northern Minnesota across the country to Nebraska, with more roads to travel. He had crossed between worlds and learned many lessons from the ancient gods of the plains Indians. Find the sacred pipe. Find the crystal mask. Unite the Seven. And defeat the Manitou, the god that had taken his soul.

They traveled in an RV that had been retrofitted into a mobile command center, or MOC for short, by the security company he had owned with his partner, Matthew Pierce. The MOC was armored and armed, and big enough to hold the people he had dreamed about. A few were with him now. There was Tony, a strange boy with Coke-bottle-green eyes who could make your blood boil—literally. He could also talk to animals. Ellie, a doctor of Native American heritage whose power to heal went beyond science. Cal was a black man and a scholar who seemingly had the patience to balance the world on his shoulders while reading Shakespeare. And there was Samson, a wolf who had befriended Tony and was almost as tall as the boy, in a motor home in the ruins of the apocalypse, to save the world.

Coming through the ruins of Hyannis,

Nebraska, Luke caught the fresh, sharp scents of burnt wood and gasoline. He could see little sign of recent damage to the buildings, but he kept a close watch on the MOC's radar, anticipating contact. The others were quiet, but he could feel their dread. Both Ellie and Cal had experience with the scavs. For Luke, combat was nothing new. He was ready. They did not have to wait long.

A small orange blip on the radar screen triggered an alarm. As Luke pressed a button on the dashboard to turn off the warning tone, radar identified the object as a motorcycle, two miles behind them and closing fast. Luke kept the MOC at a steady speed as the motorcycle closed the range. Three more blips joined it on the radar. Luke scanned military and civilian radio frequencies. He found them on a CB radio channel.

"Yeah, man. It's a fucking motor home. They don't know we're back here yet!"

"Okay. We're all set. Move on 'em. Remember, I get the first crack at the women's cracks!" Raucous laughter.

Ellie raked back the charging handle on her M4 and spit out the word, "Scavs!"

There were now ten blips behind the MOC. Luke dropped the armor shields into place and said, "I don't think we have much to worry about."

Ellie, Tony, and Cal watched in

amazement as video monitors came to life. The screens gave Luke clear views of their front, rear, left, and right.

Cal asked, "You can drive by those?"

"Easily. And more. "

Luke raised the firing control stick from the console. Readouts on the computer screen showed the status of ammunition and bearing on targets. He gripped the stick, and a firing cursor appeared on the rear video monitor. As Luke moved it across the screen, the range to target appeared in the bottom corner. Too far.

"Let them come."

The scavs quickly closed the miles between them. He zoomed in to get a better look at their pursuers. All had weapons they could fire one-handed; Luke saw pistols and sawed-off shotguns. Then the radar picked up a new, larger object ahead of them as they rounded a bend in the highway: a battered pickup truck by the side of the road. As they rumbled by, a hail of bullets spattered against the MOC's side. Ellie and Cal ducked reflexively. Luke watched Ellie carefully. Though pale, she was not overreacting. Good. They watched on the rear screen as the truck pulled onto the highway to join the motorcycles.

Luke slowed their speed until they were surrounded by scavs. Separate alarm tones filled the MOC with urgency. The screens were filled with targets. Bullets spanged off the armor as the scavs tried to stop them.

He grasped the control stick again and said, "Now we fight back."

He put the crosshairs on the scav who was furthest away and touched the trigger. A short burst of the heavy .50 slugs tore the biker in half. Moving quickly, Luke brought down each target with emotionless determination. Cal and Ellie winced as the .50 boomed overhead, raining down death all around them. Return fire rattled off the armor.

Twice, Luke steered hard left and right to crush scavs on bikes beneath the MOC's wheels. The maneuvers brought cheers from Tony. As he destroyed his enemies, Luke's thoughts touched on the lesson of the Spirit World buffalo hunt. Without the MOC, they all might be dead now. Though in the future there might be no place for guns, he needed them now. Everything in its own time and place.

The alarms became strident as a rocket-propelled grenade was launched from the pursuing truck. Luke yanked the wheel hard left, then right, bringing the MOC up on its right-hand wheels momentarily, swerving at the last instant to let the projectile streak past them. Ellie, Cal, and Tony clung to their seats. The projectile bounced off the road ahead of them and exploded. As the MOC lurched back down on all wheels, he set the targeting cursor on the truck's grill and pumped the vehicle full of jacketed bullets the size of his thumb. The truck spun and exploded in a fiery ball. No more threats.

The radar still sounded a tone, and Luke flicked his eye over the forward screen. A large mass of metal sat directly on the road a few miles ahead.

"What is it?" Cal asked.

Luke answered, "It looks like a roadblock of some sort. Cars, maybe. Let's see."

He slowed to a crawl and stopped a few hundred yards from the roadblock, engine idling. He was right: a tractor-trailer and a few cars had been pushed together to form a barrier. "Can we go around?" Ellie asked anxiously.

Luke examined the terrain. The ground rose sharply on either side of the roadblock. The scavs had chosen wisely.

"No, we'll tip or get stuck. They've set a nice trap."

She dug out a map. "Let's back the hell out of here and take another route, then. We can blast the bastards if they follow!"

Luke smiled. "We don't need them following, not where we're going. I think there's another way."

A fusillade of bullets struck the MOC. This time Ellie didn't flinch. Luke set the .50 to automatic, and immediately it fired several short bursts at targets they could not see. He put the vehicle in park and went to the back bunks. He lifted the mattress on a lower bunk and withdrew a four-foot-long gleaming black cylinder with a box on one end. Luke removed the covers from each end. He turned the munition on, and a string of LCD lights glowed green on the side. He asked Ellie to press a button on the panel of the MOC, and a sunroof opened on the ceiling between the two front seats.

Luke moved beneath the sunroof. "This is a variation of a US military Stinger missile. It's very fast and powerful. It is made to stop tanks and should take care of this roadblock."

Sunlight streamed into the MOC. Luke stopped the .50 roof gun. A voice came from somewhere beyond the roadblock.

"Give us the motor home, and we'll let you live. We have you trapped!"

Hoots of laughter echoed across the roadblock. Luke braced a foot on either front chair and brought the Stinger through the opening.

"I don't think so," he said, settling the tube on his shoulder as he brought his eye to the sight. The center of the roadblock was clear in the crosshairs. Luke pressed the trigger, and the Stinger rocketed from the launch tube with a loud whoosh. He kept his eye on the trailer, guiding the missile, and dropped back through the sunroof as it hit.

They felt the explosion even inside the armored vehicle. When the smoke cleared, the trailer and cars were cleared from the road, and

THE DIVIDED MAN BOOK TWO

motorcycles had been thrown to the sides of the road like children's toys. There were no more shots or voices.

"The subtle diplomacy of a clenched fist," mused Cal as Luke put the MOC in drive and trundled through the burning wreckage.

"Not so subtle," Luke replied, "but it works."

Luke and his party were not the only ones to encounter scavs. At the I-80 bridge over the Missouri River in Council Bluffs, Iowa, Brother Jed and his army of holy warriors were attacked by a force much better armed and trained.

The march from Minneapolis had done him well. The weeks following the shooting, of long walking and sparse food, had leaned him down. Jed had rediscovered bathing, and even he noticed the difference in how he smelled. These things made him feel good and lent strength to his divine purpose: destroy the devil, Kimball!

God spoke to him often, sometimes in his head during the day, and always in the evenings when he went aways away from his soldiers to pray.

He had seen God, his green glowing eyes, sometimes as a four-legged beast, sometimes as a man. Always in shadow, and always with the strange, twisted antlers, which, he reasoned, must symbolize the thorns Jesus had suffered on the cross. God was strong and encouraging, giving him visions of his success and glory. Blood. Feasting. Jed in flowing white robes, standing on a mound of his enemies.

Even his voice had regained its godly, compelling strength! If he closed his eyes and concentrated, he could feel the devil to the west, pulling him ever on as a lodestone pulls the compass needle. They had walked, forsaking other transportation because this was a holy quest, and pilgrims always traveled by foot.

For guidance, they had a Rand McNally road map (with 18,116 reasons why they needed that road atlas). It had led them unfailingly across highways littered with rusting cars and trucks and the moldering bones of sinners. They followed the red and blue map lines through towns and villages, where they foraged for unspoiled canned food. In fields, they found corn gone wild, and Jed used it as a sacrament for the mass he held every day at sundown. Though he secretly craved the Body and Blood, he needed every one of his warrior priests for his Holy Mission. But that would not stop him if they found other living souls . . . which they finally did, though the encounter was not what they had wished.

The bridge across the Missouri River had appeared deserted, filled only with a monstrous jumble of cars from the very last traffic jam. The attack came when they were mid-span on the structure. A withering hail of bullets mowed them down. Where Jed's warriors had assorted deer rifles for weaponry, their attackers were equipped like an army.

Jed heard the roar of heavy machine guns, bullets parting the air over his head like angry bees. He found a spot behind a car tire and hugged himself into a ball. Small arms fire chattered all around him, and his men fell, dying. The shooting lasted less than a minute. When it stopped, Jed raised his head just high enough to see that most of his men were dead. While he felt sad that his army had been defeated so early in his quest, he felt no remorse for their deaths. This was a holy quest. They would go to Heaven.

Seeing the blood and wasted meat around him, his mind screamed out for sacrament, and he struggled to make it quiet.

Then he heard the scratching of a PA system, and a voice asked, "Is there anyone left to surrender?"

Raucous laughter echoed across the bluffs. From the laughs, Jed could tell that there were many. A better army for his cause? The speaker sounded strong, but he did not have the Voice of God! He felt God's will strongly and had a vision of himself marching at the head of this new, stronger army.

"*Stand,*" God's voice whispered in his head. "*Take your new army.*"

Jed smiled and stood, empty hands in the air.

"I am unarmed. Warrior priests, lay down your weapons and stand." As they did, Jed counted. He had twelve left.

"We surrender. To whom do we relinquish?"

All around them, men began to emerge from shallow trenches in the ground and other obstructions. Soon almost two hundred surrounded them, each armed with modern weapons. They were a dangerous-looking group, dressed in dirty black leather and many colors of combat fatigues. Every one of them was festooned with weapons. They wore their hair long or short, in mohawks and braids. Many had carved scars or tattoos across their faces. They looked eager to kill.

Some individuals wore radio headsets. Advanced communications. He saw three or four big machine guns mounted on pickup trucks. But even with the disarray of gear, they held themselves like professional soldiers. One of them swaggered forward, rifle held ready as he approached Jed.

Jed was pushed to the concrete from behind. His cheek was cut on the rough surface, but he did not struggle. Instead, he tried the Voice.

"Be gentle with me." He felt his captor pause. "Bind me, but do not hurt me. You will be well rewarded."

He could almost see the Voice weaving a

net around the soldier. Jed smiled as his wrists were gently tied.

"Now help me up. Please."

He was pulled to his feet with no slaps, kicks, or bruises. Jed turned to the warrior and memorized his face. The warrior's eyes had the faint glaze of those under the Voice. This one would soon be his.

"Very good. Now, take me to your commander."

Others surrounded him and his priests as they were marched over the embankment and down beside the bridge. Completely invisible from the road, a small camp had set up, complete with cooking fires, women, and even a few children. Everybody he could see was well-armed. His captors maintained silence as they brought him to the largest tent in the center of the camp.

Armed guards surrounded the broad canvas structure. Even though everybody looked relaxed, Jed felt like he was surrounded by poisonous snakes. They stopped outside the tent, and moments later, their leader appeared. He moved with the same deadly economy that Jed had seen in the devil Kimball.

The man was tall, over six feet, with dark thinning hair pulled into a single braid that fell past his shoulder blades. Patches of gray marked each temple. He wore a black leather jacket with cut-off sleeves, some kind of armored vest over it, dirty black fatigues, and well-worn black combat boots. There were automatic pistols strapped to his belt and a large, curved knife of some strange design.

As the leader glided close, Jed saw a cold, vicious glitter in the man's brown eyes. His face and visible musculature were planed and hard. A gray-streaked beard and mustache made him look even more deadly.

Someone hit him behind the knees and brought Jed kneeling to the ground. The leader towered over him. He radiated power like waves of heat from molten rock. But Jed was not afraid. He would have to be very careful in taming this lion. He felt the hard eyes study him and his men. He did not meet the man's eyes and then realized belatedly that it was a mistake, for the man said, "Shoot them" in a clipped British accent, then turned his back and walked away.

Hands grabbed Jed from behind, new ones that threatened to rip his arms from their sockets.

"Wait!" he yelled, then screamed in pain as they jerked him to his feet.

The man kept moving. So, he fought the pain and used the Voice.

"I can give you what you want!"

The man stopped and turned slowly. His face showed amusement. This one would never succumb to the Voice. He needed another way, then.

"What could you possibly offer that I want?"

His captors stopped, waiting on the command of their leader. Jed locked his eyes on those of the leader, and his heart missed a beat. At that moment, he saw something: a connection, a duality of purpose. What this man needed.

"I offer you two things. First, unlimited road power," he gasped.

The leader shrugged. "Two things? Talk fast or die." He pulled the strangely curved, glittering knife from his belt and began to spin it across his fingers. The blade had a bend halfway along its length and whispered a song of death as it moved.

Jed rambled, "A motor home loaded with some of the most sophisticated weapons ever made! Armor-plated. Unstoppable! An MOC!"

He described the vehicle with a detail he did not know he possessed. As he spoke, the leader began to frown. When Jed gave the driver's name, the leader's eyebrows shot up, and his hand snaked out to grab Jed's chin.

"God help you if you're lying," the leader said and spun him around.

The knife flashed, and his bonds fell away from his hands. Jed turned around to face him.

"I know where you can find him. I can lead you to him. I can give him to you."

The leader sheathed his knife. "Tell me

more. You and your men will remain alive . . . for now."

At the entrance to the tent, the leader turned and said, "Luke Kimball? You will tell me where he is and how we will find him. My name is Pierce."

Jed smiled. In his mind, he could hear God speaking to him again, in his chambers, telling him of the army that would be his, if only he could get Luke Kimball. In his head, he heard the triumphant marching of thousands of booted feet, voices raised to God, to him, as he entered Pierce's tent.

THE ONE-EYED
MAN NEEDS YOU

Almost from birth, Michael Narajian had been a master of every musical instrument he touched, especially the twelve-string guitar. He had taken the instrument and played it in ways that made classical guitarists cry and his fans worldwide rave. His skill had brought him to the pinnacle of rock 'n' roll success with a series of platinum albums. Whenever everything else had gone bad, he always had the guitar for comfort. He played it now, sitting on a bluff overlooking the highway on the outskirts of Holyoke, Colorado, waiting to kick some ass.

Mike was lean, menacing, and wiry with a raven-black mohawk, short bristly hair on the sides, and a vicious scar running across the bridge of his nose to his right ear. Mike had been shot three days ago. The bullet had hit him in the side, just below the ribcage, and punched right through. Blood still seeped through the compression bandage.

Mike felt like shit. He supposed he was dying from infection, but didn't give a rat's ass. He sat on a Harley Softail, strumming the twelve-string and waiting for the scavs to come his way. He had a little surprise waiting for them on the road below. The pain in his side was a fire Mike kept under control by popping pain pills he had pillaged from a Nebraska hospital. He stopped playing long enough to swallow one, washing the pill down with a swallow of warm, stale water.

"Isn't life wonderful?" he asked himself.

The most memorable thing about Mike was his eyes, currently hidden behind a pair of battered sunglasses. His producers had featured them on the covers of his first three albums. Studio graphic artists had captured the electric blue orbs on video and played them into the hearts of young girls across the world. He had been a rock 'n' roll legend with a future made of gold.

But the war had changed that—had changed him. He had been kind, naive, and innocent of the horrors that could befall mankind. He had believed that you could live happy, safe, and free. He and his wife, Susan, had a New York penthouse with expansive views of the city. His career was going like wildfire, he was in love, and his music was good. They were happy and wanted for nothing. Then the war came as they were flying home from LA and the wrap of his *Blue Steel Silk* tour.

The electromagnetic pulse (he found out what it was later) had knocked out the electric power on their private jet. It sank like a rock into the Blue Ridge Mountains. In shock, surrounded by flames, Mike managed to pull Susan and his guitar from the wreckage. They were the only survivors. She had never gotten over the trauma. They didn't even know there had been war until days later.

They spent the night near the wreckage, waiting for rescue. The sudden impact of the crash had bruised them both so severely that they could hardly move. They were lucky it was summer and warm. Mike held Susan through the night as they mourned their friends who had perished in the crash. He stroked her silky blonde hair, streaked with soot and reeking of jet fuel. Susan drifted in and out of consciousness. Once she gripped him tightly and said, "The door is opened. They're all coming back."

At the time, he thought she was delirious. There was a knot on the back of her head, and her pupils were different sizes. Not knowing what to do, Mike held her closer, afraid of what had happened, of what could happen, trying to keep her safe in the night and waiting for daylight. But the day came and went, with no sign of rescue.

Hunger drove them to move shortly after dawn. They wandered in a daze. Mike tried to keep them moving downhill as much as the rough terrain would allow. He used the sun as his compass until ugly black clouds began to shut it out. They stumbled for two days, wondering where they were. As deep despair began to set in, they limped through the tree line into a plowed field. They stopped and gawked at row after row of tall corn. They were in a valley, trees ringing them on all sides.

The rough, ugly sky made the corn shine even more golden, and Mike broke off several ears. They gnawed the raw corn, savoring the sweet, nutty taste, a salve for their ravenous hunger. Where there was corn, there must be people, so they set off looking for the farm. The fields (there were two) were not very large. But the farmhouse was spacious enough for the Franklin family.

The Franklins met Mike and Susan with shotguns and rifles ready: Grandpa and Grandma Franklin, Marcus and Dianna, and the three oldest children. They listened with skepticism to Mike's story until one of the youngest children toddled out of hiding with Mike's first CD in hand. Right there, surrounded by guns, strumming his guitar with trembling fingers, Mike gave the shortest and best concert of his life.

The Franklins turned out to be good people. Their knowledge of the war was scant. They knew that bombs had fallen and that fallout was poisoning the skies. They did not know if the war was over or who had won or if the communists had invaded America (but if the commies did come, the Franklins were ready). They had been busy harvesting corn when Mike found them, getting the crop laid up in the barn to feed them and their small herd of cattle during the "nuclear winter," which turned out to be no worse than any other winter Grandpa Franklin could remember. The Franklins took Mike and Susan in and treated them like family. He helped bring in the rest of the corn and gladly pitched in with the chores of the farm.

In return, Mike taught their children to play the guitar. One night after dinner, when he was giving lessons, Diana Franklin broke into tears.

"You have brought music back into our house," she said.

The next day, Marcus brought a dulcimer out of storage. From then on, the nights were filled with the sweet sound of music. Mike and Susan took over the loft in the barn. During the first winter, his hair grew longer, and he grew a beard. By spring, he looked like a mountain man.

Marcus taught him how to shoot a rifle, shotgun, and pistol. It was a matter of precision, like picking a complicated rhythm, and Mike was a quick student. Much of their protein came from deer and wild hogs. Mike learned to love the quiet and solitude of the hunt. But where he adapted to life in the country at a very rapid pace, Susan had difficulties. As a native New Yorker, country life took her way out of her element. She grieved for the people and things she had lost. The tasks she had to perform were sometimes beyond her comprehension. It led to frustration that drove Susan into a deep depression. At night, she clung to him, afraid to let him go, and her pillow talk was about the way things had been before the war.

The changes in Susan saddened him. Mike noticed that periodically, one of Susan's pupils would become larger than the other. She developed headaches that Grandma Franklin soothed with herbal teas. She was no longer the self-confident, cocky girl he had married. He believed she had suffered some type of brain damage during the crash, and there was nothing he could do about it.

There were no doctors anywhere near the Franklin farm. They only had three neighbor families within twenty miles. From their occasional visits, they learned some of the horror stories about the radiation and plagues spreading across the land. To leave would be certain death. All he could do was love and care for Susan as best he could and hope that one day she would be better.

Instead, Susan slipped further and further from reality. One night, she woke him from a sound sleep.

"Michael. Get up. We have to pack our things now."

She wanted to go out west, to Washington state. There was to be something she called a "Ghost Dance." Mike had heard the term before, but he couldn't remember in what context.

"Why," he asked as he stroked her hair, "do we have to go there?"

Susan whispered, "The one-eyed man needs you."

He did not know what to make of this. "We can't go yet," he whispered to her. "It's too dangerous. We'll go as soon as it's safe. Now sleep, my love, and dream of sheep."

Susan slept on her side and Mike rubbed her back, singing softly until her breathing had fallen into a deep, restful rhythm. Then he rubbed tears from his eyes. Sleep, for Mike, was long in coming.

Her fascination with the West continued to grow. He found out what a Ghost Dance was from one of the children's history books, some kind of ceremony that had been done at Wounded Knee before the cavalry nearly wiped out the Sioux Indians.

Her desperation found its way into his music. The Franklins knew they were having problems, and he even went so far as to discuss taking Susan west. But they all agreed that they were safest here, in the valley in the mountains. Mike truly believed this—until the day Susan and the Franklins died.

The scavs came almost a year and a half from when they had first wandered into the Franklins' valley. The day was the finest Indian summer Mike had ever seen. He was coming down the mountain with a large tom turkey slung over his back, shotgun in his hand, feeling about as good as a man could feel.

Mike heard the first shot when he was still a ridge away from the farm. It was followed by a flurry of shots that made his steps falter. More gunfire crackled in the air, and he was running down the wooded mountainside. He dropped the turkey and shoved shells into the shotgun, horrible pictures in his head.

He broke through the clearing at the edge of the field and saw smoke rising from the house. A strange sound, a feral growl, ripped from his mouth, sweat streaming off his face, corn stalks whipping him on as he thrashed through the field. Mike now smelled smoke. He heard screams as he reached the yard. The house was an inferno. Bikers, or so he thought then, in dirty black leather were running through the smoke.

It seemed to Mike that there were at least a hundred, though there were only seventeen. The bodies of the elder Franklins lay in the yard. Blood darkened the soil around them. Marcus lay closer to the burning house. He had been beheaded. Mike pointed the shotgun in front of him and looked around wildly, uncertain of what to do.

Susan! Where was she? Mike saw a knot of the scavengers and a flash of white leg. There was a scream, and he recognized Diana's voice. They held her down as one rutted on her. He wanted to help her, but he had to find Susan! Then he heard her cry from the barn and ran, finger on the trigger of the shotgun. Mike had the element of surprise and gunned down three of the scavs before he reached the barn. It was the only reason they let him live.

They had Susan tied to a post and had torn off her clothing. Their leader smiled as Mike lifted the shotgun, and he held a very long knife to Susan's throat.

"Go ahead, man. See if you can shoot me before I cut your lady's throat."

Bars of sunlight lit the interior of the barn. He held the shotgun steady. The leader moved the knife a fraction. A trickle of blood seeped under the blade, and Susan whimpered. There was nothing Mike could do. He heard—and would always remember—the sound of hay dust trickling through the rafters.

A fighter would know what to do, Mike thought. *But I am no fighter.*

With a sigh that was almost a sob, Mike lowered the shotgun. It was torn from his hands. He was grabbed from behind. Handcuffs closed on his wrists, and he was harshly roped to the post opposite Susan's.

"Just let my wife go," he pleaded. "She's not well."

The leader was almost seven feet tall. Dark keloid scars marked his face like a tribal mask. His hair had been oiled back and cut in an *ichomage*, the trademark haircut of the samurai. His arms bulged like timbers. He grabbed Mike's face and squeezed until the bones in Mike's jaw flexed. Then he smiled, and Mike saw through the pain that the man's teeth had been filed into razor-sharp points like that of a shark. His voice was high-pitched and filled with a mania that made Mike's blood run cold.

"Sorry, man. You just took down three of my boys. You're a brave little cock, but you gotta pay. Do you love your wife?"

Mike nodded desperately. "She's all I have. Let her go. Please."

The leader shook his head. "No way. She's all you had in this world. Watch."

They held Mike's head so he could not look away. The leader raped her first. The others followed. Each time Mike tried to close his eyes, they hit him. At first, Susan screamed and called to him. But then her screams changed, became mindless. Her eyes grew dull. Mike felt her slip away forever. He screamed and struggled against his ropes until his wrists bled. The leader patted Susan on the cheek and said, "Was it good for you too, honey?"

He slapped her harder. "Hello? Is anyone

home?"

The other scavs laughed. It was then that Mike began to pray for survival so he could have revenge. He made it a vow. Shark Teeth took a handful of Susan's hair.

"Well, I guess we'll just have to put her out of her misery."

He smashed her head hard against the post, exposing her throat, and sunk his teeth deep into her. Susan collapsed against her bonds as blood arced from the punctures. Mike screamed. Shark spat a wad of flesh to the ground and used the back of his arm to wipe the bloody clown's mouth from his lips.

"Now, man, it's your turn."

Shark began to hit him methodically, fists like hammers, pounding Mike's face, chest, and arms. As he beat Mike, he called out, "Bad boy, bad boy," over and over.

Mike felt no pain after the first few blows. When Shark stopped, Mike's face was hamburger. He could feel ribs grating as he breathed. He was surprised, in a very distant way, that he was still conscious.

Shark pulled out his knife and held the glittering length in front of Mike's face. He drew the razor edge along Mike's nose to his ear. Blood sheeted Mike's face. Mike kept his swollen eyes riveted on Shark's. Shark flipped the knife into its sheath and cocked his fist.

"See ya 'round, man," he said, and poleaxed Mike between the eyes.

He came back to life at dusk. The falling sun was warm on his face. They had put him outside, laying Susan's body across him as a final gift. He slid painfully from beneath Susan and lay there, floating at the edge of painful, dark thoughts.

He must have passed out. In the morning, he kept his focus as narrow as he could. Broken and battered, he forced himself to move, to do what needed to be done. He buried Susan at the edge of the cornfield. He left no marker on the spot. He needed none; it was burned into his memory. Mike did not have the strength to dig more graves for the Franklins, so he rolled them onto a tarp and pulled their bodies to the barn. Their children were in the hayloft where Susan and he had stayed, both shot in the head. He covered them with sheets and set the barn on fire.

The scavs had left their own dead. Mike ignored them. In the back of the charred skeleton of the house, he found his guitar, lying in the dirt, miraculously intact and unharmed. He sat by Susan's grave and picked out "Hallelujah" as he remembered her, sad and bittersweet.

He grieved as the sun fell, tears coursing down the bruised, bloody flesh of his face. And as he cried, he felt, for the last time, the whisper of Susan across his mind, the word "West" in her voice. The fleeting image of an eye patch. Then nothing. She was gone.

A terrible rage colored Mike's vision. The scavs had left behind a Yamaha superbike because there was no one to ride it. It started when Mike hit the switch. He rode it around the yard to get a feel for the gears, ignoring the sharp pain in his chest from the broken ribs.

He used a length of barn twine to sling the shotgun across his chest. The guitar was strapped to the back of the bike. After cleaning himself with water from a cattle trough, Mike knelt by Susan's grave and began to hack at his hair, working by feel. When he finished, all that remained was a mohawk strip down the center. He buried the cuttings in a small hole by her grave.

"I'll never forget you, babe," he whispered, and left to go hunting.

The scavs were easy to follow. They pillaged and burned where they pleased, making no effort to hide the signs of their passing. Mike followed them for weeks, staying far behind them, letting his wounds heal, stopping at sunset, rain or shine, to play a song for Susan. He searched the towns after the scavs left and found better guns and ammunition, clothes, and food. He left the Yamaha when he found a larger and more stable Harley.

By watching the scavs, he learned their ways. They were surprisingly stupid. Marcus, who had taught them to make every shot count, would have laughed at the way they wasted ammunition. They seldom posted guards, and when they did, the guards usually ended up asleep. Whenever they found liquor or drugs, the scavs stoned themselves senseless. It was this behavior that gave Mike his opening.

He followed them west into Tennessee. A road map he found in a gas station showed the next towns in the direction the scavs were traveling. Mike skirted the band on side roads to get there first. When they came, he was in place. They looked for women but found none. Next, they went from store to store, looking for canned food and alcohol. The scavs found both and began to drink as they looted. As the day passed, they became progressively drunker. It was easy for Mike to just walk in and start killing.

Mike took the first one with a knife, holding his hand over the scav's mouth as he cut the man's throat. He did several more in the same way. When the drunken scavs began to fire their weapons in the air, his job became easier. Each time he pulled the trigger of the AR-15 carbine, the sound was masked by other shots. Mike moved as fast as he could, reducing opposition before he was discovered.

As it turned out, the remaining three scavs never realized they were being hunted until Mike shot them down. Mike ripped out a fast series of bursts to cut the legs out from under the last one, Shark. He slapped a new magazine into the weapon as he approached the wounded scav. Shark recognized him.

"You!" he said.

Mike stood over him, not knowing what to say. He wanted to say so much, yet none of it could convey what he felt inside. He aimed the carbine at Shark's chest.

"Fuck you, Shark," he said, and fired until the weapon was empty.

Mike looted the bodies, taking everything he thought might be useful, and was gone before the sun fell. It had been the start. From then on, he had moved slowly west, unconsciously following Susan's wish. As the scavs preyed on the wounded remains of humanity, so did Mike prey on the scavs.

There were small bands of scavs roaming the land, few and far between, gleaning sustenance from the carcass of America like cockroaches. He learned how lucky he had been with the first group. Most of the bands he hunted were smarter and much more vicious. As he became battle-hardened, he accumulated an impressive collection of scars. He lived much like his enemy, ransacking buildings for food or clothing. Leather was more practical than cloth because of its durability. Soft armor was more flexible than hard plates. Motorcycles were the most efficient means of travel. They were very mobile and balanced the need for speed, maneuverability, and fuel economy. Ethanol-free gas burned better than ethanol and lasted longer. Lessons learned. But he lived only for one thing: killing scavs.

Occasionally, he encountered good people. He was quick to back off, to not pose any threat. Twice he had played the guitar and sung for his supper. But most people saw his Harley and guns and either fled or opened fire. He could not blame them.

Sometimes, especially when he was weak and tired, Mike would forget why he was doing this. He mourned for Susan every sunset, playing "Hallelujah," tears wetting his eyes, though he could no longer remember her face—only the warm, soft glow of her hair.

In his solitude between battles, Mike found a purity of music that was more powerful than anything he had ever felt. His ability to play stripped him down to the leanest essentials of music. It sustained him when it seemed there was nothing else left.

Mike saw many strange things on the road as he hunted gradually westward. He was awakened one night by the distant throbbing of drums. The sound quickly grew louder, and Mike saw giants dancing and leaping across the sky. They wore bizarre masks covered with paint and feathers. Some rode horses; others had wings traced with lightning. Their chanting shook the Earth and was enough to rattle the fillings in his teeth.

"Son of a bitch!" he swore and ducked behind a tree when one of them turned his way. But he must have been beneath the notice of the god (what else could it be?), because it turned away.

As they marched over the horizon, he remembered what Susan had said on the night of the plane crash, so long ago. So, he had kept west, day by day, hunting and surviving. All the way to here.

His head came up with a jerk, and he reached for the assault rifle lying across the tank of the Harley. Nodding off like that could get him killed. He took his hand off the rifle and touched the cool metal of the motorcycle beneath him. This was his fourth. The gas tank of the Harley was painted with a naked, busty wench lying on the back of a white unicorn. Mike had blasted the owner out of the saddle at point-blank range. On the gas tank in front of the rifle sat a small black detonator box. When he pressed the button, a string of claymore mines located on each side of the highway below him would blow the living shit out of anything in the middle.

Mike stretched his neck. The sun was falling, making long, fiery streaks across the purple dome of the sky. The gentle shadows of the rolling hills moved slowly across the highway over which he presided.

He would stay here all night if he had to, into the next day and the night after that, until they came. He had never been wrong before. He was the hunter; the scavs would come this way. Mike settled the rifle and strummed the guitar again, picking out the sweet, simple chords that led him to "Hallelujah."

He did not have to wait long. He heard the distant rumble of tires on pavement. Sitting above the highway as he was, Mike saw the motor home a long way off. He changed to a flamenco riff, fingers flying over the strings as the vehicle approached the ambush.

The detonator box was armed and ready, antenna extended, lights glowing, the button begging to be pushed. The motor home was cruising. The claymores would have enough force to blast the vehicle off its undercarriage.

It did not occur to Mike that the motor home would contain anything other than scavs until it stopped a hundred yards from his ambush. He stopped playing as a large machine gun extended itself from the roof. He was beyond its range, he hoped, but he made ready to drop to the ground if the gun pointed his way.

Instead, the motor home crept up until it was fifty yards or so from the hidden mines. Armor plating dropped to cover the windows and tires. The gun barrel swiveled to the road and opened up, methodically detonating the claymores up one side of the highway and down the other, finally taking out the one he had buried dead center. Mike snorted in disgust and turned off the detonator. Shit! How did they know?

When the dust had cleared, the motor home rolled past the ambush site and shut down. Mike thought of bolting, but decided against it. This might be interesting. Besides, he was bleeding to death. He had nothing better to do. So, he held steady, watching.

The armor rolled back up, and a man stepped down from the driver's side. He walked the length of the ambush, examining where the mines had been placed, nodding to himself. He then raised a pair of binoculars, sighted down the road, then turned directly to where Mike sat. The man stared at Mike; he stared back, making no move. Then the man raised his hand in greeting.

Mike returned the gesture, thinking, "What's happening here?" He sensed it was big, maybe the most important thing that had ever happened in his life. The man waited in the center of the road.

Mike shrugged, then slung the guitar across his back and motored the Harley down the hill. The man was lean and radiated battle readiness. He was no scav—at least, not like any he had fought. Mike took one look and thought, *Military*. His one eye was as cold as Mike's were electric. The other was covered by a patch.

He heard Susan's voice: "The one-eyed man

needs you. "

The man looked him over, and Mike felt as if his soul were being scrutinized.

"Nice ambush," the man said. "You've taught yourself well."

Mike was surprised. It occurred to him that this conversation was not going to end in battle.

"How did you know that?"

"I know quite a bit about you, Mike. My name is Luke Kimball. I've been looking for you. We all have."

Things were going a little too fast. "Whoa. Who are 'we'?"

Luke called to the motor home, "Come on out so he can see you. Slowly, please."

The side door of the motor home opened, and out stepped a kid, a woman, and a large black guy. When they were all within arm's reach, thunder rumbled, and they saw, felt, for a moment, the fiery Hoop of Life arc cross the sky. Mike connected with them and felt the open spaces around them still to be filled.

"The one-eyed man and the Ghost Dance," he whispered.

Luke said, "You know?"

Mike shook his head. "No. Not really. Something someone once told me."

Luke nodded. "Susan. I am sorry for your loss. You are a part of what she saw. What exactly that is will take some explaining. I'm not even sure what it all means. Together, maybe we can figure it out. We have a place for you among us."

Luke took a step closer, so they were eye to eye. "Our enemies are the same. We need you and your music. Ellie is a doctor and can patch you up. It's not time for you to die yet. Join us." And Luke held out his hand.

Mike thought, *I don't want to be alone anymore*, and took it.

Cal placed his hand over theirs. "Welcome, Mike; the Music Man has come."

Ellie joined hands with them. "For better or worse, we are what we are, together."

Mike looked down at the kid. He held out his arm, and Tony came to him.

"Yes," Mike said, "together," and he knew this was where he belonged.

WHAT HAVE
I BECOME?

The storm rolled across the prairie, an endless, dangerous thing, coiling and uncoiling from horizon to horizon with a charged, mindless fury. It stretched across the sky like a black, boiling wall, lightning arcing to the ground along its turbulent leading edge, like legs carrying the storm forward.

A cold, dusty wind led the storm. Pierce's commandos cursed it, for the dust would carry fallout. They had the vehicles circled and tents struck just as the first cold sheets of rain lashed the ground.

Pierce and the others stood in the rain. He motioned Jed out from the security of the tent, and the preacher reluctantly joined him. The storm was so violent that the wind made them stagger, and the driving rain hammered them like hail. Pierce had to yell in Jed's ear to be heard.

"The rain will wash the radioactive dust off your clothing and skin."

Jed nodded, dazed by the fury of the storm. After their clothing was soaked, the commandos stripped off their clothing and washed with bars of hotel soap.

Jed, composure regained, yelled, "Has this happened before?"

Pierce soaped his face and turned it to the sky. His body was covered with savage knotted muscle and scars that showed pale against his tanned skin. Jed was ashamed at the loose folds of skin hanging on his own ghost-white body. He looked nothing like a dangerous man, even if he did hold the Voice of God within him. Considering Pierce, he thought how intensely volatile this man was.

Over the last few days, Jed had seen him kill a man with his bare hands. He had watched with concealed disgust (and even more deeply concealed jealousy) as Pierce whored with his wenches. He had seen the warrior shred targets with the many edged weapons he carried. Jed knew that Pierce had no compulsion against killing him and that he was being tolerated only because he knew how to find Kimball.

If Pierce ever thought that Jed had nothing left to give, or that he had ulterior motives, Jed knew he would be dead as fast as the man could hurl a blade. In doing the Lord's work, Jed played the most dangerous game . . . and found to his surprise that he liked the spice it added to his life.

Pierce saw him look at the people bathing

in the storm around them. "All of us here have experienced radiation levels higher than normal," Pierce said. "Look at my troops."

In the lightning-lit half-light of the storm, Jed could see the gleaming whiteness of naked skin. Many had strange patches of greenish or red skin on their backs, faces, and arms.

"Those are scars caused by the intense heat of a nuclear blast. The rash-like scars many also have, including me, were caused by contact with grains of fallout. I will carry these marks forever."

Pierce held out an arm, and Jed saw the mottled, shallow scars. "A number of my people have nearly died from radiation exposure," Pierce continued. "We don't know how many of us will develop some form of cancer tomorrow, next week, or next year. We are all at risk. To maintain health, I will shoot anyone in this band that refuses to wash at every available opportunity. Disease or plague could spread through us all too rapidly."

Jed shook his head, letting soap wash out of his thin hair. "I didn't realize there was so much to consider. My thoughts have been dedicated to . . . one goal." *And whatever it takes to meet that end*, he thought.

Pierce laughed. "One goal. Yes. The demise of Luke Kimball."

The leader turned and strode to his tent. Jed followed and almost walked right into one of the biggest men he had ever seen. The figure was easily six-and-a-half feet tall, broad, and rippled with muscle. Strange, sinuous tattoos covered his chest and massive arms. Long black hair fell to his shoulders. Even in the darkness of the storm, his eyes shone with a menacing light. He was naked save for the assault rifle hanging from his shoulder. It was pressed against his throat before Jed could even startle. He regarded Jed down the length of the weapon as lightning cracked the sky.

Pierce called from the tent, "Billy! Bring my guest and I something to eat, please."

The giant said, "Ah," softly and eased the rifle away from Jed's throat. "You got it, Mr. Pierce."

He addressed Jed. "You want anything in particular?"

Jed cleared his throat, knees shaking. "No. Whatever is served shall be sufficient," he replied stiffly.

Billy stepped back into the twilight and was gone. Jed entered the tent, dried and dressed.

"Who was that . . . red man?"

Pierce answered him as he dressed in clean black fatigues. There was a steel edge in his voice. "Race and religion are moot here. We all fight with the same hand and bleed the same blood. That is Billy McCrae. He is the finest soldier I have. He could cut your heart out and leave you standing, wondering what had happened. Do not debase him, or I will let him."

Jed kept his voice light. Concealing his intent from Pierce was becoming easier. The man's ego was much too large. "I meant no disrespect. He is simply one of the most impressive men I have ever seen. He must be very deadly."

Pierce laughed and relaxed. "He is, and more. I trust him."

Jed smiled weakly. Too close. Pierce was unenlightened to the true ways of the Lord. He was a tool to be used and thrown aside, but a dangerous one, a sword that could twist and cut off his hand.

I will cleanse this earth of your most foul kind, Jed thought. *Your head and Kimball's will rest side by side!*

Pierce sat at the desk in the back of the tent and poured a small amount of scotch into a glass. He offered the bottle to Jed, but the preacher declined.

"We won't be able to move until the storm clears. This type of weather can be extremely violent. It usually takes a day."

"Damnation," Jed hissed, "I can feel the devil to the west. He is slipping away."

"But you can lead me directly to him?"

Jed closed his fist. "Within hand's reach!"

"Then," Pierce said, "we have nothing to worry about."

"Truly; but I feel the passing of time."

The tent flaps parted as Billy returned with plates of hot food. Lightning flashed like daylight outside the tent. Thunder cracked loud enough to make them all jump. Jed laughed nervously as they relaxed.

"Stand watch inside the tent, Billy," said Pierce. "It is too mean a night to be outside."

Billy moved to the shadows in the entryway. He shoveled warm stew into his mouth as Pierce and Jed talked. Outside, lightning continued to streak the dark sky. The actinic light and rolling thunder made him uneasy, bringing back memories from his childhood—things he had not thought about for decades.

His father had once told him, "Lightning is a sign that the gods are displeased. Have you been a good boy?"

He had been a good boy, then. As a child, Billy had believed in the gods and life in all things. He had put these beliefs aside when he left the reservation and learned the ways of the world.

But tonight, after so many years, something was happening to him. In the voice of the thunder, Billy heard his father shout his name. The name was almost an accusation, a spirit hand ripping away the black veil he had drawn so tightly over his past.

"Billy!" his father's voice thundered. "Have

you been a good boy?"

Billy's mouth fell open as his life reeled past his eyes. He saw all that had happened to him, all that he had become. And Billy felt shame, for he had not been good.

He had been born Billy McCrae on the great Navajo reservation spanning the Arizona-Utah border. His early years took place in the often-confusing space between the Navajo and *belegana*, or white man's world, learning one thing and being forced to practice another.

His father, a veteran of the Vietnam War, had been a respected medicine man. His sand paintings had always been beautiful and intricate, captivating Billy for hours on end. Sometimes the colored sand seemed to come to life with the stories his father told.

In the Way ceremonies, his father became one of the *Yei*, the gods, when he donned the costumes and masks and sang the sacred songs. Often Billy dreamed of the Navajo gods dancing across the painted desert, wings and fur and claws, their calm eyes and voices teaching him important things he could not remember when he awakened. Perhaps, if things had happened differently, he would have gone to the world, come back, and become a medicine man like his father.

Billy's father taught him respect for life. He had also tried to teach Billy the trick to surviving in the *belegana* world.

"Learn to live with them, in their ways. They are not all bad. Some will become your friends and may even come to understand the true world. But never forget that in your heart, you are Navajo."

Billy had been a good boy, then. But as he grew older, not so good.

The change came when his father died. His father had fallen off the edge of a canyon while herding sheep. Such a stupid way for a great man to die. Through the shock and the subsequent move with his mother to his relatives' house, Billy questioned why the gods his father served so well had let him die. Billy felt that his father should live, should spring from the soil and be whole again. What had happened was not right, and the gods needed to make it so. If they would not bring his father back, then he would not believe in them.

He rebelled. The custom of not using a dead person's name angered him. Billy ran into the wilds and screamed his father's name until it echoed from the canyons. He took his father's colored sands and scattered them to the winds. He was not happy living with his relatives. They thought him sullen and brooding, prone to lashing out. His rapidly growing body scared them with its size and potential for violence.

Out of concern, they held a ceremony to cure Billy of the melancholy that made him act the way he did. Halfway through the ceremony, he jumped up and screamed, "None of you understand. This isn't real!"

And he ran into the darkness, away from the numb shock and embarrassment of his people. Thereafter, they left him alone to do pretty much as he pleased.

Billy eventually learned to hide his grief. He taught himself not to care, and it gave him a calm center that became his armor and sanity. He saw that there was no future for him on the reservation. His people were no longer his people. His place was somewhere out in the world.   His first step away from the reservation was joining the Marines the day he graduated from high school. He became Private William McCrae and lost his old identity. After basic training and advanced courses in jungle warfare, now Lance Corporal McCrae was shipped to El Salvador to fight the spread of communism. It was there that he gained his real training, to kill efficiently and without hesitation, from a quiet, deadly SEAL by the name of Kiko Sloan.

Sloan had come from the confusing, bizarre subculture of the Los Angeles goth scene. Even in the jungle, he wore a short mohawk and earrings made from the claws of a jungle cat. He was lean and muscular and could move as silently as the cat whose claws he wore. He was intelligent and did so well at counterinsurgency that his superiors gave him the leeway to do pretty much as he pleased.

In the jungle, he had carved out an empire. Billy's unit was assigned to his detail. Sloan put him through hell, and the experience tempered him into a killing machine to rival his mentor. He learned many things, among them the ability to distance himself from the act of taking life.

The heat of the jungle and war melted away his past until only vague shadows remained. And those were easy enough to forget in the rare, calm moments between battles. Nothing else but fighting seemed to matter.

When Sloan died in a vendetta battle against a rebel leader, Billy felt nothing. But he came back from R & R in Tulum covered with strange, intertwined tribal tattoos across his chest and arms—a tribute to his dead mentor.

When his tour of duty was up, Billy passed on the chance to reenlist and station outside of North Korea, where a war was shaping up, and instead took his discharge and left. Now he was just a soldier on his way home to an uncertain future. His past was occasional dreams of forgotten gods, people, and storms of pure lightning and thunder. The dreams were few and far between.

Back in the real world, work was easy to find. His impressive build and military background made him desirable as a high-paid executive bodyguard. He had his pick of offers from military contracting companies. A wealthy

Southern industrialist who feared kidnapping took his contract. His employer did not need a bodyguard, but Billy took the job because the man paid well and the work was easy. He had been working for six months when the war hit. They were at home in New Orleans.

The man took the news badly. They could have survived, but instead, he ushered his family into the basement, shot them all, and then put the last bullet in his head. Billy heard the shots and came running. But it was too late to do anything but stare at the blood running down the walls.

He stood there for a while, listening to the silence of the house, and thought, *This is what it feels like to die.*

The house was rich with things he could use. Billy loaded as much food, clothing, and weaponry as he could carry on his former employer's Harley Electra Glide, a road sofa of a motorcycle. He headed south, getting to the Florida Everglades before the fallout from Miami stopped him, then back up across the panhandle and the southern US to what was left of California. In his years on the road, Billy saw things no man had ever seen, death and plague, destruction on a scale too large to comprehend, the sheer brutality one man could unleash on another.

Adapting to the brutality of post-war existence was simple. Billy crushed whoever stood between him and what he wanted, as long as they were unarmed. He fought scavs or left them alone depending only on how hungry he was or how aggressive they were to him. He had his moral code. He did not rape or murder and made it a point to exterminate those who did. Billy kept his mind free, concentrating only on survival. Nothing else mattered. . . until he met Pierce.

He knew who Pierce was. SCI had been a legend among soldiers, a place to get good employment if you had a clean service record and were up on your skills. Pierce had charisma, as much as Kiko Sloan, which was the main reason he joined up with him. But as time went on, Pierce managed to break him from some of the ice in which he had unknowingly layered himself. Pierce did not just see him as a tool. He had five men. Billy was the sixth and quickly became number one as the mobile army grew, fighting its way across the land. He came to hold Pierce in awe. Pierce was more deadly than even he. He led with a precision that was more than military. When they took a town, they didn't vandalize or pillage. It was more like a systematic dismantling of everything usable, eatable, or worth trade.

Pierce trained them to fight like an army. They ransacked National Guard armories and other bunkers for combat weaponry. Any force that stood in their way was obliterated.

And anyone who challenged his leadership was impaled on the sharp point of Pierce's kukri blade.

Life with Pierce had been better than he would have expected. As his right-hand man and bodyguard, Billy had found purpose. But . . . had he been good? As he stood in the dark of the entryway, he examined his life in the glaring lightning. And he hung his head, for there was only one answer.

Silently he mouthed the word, "No."

For a moment, all was silent. Then the sky came alive. Sheets of lightning turned night into day. The walls of the tent glowed. They pulled away from him, fading into the vast blackness of the night. The rain ceased. He stood solitary in a desert, infinitely alone. He felt the presence of others, great others, watching him, judging. There was no light upon him, but it felt as if a beam of fire had flayed him down to the essence of his soul.

The voice of the thunder, his father, made the earth tremble. Billy listened and heard his judgment.

"You have left the sacred path!" his father called. "You have taken food from the mouths of the hungry. You have slain the innocent. You have lost your respect for life and forgotten your true heart. You have walked away from your spirit. The gods weep. You have forgotten the face of your father. You cannot run away anymore. You must choose!"

Compelled by forces greater than himself, Billy held his hands in the air, equal like the balances of a scale. In his left hand, he held his current life path. He saw the roads filled with battle and conquest. He felt the pull of battle and felt the blood singing in his veins. A voice whispered in his head, soft and seductive. *"This is your calling. Follow me to your glory."*

As he looked down the path, he saw a god with green, glowing eyes and an ever-changing shape watching from every hilltop, licking its lips at every blood-soaked battle. It was sometimes a four-legged beast, sometimes human-like, always with strange, twisted antlers. It pulled at the warrior in him with the berserk of death and destruction. It was a dark road, drunk with bloodlust.

In his right hand, he saw the path that would take him away from here, from his comfort zone of fighting and making war, into the pain of his past—and maybe through it. That future had many forks that opened up past him leaving here tonight. This was the painful way. No twisted creature was watching him here, only a tough-looking guy with one eye. That guy said, "You ready to find your way back?"

And he was. He dropped his left hand, and the glow from the right enveloped him.

It was true, so true! He had isolated himself from his people when his father died. His people had tried to help him, but he had turned his back on them, on the ways of his father. That was where he had gone wrong. He needed to be set back on the right path, to feel again what it was to be of the *Diné*, to belong. He needed spiritual guidance. He might not make it on the path he had chosen. To perish would not be so bad. He had faced death for so long that it had lost much of its mystery. But to be without spirit any longer was too much for him to bear.

Suddenly, he was back in the tent. The storm had lessened to a light, steady rain. He could hear Pierce and that freak talking behind him. He felt the pull to leave. But to walk out now would be suicide. Pierce would never let him go.

So, Billy planned as the storm wound down. He knew Pierce and Jed could not have heard what was in the voice of the thunder; that had been for his ears alone. They continued their conversation as the storm settled.

Billy listened to them discuss their plans for Luke Kimball, a name he recognized from his contracting days. He had been Pierce's partner. Billy absorbed everything they said. Their overwhelming desire to destroy Kimball had led to this unhealthy alliance. It was wrong. Something about Jed made his skin crawl.

He left the tent to do a routine loop around the camp. By the time he returned, he knew what he was going to do. Pierce took his report quietly and then wished him good night, as was his fashion. Billy left, knowing he would never see Pierce again. He went to his own smaller tent, put on his leathers, then shoved food and six loaded AR magazines into a pack.

He wheeled his motorcycle to the edge of the camp and spoke briefly with the perimeter guards. They knew him well and did not question his story.

As he walked the bike out of the camp, he felt a weight slip off him, a phase of his life completed. Somewhere out in the darkness was a new life for him, a life with meaning. Out of earshot from camp, Billy kicked the Harley to life and headed west, into the trailing end of the storm. It was dark enough that he drove as much by feel as by sight. The rain plastered his leather clothing to him like a second skin.

By first light, he was sixty miles from the camp. Following instinct and some newfound inner direction, he passed the western edge of the storm by early afternoon and spent the rest of the day under a bright, cloudless sky. He crossed into Wyoming at sunset and drove through the night, bypassing Cheyenne and Laramie when his Geiger counter started to click.

By morning, he was looking at Medicine Bow Peak. At its base was a great mountain meadow. This is where he wanted to be. He set up camp in a group of trees by a stream at the edge of the clearing. His gear was soaked. Billy hung his clothes on branches to dry, cleaned and oiled his weapons, and then slept through that day and night. The next dawn found him naked, sitting on a blanket in the middle of the meadow, gazing at the mountain.

He remembered this meadow from his childhood. His father had brought him here, when he was young, as they traveled to visit one of his service buddies from Vietnam. Billy had been awed by the simple, snow-capped majesty of the peak. It was a good memory and a good place to start.

Sitting here, he felt that if he were to pray for help and guidance, this was a place where the gods would be. There were rituals he should follow, he knew, and prayers he should sing. But he had forgotten them many years ago. So many important lessons that he needed now. He was desperate to find his spiritual center. He understood what it was to have your soul be thirsty. It was more than a need; it was survival. So, Billy began to pray to every god he could remember, to every god he felt existed, for forgiveness, for guidance, for help.

Sun warmed the meadow basin as the day grew older. Billy grew hoarse, his prayers coming forth in whispers. The sun beat down on him like a hammer, burning into his bones, pounding him on the great anvil of the earth into shapeless, spiritless metal. The sound of his voice grew in his head like the roaring of the wind. The sun seemed to hang forever at the top of the sky. Billy stared at the molten orb until its brilliant light became blackness.

He blinked, and it was night, stars hurtling across the sky like the brightly colored lights of every carnival that had ever traveled the earth. He looked into their depths and saw men sailing between suns on gleaming, metallic ships open to the heavens. Among the stars, he turned and saw himself far below, a tiny speck on the face of a tiny world, one of millions of worlds, sitting in one of a million meadows.

Across the American continent, he saw people on the move, pitifully small groups of survivors, all heading to the same place in the northwest. A god saw him. He felt, more than saw, the unique shape of one of the kachina. The god reached out. A giant hand swatted him back towards the earth. He rocketed into his body and opened his eyes. Morning sunlight dazzled him, only to be blotted out by a great golden eagle. The bird of prey screamed its war cry and slashed his cheek with a talon as it passed. In that instant, Billy looked into its eyes and saw a man.

He was shorter than Billy, just over six feet, with close-cropped white-blond hair and one blue eye the color of winter ice. The other was covered with a black patch. The man seemed chiseled from stone, with harsh, angular planes building his face and muscled torso. The man looked at him for a long moment, then stepped aside. Beyond him, Billy saw a motor home with four people next to it. The man held his hand up, palm out—a sign of peace.

"Find me," the man said, and then vanished.

In his place was the bone-white mask of Talking God. The mask turned to him, ancient wisdom burning deep in its empty sockets. "Go to this man," Talking God commanded, "and help him help the *Diné*. In this way, you may find your spirit again."

Talking God reached out to touch him, and Billy saw the eagle feathers on the rim of his mask. As the god's hand touched him, Billy reached out in a desperate grasp and plucked a feather from the tail of the giant eagle. His world exploded, and for a time he felt nothing.

He came back into his body as the sun dropped over the western mountain. Blood ran from his cracked lips, but Billy smiled anyway. In his hand, he held a golden eagle feather. The slash on his cheek was matted with dried blood. And a name was imprinted in his mind.

Billy smiled again as he lay back on the blanket, relishing the cool mountain air, and whispered the name: "Luke Kimball."

Once again, his life had a purpose.

THE THUNDERBIRD

The MOC was parked at the edge of an alpine meadow a few miles off the road, south of Alamosa, Colorado. There was a stream crossing the meadow. Luke had made Tony a fishing pole, and the boy had caught a few rainbow-hued trout. It was a good spot to rest for a few days, secluded and miles away from any chance of human contact.

One day of rest had already made a difference in them all. Cal's back was healing nicely, and Mike had regained his color. Luke sat far out in the middle of the field on the white buffalo hide, watching. In getting to know them, Luke could see why each was so special. Their strengths made their auras shine like diamonds.

Tony and Mike stood straddle-legged an arm's length apart, playing mumbly-peg. Mike flipped a knife from his fingertips. It spun lazily in the air and stuck in the ground between Tony's legs. Tony picked it up and tried to do the same.

The knife skidded in the dirt.

Mike laughed and said, "Try to roll it from your fingertips, like this."

It worked, and Tony hooted in delight. Cal and Ellie sat by the MOC, embroiled in some debate. He was leading these good people to their destinies, to a future, that even he was not sure of. He only hoped he was not leading them to their deaths.

High overhead, a golden eagle soared in the warm air. Luke tilted his head back to follow its flight. It led him to face the towering wall of mountains. He took the pipe in his hands. It was almost complete, lacking only the eagle's feather. With it and the crystal mask, he would have the tools he had first dreamed of . . . maybe.

He gazed up at the eagle and knew what he desired, what needed to happen. He held the pipe high with both hands, staring now into the sun, and concentrated, feeling the warmth of thermal wind on his arms, his legs . . . his wings. There was a moment of intense pain as his body contracted and stretched into new shapes. Then he was flexing his wings, soaring into a tight thermal current to gain altitude.

When he reached the level of the other, the eagle cocked its head at him and said, "Well done. Took you long enough though."

Luke laughed and heard the sound of his laughter under his eagle's cry. They flew higher and soared south, over the mountains.

"Who are you?" asked Luke.

Multicolored fire spread along its wings. The eagle grew until its wingtips brushed the horizons, a flaming, multicolored bird with a fierce beak and talons like titanium. Its voice shattered the sky. "I am Thunderbird. Across the world, I have been known by many names: Phoenix, Quetzal, and Firebird, to name a few. Mine is the power to rise anew out of the ashes of the old. Rebirth. It is a fitting power for what you are to do. I choose to help you."

Thunderbird continued, "When the earth was young and man was evolving from the early beings, he was a very powerful creature. The divine was in his nature, as was an overwhelming childlike curiosity to know and shape the world around him. To seek the answers he needed, man gave birth to the gods to help explain why things were. So strong was his imagination, his belief, the power of his intention, that we, the divine inner nature, became manifest in our forms.

"As man evolved, so did his gods, all across the world! We developed the ability to reason and influence man's destiny. Through the ages, we were revered and worshipped. But eventually, mankind's beliefs changed. Their intention went to new gods, then no gods. It went to *things.* And with no belief to sustain us, we slowly faded from this to another world, the Spirit World. You know how bleak and desolate it can be."

Luke nodded. He had been there.

"It is also a place of peace and great beauty. But that is for another time. The loss of belief was new to this world. It was set adrift from the balance of all things. Chaos reigned. But the war between all men shook the very foundations of the universe, rent the fabric of reality. First, the prayer of the Ghost Dance found you, the one prophesied to reunite man and god. When you reached through and touched the Manitou, the contact created doorways we could pass through. And the belief of the people who are left is enough to sustain us ... for a time. This is what has happened."

Luke was stunned by the chaotic possibilities. "So, all of the American Indian tribes ... their gods ... have come to life?"

"Not just theirs. All gods. See for yourself."

They soared over the desert. The air below shimmered and began to coalesce into a thousand shapes, colorful, winged, and horned, wearing skins and robes or nothing at all, painted and plain, hoofed and human-footed, peaceful, loving, and ferocious, of good and devious intent, human and inhuman. They danced in a complex spiral that seemed destined to wind into itself, yet never did. Occasionally one of them would glance up at him, aware, and Luke felt they were looking through his eagle form to the very heart of his soul. He could hide nothing from them.

"This is the Hoop of the God Dance," said Thunderbird, "and before you is the pantheon of the gods from the world you call Earth. This is the dance people danced at Wounded Knee and called the Ghost Dance. It has been danced in different forms by all peoples across the history of humanity. It connects us all, backward and forwards through time, and across the planes of existence. Its pattern is circular and eternal. Look well, for there are those who shape your destiny. Hopi. Navajo. Sioux and Ojibwa. Crow and Zuni. Algonquin. Mohegan. Seminole, Aztec, Norse, and many more."

Thunderbird chuckled. "Pray to a god now, and he or she just may come to you. Or a god once worshipped by one tribe may appear to any human. Some gods are pranksters. Some are what you would call evil. This has happened all over the world, and each people has their sacred dances and gods. And all of us, god and man, tie back to one central hub where the Hoop turns. The point is, here you see the scope of what has come to be. This is the world in which you must now live . . . in which all men must live."

"Why are they dancing?" Luke asked.

"Through the dance, the power of their attention, their energy, drives the turning of the Hoop of Life. But their ability to do so has faded without the power of belief. Now they wait for you to complete the Key of Seven and bring it to the sacred place. If you do, the power of man and god will unite in the turning of the Hoop. But fail, and man and god will eventually fade away. This is what your enemy seeks. You are the driving force. Your enemy is the opposing force. There may not be one without the other."

Luke surveyed the moving, twisting pantheon carefully. "The Manitou is not there."

"No," Thunderbird answered. "He dances alone in the world of man, your world, working his plans. You have many hardships to overcome yet, and the Manitou will be the most difficult. You cannot succeed as a divided man. Come."

They flew on. Luke soared in silence, considering what he was seeing. He had never known there were so many gods. But who led them? If the gods had sprung from the minds of men, they would share certain traits with man. Just about every mythology had stories about wars among the gods. Luke questioned Thunderbird.

"It is true that gods have fought each other, and will most likely do so again. We were created in the image of man, after all. But we do not battle each other now; that challenge is for the Manitou and you alone. Your quest is enough to stop even the fighting of the gods. Now do you realize the importance of what you are doing?"

Luke understood . . . and liked it not at all. "All I wanted was to regain my humanity, to be able to live in peace. Why was I selected? Why me?"

Thunderbird's tone was matter-of-fact. "Because you were fated. Your readiness to take the blame for the deaths of your loved ones moved you into the path of this destiny. The Ghost Prayer needed a savior to fulfill it, and you needed to be fulfilled. You have a special gift, Luke. What it is, I cannot tell you. You must find it within yourself."

Oceans flashed beneath them, then the icy expanse of the North Pole. As they soared southward over Canada, Thunderbird said, "The pipe you are creating is an ancient symbol of peace and unity. You still need the feather. Find it and the crystal mask . . . and you will be ready to face the Manitou. Observe. Understand."

Luke saw the mountain and a meadow much like the one the others now sat in. In the center sat a man on a blanket. Luke circled closer. The man was large and muscular, with long black hair and intricate tribal tattoos. His head was thrown back towards the sun, eyes open and focused on infinity. A hoarse whisper came from the man's throat.

Luke heard the man's impassioned plea for salvation and empathized with his desperation. He had dreamed of this man. But what was he doing here? Luke needed him! He banked and dropped like a missile, screaming a fierce cry. The man looked him straight in the eyes, and Luke knew the man was seeing him as his true self.

"Find me," Luke spoke into the man's

mind, and his talon brushed the man's cheek as he passed.

He felt a tug as the man reached for a feather. It fluttered into the man's hand. As Luke winged back into the sky, he saw the man clutch the feather and whisper his name.

"Now you see," said Thunderbird.

"Yes," answered Luke. "Small pieces complete large puzzles, hoops within hoops. "

"You see," agreed Thunderbird. "You have my blessing. I wish you well. Can you find your way back?"

Luke knew he could now become an eagle at will. "Yes. I want to soar for a while, to think."

"Sometimes it is good to be alone. Farewell, Luke Kimball. We shall meet again, in the moment between the lightning and the thunder."

Thunderbird veered away and was quickly lost in the distance. Luke climbed higher until he flew in and out of the cloud tops. Here the only sound was the wind in his feathers. The music of the life below was too rich to listen to. He was content with this windy silence and his thoughts.

How many others, he wondered, felt the westward call? What kind of people were they, and what would they be . . . if he completed the Key and defeated the Manitou? What would the world become?

He had seen unicorns and gods. What

other kinds of mythical creatures wandered the earth? The complicated possibilities of the future all hinged on his completing this quest, leading these people to the sacred place, defeating a god in battle, regaining the lost parts of his soul. All Luke could do was play out his hand the best he could.

The sun was rapidly dropping to the western horizon. Luke rode the upper currents south to where the MOC sat. Smoke rose from a cooking fire. Far below, he could see Tony, Cal, and Mike eating by its light. Samson lay curled at the boy's feet. He searched for Ellie and found her sitting in the meadow at the edge of his robe, arms hugging her knees to her chest. Waiting.

Luke circled, watching her from afar, and realized how beautiful she was. Such an awesome blend of fragility and iron, vulnerability and strength. She reminded him of Reiko, gone from him for so long. A gust of wind blew hair across her face, and Ellie shook her head, throwing back the thick tresses. He realized that if he could love anybody again, it would be this woman. If only he could succeed in his quest, he would have a soul to touch hers. Holding this thought, Luke spread his wings and dropped to the robe.

Ellie watched in fearful astonishment as Luke changed from eagle to human form. *What kind of man has Luke become?* she wondered as the strong shape of his shoulders emerged from feathers. *Is he a god? And why now, after all that has happened, am I coming to love him?*

Luke sat up and pulled the robe over himself to cover his nakedness. He watched Ellie calmly, seeing a wild mix of emotions in her eyes: fear, wonder, and yes, even . . . love. Her voice trembled.

"What are you?"

"A man, Ellie. Just a man. A tool of the gods, maybe, but still only a man."

"But I saw you change shape. . ."

"I can do that now, and more. But all I can do is nothing in the face of what is happening for all of us."

"What do you mean?"

"You, Cal, Mike, and Tony, and a few people we have not yet met, have become something magical. You may not feel all of it yet, but when all of you come together, you will. The world will build on whatever magic we make together."

Ellie studied his face in the last moments of daylight. "Why are you doing this instead of one of those gods?"

"Let me tell you a story," Luke replied. "Once, long ago, I loved a woman very deeply." He smiled. "She was as wonderful as you. It was during the Gulf War. The problem was that I felt that everyone I loved or cared for would die. I was very selfish. . ."

Luke told her about Thomas, Reiko, and

Trinkla, his years of loneliness while building SCI, the coming of the Manitou.

"I built great walls and refused to love anyone out of fear that they would be taken from me, but I still could at least feel love. The Manitou took that from me—the ability to love, to care, to feel. I walk through life now missing the most important parts of me and only too late realize what is gone. I remember what it feels like to have emotions. But it's as if the memories belong to someone else.

"If I can find the Seven and bring you to a certain place, I have a chance to get back what the Manitou took from me. Right now, I have nothing. Nothing except you. You don't know how much I need you. We Seven are the hope of the world. But you are my only hope . . . my salvation."

Luke saw the gleam of tears on her face. Ellie reached out a trembling hand to touch him.

"I'm so sorry," she whispered.

She moved closer, wanting, and Luke opened the robe so she could come in with him. Luke held her as she cried, grieving for them both, for what he could not. They lay back in the grass as the stars grew strong, illuminating the mountains with their pale light. His muscles were strong and hard under her hands. Ellie kissed him, and Luke responded, feeling the power of his body's animal response.

He unbuttoned her shirt and slid his

hands over her back, feeling her hot, lithe grace. They explored each other as she shed the rest of her clothing, with hands and mouths, clinging and twining. Luke rolled the buffalo robe flat and brought his mouth to her neck, then her breasts and lower. She savored the feel of him on her, then arching up, she pulled his face to hers and drew him down into her body. They made love under the stars, Ellie moaning with need and the fulfillment of that need, rolling him over to ride him, bearing down with a desperate hunger for love, to feel his need, his heart.

Luke responded to her with cries of his own, feeling the animal lust of his body as they crested the wave of passion together. As they panted, breathing in each other's breath, he missed the emotional intimacy that made love truly real and vowed anew that he would defeat the Manitou, if only to love this woman as she needed and deserved to be loved—as he so desperately ached to love her.

THE WOMAN WITH THE POWER OF THE SUN

From where Mindy Barsky sat in the warm sand, the Gulf of Mexico seemed to go on forever. On the beach at the southern edge of Padre Island, Texas, the purple curve of the island to the north and south was lost in the distance of evening haze. The sun, almost past the western horizon, lit the sky in a flaming post-nuclear sunset. Mindy dug her toes deeper into the sand at the surf's edge, hugging her knees, not minding the dampness soaking her denim shorts.

She was beautiful, an exotic woman with silky mocha skin, golden, tawny hair, and flashing emerald-green eyes. A green-eyed lioness. Mindy was lithe and trim, in excellent shape and tone from daily exercise. The evening breeze whisked her hair across her face. She threw it back with an impatient shake of her head, waiting . . . both dreading and yearning for what she knew was about to happen.

At thirty-one, Mindy didn't know how much of her life remained. The war had left too much uncertainty. Residual radiation. Plague. Chemical toxins. The scavenger scum. Death waited at every turn. She had seen it happen many times over the last three years, from the safety of the Padre Island Solar Habitat: scientists and their families who tried to leave too early or who chose to end it on the beach, by exposure to the plagues that had drifted up from Mexico over the first two years, or by faster, more personal means.

There had been three hundred in the habitat before the war. Now there were only fifty. Her staff. The deaths had been enough to harden even her, at least on the surface, so that she no longer broke into tears when they buried another body in the makeshift cemetery farther up the island.

It was safe to be outside now, and had been for over a year. The gleaming, white-domed buildings of the Habitat were behind her, nestled in the dunes. They had been designed to blend in with the environment, to direct attention away from their existence . . . and to hide the larger and more complex level hidden beneath the surface. The Habitat was filled with what, to Mindy, was wondrous science and a bit of magic: the power of the sun.

When the government, which no longer existed, had named her director of the Habitat more than four years ago, she had dubbed the scientists, solar technicians, and their families living in the Habitat the Children of the Sun. She thought it a fitting title for those who were going to deliver the power of the sun to the people. Now, almost like a god, Mindy had the power of the sun ready to hand down to the people. But there were none left to use it. The war had made it an empty gift.

Mindy turned to look at the sinking sun. It was almost time.

Once, Mindy had been among the world's most brilliant solar scientists. Her life had been dedicated to bringing the light and warmth of the sun to the people, a gift of unlimited electric power. She dreamed of making solar power practical and affordable, to take the light of the sun and convert it into pure electric current to power the engines and machines of man. Mindy imagined a world rushing by at incredible speeds, wheels blurring to invisibility, jets soaring overhead, assembly machines racing in high gear, and all of them silent, imbued with the quiet strength of the sun. No hydrocarbons or greenhouse gasses. No more global warming. No danger of radiation. Just pure, clean power to make things live and grow.

The dream had been hers since she was a ten-year-old girl growing up in Los Gatos, California. It had carried her through UCLA and then Berkeley on a full scholarship. She had completed her doctorate with the development of a revolutionary solar power system for a government satellite, smaller and more powerful than its predecessors.

A year later, the Padre Island Solar Habitat was completed. They gave her free reign to design and direct as she wished, to bring them the power of the sun, as long as she produced results. And she had. Mindy had always known the direction her research would take. Crystal was the key. She touched a thin gold chain around her neck. Suspended from it was a perfectly formed octagonal crystal spar an inch long. It was clear as water, without even the slightest imperfection. A spiderweb-thin trace of gold wire cradled it and looped onto the chain. It was the only tangible connection she had to her parents.

Her parents had been wonderful people, intellectually secure artists who taught sculpture and painting at Stanford. Her mother had been black, her father white. They had been color-blind in a world where something so minor as pigment could become so great an issue. Their home had been a haven for artists, writers, and all manner of intellectuals, of all colors, proclivities, and beliefs. Mindy had been privileged to hear their debates, and when she was older, to participate. Her parents taught her to take pride in herself and the potential of what she could be.

"You cannot change the origins of your birth, nor should you ever want to," they told her, "and what you are is beautiful. You are what art and life should be: a blend of everything good. The rest of what you are is up to you."

Once, someone had called her mulatto. Mindy had laughed. "I'm not mulatto. I'm the world!"

They had given her the crystal when she was four. When Mindy held it up to the sun, the rainbow light that reflected on the walls and ceiling, in her eyes, was clear and . . . pure. In it, she saw and felt the same essence that her parents found in the mediums of paint, clay, and steel.

Her parents had encouraged her fascination with light and later with physics, as she tried to define her passion and bring it into reality. Her desire to evolve the power of light led her to the theory and miracle of solar power. It became her art form: the art of sunlight. How ironic that her parents had vanished in the scorching nuclear "sunlight" that had burnt the San Francisco peninsula to dust and rubble.

She had accepted the fact of their death a long time ago, but Mindy missed them every day. In a very significant way, all she had accomplished at Habitat was a tribute to them. Light . . . and crystal. Through crystal, she had found a way to make solar power practical.

It happened just months after the war. They were running at full capacity, and Mindy drove her research staff relentlessly to keep their minds and hands occupied and off the fate of the world. Exploring crystal matrices, they created a molecular crystal lattice that generated a substantial electrical current when exposed to light. Grown under a magnetic field, the crystal could be shaped into micro-thin sheets. They bonded the crystal to a simple capacitating circuit and had the world's first practical grown solar cell. She had named the crystal LightForm.

LightForm was easy to grow under basic lab conditions. They quickly made Habitat completely solar-powered, cutting their dependency on outside power sources. She doubted the government would ever let her discovery go public; it would have put the world's oil companies out of business.

While happy that her life's dream had been brought into reality, Mindy was saddened that it had come too late. She had found a way to bring light to the people—only now there was no way to give it to the few who were left.

Life at Habitat had become bleak. She was now the director in name only. Though they could live here forever through hydroponics gardening and solar power, Mindy had lost her hope for the future. She thought about suicide, an option many at the Habitat had taken, but the fact was that she had come too far to just end it now.

Every day was a choice to keep moving. In the end, what kept her going was the overwhelming sadness she felt at every sunset.

Mindy had been a scientist too long to disregard the paranormal. She believed that all people were psychic to some degree. The first time she had felt the sadness, she thought she was going insane. She tried to shut it out of her head, but the emotion was so strong that she had to scream, to cry, to rage. It only lasted for a short time at each sunset: the sadness and the music. Always the same song, just simple chords on a guitar. When it was over, Mindy always felt drained, the melody etched in her head, lyrics she would find herself whispering, and she was moved in a way so profound that she could not fully comprehend it.

She had come to live with this episodic sadness, both dreading and hungering for it. Each evening, she removed herself from her people and sat on the beach, rain or shine, riding out the wave. In the year since it had begun, Mindy had learned much about the source of it in the other emotions that ran through it like individual threads of a much larger weave. She felt that somewhere, a man grieved for a woman he had loved. Mindy believed that she was psychically tuned to him, on his mental wavelength. His sorrow was constant, but he kept it in check. Only at sunset did he allow himself the luxury of grief, when he sat away from the world and strummed his guitar, mourning what he had lost.

The man had been moving across the country. Sometimes she could even see through his eyes, quick snatches of roads or fields. Often she could feel in her hands, for an instant, the wood and steel strings of the guitar he played. It was always the same song, of sadness and loss, a melody so bittersweet it made her ache. It echoed in her so strongly that Mindy cried out to comfort him. Never had she felt such a resonance of compassion. She had no idea who he was or what he looked like, but she loved him. He had to be an extraordinary man to survive the war and still carry such love in his heart.

But their channel was one-way. She was the receiver of his broadcast, but knew he could not feel her in return. As her shadow grew longer on the beach, Mindy heard the first few notes of his guitar. She grew slightly dizzy as her mind tuned to his wavelength. She felt he was north of her tonight, and she shifted to face him. She could feel her/his fingers sliding over the hard, shiny strings of the guitar. A cool whisper of wind touched her face, and Mindy saw a high shadow wall of mountains against the darkening sky. She could feel the sadness and sorrow approaching her like a tsunami, emotions like the sea pulling back from the beach of her mind, towering over the calm surface, strong enough to overpower her and carry her away.

The wave collapsed over her. She was part of the sorrow, the anguish—part of him. Mindy floated free in his grief, then decided to go deeper. She dove, her mind no longer completely her own, and saw for the first time why this man grieved so. With his arms, she held a beautiful blonde-haired woman. His wife. In the space of heartbeats, she saw scenes of their life together: he on a stage, seeing her in the audience; dancing on a balcony overlooking the ocean; their fights; even their lovemaking—everything about her that he had loved.

Mindy felt a flush of embarrassment at sharing his life so intimately, yet had an even stronger curiosity towards the man whose anguish she shared. She lived with them on a farm after the war, feeling his love and desperation as she slipped away. Then the raid of the scavengers, smoke, and brutality... His pain, rage, and sorrow peaked. Mindy sobbed at the intensity of their feelings.

Now he cried for his loss as he sang. He was sad and so lonely, so ... alone. He did not like what he had become, but he did not know how to stop hurting.

"Well, maybe there's a God above,

But all I've ever learned from love
Was how to shoot somebody who'd out-drew
ya.

And it's not a cry that you hear at night,
It's not somebody who's seen in the light,
It's a cold and it's a broken hallelujah..."

His hurt was more than she could bear, and Mindy reached out, discovering a part of herself she did not know was there, and she felt him, held him tightly.

"No," she sobbed, "you're not alone. . . I'm here!"

The wall between them shattered. For the first time, their minds touched, and his sorrow stilled her being, their minds groping in wonderment at the presence of each other. They came together, encapsulated in a single moment. Everything else fell away. She felt his surprise at the discovery of her.

"You are not alone," she said. "I hear you. I feel you. I feel . . . for you."

His fingers stopped moving on the strings. "Who are you?" he whispered in amazement. His voice was musical in her mind. She saw his face: black mohawk, harsh and angular, scarred and beautiful. Mindy knew he could see her just as clearly.

"Who are you?" he asked again.

She knew what to do. "Look," Mindy answered, "see me." And she opened the door to herself.

Her life rolled through his mind, every moment, so that he knew her as well as she knew him. It was more intimate than any lovemaking could ever have been. She offered him comfort, and though he was hesitant after grieving so long, he felt the love of her embrace and gave himself up to her. The memory of Susan was strong in him, but Mindy showed him how to live with the memory of that love—how to love again and have hope.

She could see where he was, high in the Colorado mountains. Far, but not so far.

She whispered, "Michael, I will come to you."

"Yes," he answered, "but be very careful. The way is dangerous."

Images of scavs flashed through her mind. She felt his hatred of them, and more, a download of experiences, emotions, history, and knowledge. Through their sharing, she learned how to handle a rifle, to ride a motorcycle. They were mirrors, no longer alone.

"I'll be careful," she promised. "I'll be with you soon."

"Yes. You're only a few days away. Be careful and timid."

"I'll bring you the power of the sun."

"Mindy," he said, and she saw him smile through his tears.

"Michael," she answered—and then he

was gone from her mind.

Mindy wiped salty tears from her face as the sea gently lapped the beach with waves of green phosphorescent fire. The stars above seemed close and friendly.

She reached up and touched her hair, long and soft. Her hair. But Mindy felt a hardness in her that had not been there before, an edge as sharp and keen as a fighting blade. But it was not a bad hardness; it was the heart of a defender. There were other differences too, she knew, that she would discover in time. She could feel them settling in her, creating the new, stronger person she needed to be. Stronger, yet still half a person without Michael. Together, they would be one.

Mindy sat until she had regained her composure, then went back to the Habitat. She called an emergency meeting with the occupants and announced her intention to leave. She beat down their protests with determined silence, waiting until they had nothing more to say.

"I love you all. You have been my family. But now it's time for me to see what's left in the world. If there is anything good, and if I survive, I will return."

At her insistence, they voted in a new director. She spent the rest of the evening saying her goodbyes. Maybe one day she would come back. But all that mattered to her now was Michael—Michael and LightForm.

First light found her on the mainland,

walking the highway in jeans and boots, carrying a rucksack filled with dried food, four LightForm cells, and a portable hard drive with all the information she needed to grow the crystal again. She carried a small LightForm-powered Geiger counter clipped to her shirt. A Glock 9MM was holstered at her side.

In the empty husk of Rudolph, Texas, she searched from house to house until she found a Yamaha superbike small enough for her to comfortably ride. Drawing on the skills she had learned from Michael, she scavenged a helmet, spark plugs, a battery, and some tools, and overhauled the cycle. In the closet of the same house, she found a leather jacket that was in wearable condition and fit her well. The sun was falling when she kicked the bike to life.

She spent the night in Rudolph, and the next day, searching further, she found a scoped deer rifle, along with enough ammunition for her to practice with it and still have a box in her backpack. She left when the sun topped the eastern horizon, rifle slung across her back. Every mile would bring her closer to Michael. So, with the wind in her hair, Mindy rode.

THE TURNING
OF MANY
HOOPS

Luke and his party had passed through Telluride, Colorado, a few hours before and were making good time toward the Utah border. Mike rode ahead, scouting, wanting to be alone for a while.

The mountain highway was clear, with not a rusted car or truck in sight, and the road cried out to be driven. Mike obliged and hammered the throttle on the Harley, enjoying the bright, sunny sky and the wind in the short, prickly hairs of his mohawk. Ellie had trimmed it back. The bullet wound in his side was healing well. He was fit.

Static crackled in his radio headset. *"Don't get too far ahead, Mike,"* Luke requested. *"There are enough low hills that I could lose your signal."*

"Don't sweat it," he answered, feeling good and cocky and alive.

As he rounded a bend in the highway, Mike saw a small collection of dusty, deserted buildings. He downshifted and pulled the M4 from its scabbard, holding the weapon in his left hand as he steered with his right.

"We got a town here," he said into the headset. "More of a crossing. Old gas station, a general store, couple of houses. Sign says this is Paradox. Looks deserted."

Luke said, *"Take a look at the fuel pumps and see if they have diesel. We could use more fuel."*

Mike idled over and shut down the motorcycle, scanning the windows of the station before dropping the kickstand. He got off the bike, eyeing the dust and dirt over the driveway for tracks. None. But something did not feel right. He felt . . . watched.

He ambled over to the pumps, keeping the battle rifle ready. The pumps were faded with a fine patina of rust. After three years, the legends were still readable. The fuel was from a company that had spilled enough oil once to ruin the Alaska coast. Mike laughed at the label on the pumps: Environmentally Safe Fuel. A lone pump at the end with a dusty green label read, Diesel Fuel No. 2.

"Yup. We have diesel," he said into the headset. "The pump doesn't look touched."

Mike kept his eyes moving over the area, looking for anything that was out of place.

"Good. Hold tight," Luke replied. *"We'll be*

there in a few minutes."

Mike suddenly felt exposed. "I'm going to look around a little. I'll meet you at the station."

"Roger. Don't go too far."

The station was a two-part building, a front counter room with a washroom and storage attached to a two-port garage. The glass in the entry door had been shattered long ago. Everything lay under a thick layer of dust. It was undisturbed. Mike slipped catlike through the doorway into the garage, rifle ready. Nobody. The air in the garage was dry and cool, heavy with the smells of motor oil, gas, and rusting metal. The bay doors were so dirty that they were opaque.

The door at the back of the garage was sticky and did not open easily. He shouldered it open. In the light from outside, he saw another set of tracks on the floor beside his own. Fresh. Boot tracks. A hot, slick guitar riff began to play in his head. Mike smiled and studied the floor closely. There was one set of tracks, big, from a man well over six feet by the length of his stride. He had come through the back door and stayed near the back of the garage. A careful man.

The mechanics' toolboxes had been picked through carefully, everything laid neatly back into place, only the telltale gleam of newly uncovered metal offering a clue. Other things appeared to be missing from the walls: belts, hoses, and clamps.

The man had walked out the way he

came, almost in the same footprints. He had known exactly what he wanted. While there was nothing to give him any indication of what the man was about, something in Mike's head screamed, *"Scav!"* over and over. He clicked the fire selector switch to full auto, readied the knives and pistols holstered on his belt, and peered out the back door.

Scanning the ground, he saw that the man had walked on dried grass to cover his footprints. Mike studied the clumps of grass with a monocular. They were scattered between here and the houses. He was rewarded with the partial track of a boot heel. Mike was certain the man was in one of the houses.

He keyed the headset. "Luke, hold tight a few minutes. I think we got company here."

"You want backup?"

"No. It's only one. A scav, I think."

"Don't kill him unless you have to."

Mike heard the command in Luke's tone and thought, *Fuck that.*

"I'll let you know," he answered.

Any scav he saw was dead meat. Mike turned off the headset. This was his hunt.

He went back through the front of the garage and ran like hell to the front of the general store. There he crouched low, below the line of the glass display windows fronting the store. The back of the building was only a few yards from the first house. The door was locked. Mike used the butt of a fighting knife to tap a small hole in the door glass—enough to get his hand through. The glass tinkled as it fell, noticeable, but not too loud. He reached the lock and twisted it open, then swung the door wide and rolled through. He ended up on his feet and ran to the counter on the right side of the store. Mike cleared it in a leap, rifle casting back and forth for a target. There was nobody behind the counter. Using it for cover, he scanned the rest of the store. It was empty.

An open doorway at the rear of the store led to a stockroom full of cans. Mike picked one up and examined the label in the dim light. Peaches, nitrogen-packed, with a shelf life of ten or more years. Survival stuff, still good. He looked at the wealth of food around him, put down the can, and eased open the door at the rear of the stock room. Light flooded around its edges. Mike opened it further. He looked closely, but saw no signs of life around either house.

The scav had to have heard the Harley. But where was the bastard hiding? Mike had a momentary thought that maybe he should be careful and wait for Luke. But his hatred of the scavs was too powerful.

The guitar was now roaring in his head, drowning out all save the desire to take down his enemy. He waited for five beats, counting under his breath, shoved open the door, and ran for the houses, cutting left and right as erratically as he could to make himself less of a target.

The first house was a two-story, dirty white stucco box with a black tarpaper roof. Mike threw himself up against its back, below the window line, and waited silently. Nothing moved or seemed out of place. He checked his watch and knew that Luke would be trying to call him.

Mike took a fast look around the corner, to the narrow corridor formed by the two houses, and saw a motorcycle hidden under a tarp. It was clean. Curtains fluttered through the broken first-floor window of the other house. Mike crept to the motorcycle, ready to explode into action.

As he touched the bike, he heard a strange rustling sound behind him, followed by a voice, so quickly that he had no time to respond.

"Bang, bang! You're dead."

Mike stood still as a statue, knowing that to make any sudden move was death. He slowly turned his head until he could look over his shoulder.

The scav was one of the largest men Mike had ever seen, over six-and-a-half feet, ripped with solid muscle. His hair was long, raven-black, and flowing, framing the solid, armor-like bones of his face and flattened nose. A fresh, thin scar traversed one of his cheeks. He was bare-chested, wearing only stained OCP fatigues and calf-high riding boots. Strange black tattoos flowed along the musculature of his arms and chest. The M4 carbine he held looked like a toy in his massive hands. The scav grinned, and Mike knew he had fucked up big time.

Even before Mike could try anything, the scav said, "Make a move, and I'll end you. Drop the rifle and turn slowly, hands as high as you can get 'em."

Mike let the rifle slip from his fingers to the ground. After he turned, the scav made him drop every weapon visible on his belt. He looked at the window the scav had come through.

"You should have checked the houses first. You were doing very well until you saw the bike. It was bait."

As his last knife hit the ground, Mike spit out, "Fuckin' scav!"

The scav's eyes narrowed. "Maybe I was. But I found more important things to do." He examined Mike with a critical eye. "You could be road scum yourself. You've got the right attitude. Who the fuck are you?"

Mike smirked at the scav. "I kill scavs. The only thing you got on me is your gun. Without it, I'd tear you apart."

The scav grinned again. "Oh, yeah?" He pointed the rifle barrel at the ground. "Pick up a blade. Any blade, your choice."

"Ha!" Mike laughed. "You'll blast me as soon as I touch it."

The big man lowered the M4. "What's the matter, boy? Ain't you got balls?"

Heat prickled Mike's brow. The scav watched as he knelt and picked up a Bowie-style fighting knife. Their eyes stayed locked as the scav put down his rifle and moved away from the pile of weapons. Mike followed so that the scav remained facing him. The scav's hand whirred, and the double-edged blade of a butterfly knife appeared. He flipped the knife again, and it flowed like molten silver from hand to hand.

"Come on, boy. Let's see how good you are. Cut me up!"

Mike came in fast with the blade inverted. He lashed out twice and tried to stick the scav with his backhand, moving like a cat. But the scav was much, much faster. He blocked each of Mike's attacks and then backed up a step, waiting for Mike's next move. Mike attacked again with redoubled fury, slashing and stabbing, forcing the scav back against the wall of the house. But even though the scav gave way, he blocked each of Mike's attacks.

Just before his back touched the wall, the scav's hands twitched, and Mike felt a line of fire on his left arm. He backed away, cursing, as blood welled from the slash.

"You're very fast," said the scav. "But your attacks lack focus and direction. You'd be much more lethal if you stopped being so berserk."

The scav darted in close, swatting aside Mike's defense, slapped him in the face, and backed away. As he did, Mike felt pain in his chest and saw the widening line of red extending across the front of his shirt from nipple to nipple.

"Never let yourself get distracted. It could mean your life."

Mike wiped the blood from his front and knew that this scav could take him at any time. He had the choice of delaying long enough for Luke to get here to pull his fat out of the fire, or giving it his best and going down with blood on his hands. Then he would be with Susan again. Isn't that what he had wanted for so long? This was his day to die. With that thought in mind, Mike said goodbye to life and drove in for the kill.

He came in low, reversing the blade and thrusting upwards, aiming for the heart. The scav grunted in surprise as he just managed to block Mike's attack, but not before the Bowie slashed him. Blood welled over the cut running from his wrist to his elbow. Mike kept close, pushing the scav back. Their hands locked on each other's wrists, and Mike screamed in anger as he tried to break free. He stomped on the scav's instep and tried for the knee, but the scav had the advantages of strength, weight, and experience.

The scav let go of Mike's knife wrist and clubbed him with a fist like an anvil. The blow made the earth and sky wheel. Mike felt the ground collide with his head. He lay there, stunned, feeling blood on his face, trying to push himself up. The outline of the roof was hazy against the sky. He saw the scav approach him through doubled vision, the butterfly knife flipping open and closed, open and closed.

"You put up a good fight, boy," the scav said, "but now the lesson is over."

"Then kill me, fucker," Mike croaked, anger brightening his eyes.

The knife flicked open. "I'll say one thing for you, man," the scav said with respect, "you do know how to hate well."

The scav knelt and tugged at Mike's mohawk, pulling his head back. "I promise you it'll be fast," he said.

As he raised the knife to slash, Luke's voice rang out between the houses. "Kill him, Billy, and you will never find what you're looking for. Plus, you'll be dead as well."

Billy looked up at the face from his dream. He dropped the butterfly knife and scrambled back, leaving Mike room to roll over and come to his knees. Mike reached for the knife, but Luke's voice stopped him.

"Drop your fight, Mike. This man is one of us."

"No," Mike whispered. "He's a scav. It can't be."

"It can," Luke answered, "and it is."

The others came into the space between the houses. Cal extended an arm to help Mike off the ground. He stood groggily and let Cal take his weight.

Luke put out his hand to Billy. "Do you

have the strength to take it?"

Billy hesitated, thinking about what he had done . . . what he had been. Fighting was all he knew. But the promise of the future was what he needed. Salvation, here, within his reach. He took Luke's hand and let himself be drawn into proximity with the others. He gasped as he felt the click of bonding between them. Briefly, he shared their spirits. He felt Mike's sadness and knew his hatred for the scavs. He felt shame, and the others felt it too, as well as his desire to atone, to find salvation, forgiveness.

But only one could grant it: Mike. He saw the depths of Billy's spirit and knew the honesty of his desire. If Mike could not find it in himself to forgive Billy, the Navajo would never be one of the Seven, and their task would never be complete. The fate of the world hung on his decision. Mike looked into his own heart, at his black desire for revenge. It had been an ineffectual journey to end his pain. And now the weight of this was on him. There was no justice in it.

He saw how empty he had become. It was time to put aside hate and learn to live again. This was the fire in which the steel in him would be tempered. So, though it cost him as much as it had to lose Susan, Mike granted Billy forgiveness with a cry that saddened them all. Then he staggered away under the turmoil of emotions he carried, beyond the edge of the town, until they were far away and he could grieve.

Luke said, "Let him go. He needs to be alone."

Billy rubbed his eyes. For the first time in years, he felt hope. "Luke, we have to talk. You're in more danger than you know. Your past is coming back to haunt you."

"Hold it for now," Luke answered. "First we eat, then talk. Search the store," he called to Ellie, Cal, and Tony. "We'll stay here tonight."

They dined lavishly on food meant to last for years, canned meats and vegetables that were full of the fresh taste of earth and sun, nostalgia from a world now gone. One of the houses had a gas range with propane still in the tank. The screened front porch made a comfortable place to eat. Mike stayed away, still entrapped in his emotions. Ellie brought a plate to him, but he didn't eat, keeping both hands clenched on his guitar.

"Don't worry," Luke told her. "He'll come around."

Dessert was instant coffee and a large cherry cobbler made by Ellie and Cal, who turned out to have quite a talent for baking from scratch.

"Do you think we'll have fresh coffee again in our lifetimes?" Cal asked.

"It's a long way to South America and Hawaii," said Luke. "If you ever make it there, you might. Maybe someday, there will be enough people again to make trade routes."

"Cal, go down there and bring back some living coffee bushes and start a coffee plantation," said Ellie. "Become a sailor, scholar, and trader."

"Ha!" laughed Cal, pleased with the idea. "Captain Cal, the black terror of the seas!"

Tony ran in with a book and gave it to Cal. Cal had begun to read to the boy, everything from Dr. Seuss to Shakespeare. Tony listened with a hunger, always wanting to hear more, curled up in a ball next to him, reassured by the man's presence.

Luke nodded his head at Billy. The Indian had been quiet during dinner, keeping apart, hesitant to intrude on the familiarity that had grown between the others. The two left and walked towards the road, watching the sun fall behind the mountains towering over Paradox.

Luke said, "I know something of your past from the vision. Though I can do some extraordinary things, I cannot read minds. You said my past is coming back to haunt me?"

Like the soldier he was, Billy delivered the briefing he had been building in his head ever since leaving Pierce and the preacher. He detailed the strange bond between the two: a mutual hatred of Luke.

"I can understand why Jed hates me,'" said Luke. "We had a run-in in the ruins of Minneapolis. But why Pierce? It's amazing that he survived, though it should be no surprise. He is a highly capable warrior and leader. We were close friends."

"As I understand it, you were partners. Pierce went to Las Vegas. The war nearly killed him. The fact that he lived and you had been lucky enough to die started his resentment. It became hatred with no outlet. Had you gone to Vegas with him, you would have survived together. But you were not there to watch his back. His hatred grew until everything he destroyed was an effigy of you. It's pretty obsessive, the only thing he gets crazy about.

"Then Jed showed up with his wild tale about you and the motor home, the 'MOC,' as Pierce calls it. He wants your head for revenge, and the MOC as his command post. Jed has some way to track you. They know where you . . . we . . . are now. I don't know where we're going, but we better get there fast. You know how Pierce leads. His troops are very good."

Luke answered, "But we have resources they don't."

Luke saw the puzzlement in Billy's expression and said, "Never mind. You'll see when the time comes."

Billy reached inside his shirt and withdrew a rectangular package of deer hide. "I also have this for you."

Luke took it and felt the powerful fragility of the eagle's feather. "Thank you. I know it has taken courage to come here and be with us."

As Billy turned into the night, Luke stopped him. "Billy, I can't promise you life, and I can't promise you a future. But the road we all travel can get you where you want to be. There is hope here for you."

Billy sighed, and Luke heard the raw emotion in his voice. "Hey man, it's enough for me. It's enough."

Luke listened until Billy's footsteps faded into the twilight. He could sense the hoops of his life shifting and coming together as they completed their revolutions. There were so many, decades in turning, spanning everything that was him.

Jed was a small hoop that had turned in a matter of weeks. In him, Luke felt the sly, deadly touch of something that seemed familiar, like the déjà vu of a nightmare that fades as you wake up. In the light of what he knew now, it felt God-driven. But which god? There were, he was coming to realize, so many.

Through Jed, the might of Pierce's commandos was now directed at him. And sadly, the hoop of years had brought his old friend back into his life this time as an enemy. He knew Pierce as well as he did himself. Matthew would stop at nothing to find and confront him. Even with what Luke had become, he would have a hard time defeating Pierce. When—and there would be a when—they did battle, it would be to the death, hand to hand, knife to knife.

The last, smallest hoop was Billy. He had brought Luke the feather, the final item he needed to complete the pipe. He gently opened the package and beheld the feather. It glowed in the last light of day. Billy had wrapped the quill end, leaving a string so it could be fastened to the pipe. As soon as the pipe was complete, Luke would be holding a powerful piece of magic—a magic that was still beyond his understanding. He had so much to do, so much to understand, and so little time.

Though the air was warm during the day, nights from here on out would be cool, and early winter was not far off. He was much closer to where he had seen the people going in the Dream. He could feel it. He had to have his people, the Key of Seven, complete and in place before the first snow fell. But where was the place? What about the mask and the Manitou? Too many questions. Bringing the pipe and feather together would bring him answers.

As the sun fell behind the mountains, Luke heard Mike cry out, "Mindy!"

There was joy in the music man's voice. As he heard the name, Luke saw the girl's face. He had not dreamed that she and Mike would touch each other across the distance. Here too was a hoop. If she and Mike were now connected, she would find them in a few days. Luke put the hide-wrapped feather inside his shirt. At dawn he would assemble the pipe . . . and meet whatever came next.

He left hours before sunrise, hiking across the dark, rocky land until he came to a low mesa. Luke used sagebrush to sweep clean a circle on the rock, then stripped and rubbed himself with the pungent leaves to purify himself. He sat, pipe in one hand and feather in the other, waiting for the sun to top the mountains. It came slowly, creeping over the jagged peaks. When there was enough light to see, Luke tied the feather to the pipe.

Complete, the pipe began to glow and tremble in his hands. He felt the awesome power of it course through his body into the earth, like a charge of lightning. Luke stood and held the pipe high, first to the east, and called out, "Grandfathers, hear me!"

He faced south, then west, then north, repeating the call in each direction. The mesa shuddered, sending small rocks skittering across its surface. The sky hissed with fire as the Hoop swept down from the sky and pulled him in.

In his hands, the pipe shone as if made from platinum. It hummed with energy. For the first time, he felt the deep-seated, truly spiritual meaning of *Wakan*. Luke held the pipe to the compass points twice more, calling out at each quarter, "Hear me! This is my prayer."

As he finished, a faintly glowing path formed on the mesa, leading down into the canyons on the far side. He had left at dawn; here it was twilight. Holding the pipe firmly in both hands, Luke stepped onto the glowing path and let it lead him into the night.

It seemed only a short time before he arrived at the mouth of a canyon. The opening was so narrow that two men could barely pass abreast. Yet when he entered, the canyon was immense, an amphitheater as great as the Grand Canyon. But it was what the canyon held that took his breath away.

At the center was a bright, eternal fire ringed by thousands upon thousands of figures of different shapes and sizes. Some were beautiful. Some were horrifying beyond belief. Some were man-sized and smaller. Some were so great that their features were lost in altitude. A small, furred creature with a humped back, about the size of a house cat, sped past him, stopping briefly to blow a few notes on a flute. "Be humble, yet be courageous!" the notes said. Each of the beings regarded him silently, expectantly. For the first time, Luke beheld the complete pantheon of the Amerindian gods.

There was a sense here of agelessness, gods young and old encompassing the spread of indigenous peoples from the Bering land bridge across all of North America. Some gods had been worshipped by races of men that were no longer in existence, their essence merged into other gods through myth and stories, carried forward in the fabric of the story that each generation had woven to help define who they were.

Luke studied the circle of gods carefully and found a gap three-quarters of the way around the circle, seemingly miles away. The gap was just wide enough for him to fit in. Since he was bringing the pipe to the party, it only made sense that he should be sitting at the fire.

Luke walked clockwise around the innermost circle of gods, knowing it was the right direction to go, feeling them study him with senses greater than mere sight. Though the circle was miles in diameter, it seemed as if he only took a hundred steps to reach his place in the circle. The fire warmed him the entire way.

To the left sat Thunderbird. Luke nodded in recognition. Elsewhere, he saw Stone Smith and Buffalo Woman, smiling warmly at him. To the right sat Teacher Oldman, eyes bright with humor, intelligence, and expectation. He smiled at Luke and patted the ground beside him in an unmistakable gesture: sit. He did, and the old man placed a square of white hide on the ground in front of him.

Luke placed the pipe on the hide and waited for something to happen. Nothing did. All the gods looked at him, waiting for something. Helpless, Luke turned to Thunderbird. Its face was expressionless, but the meaning was clear: figure this out. He turned to Teacher Oldman.

Teacher winked and whispered, "Speak to them."

Luke nodded and bowed his head as he collected his thoughts.

"I am a man. I come before you, outside of the races and creeds that brought you to life . . . or that you brought to life. In the visions you have given me, I have seen just how few humans are left. I see how mankind must band together if we are to survive. I understand that your survival depends on ours. With each day, what you have asked of me becomes clearer. Yet I fail to understand, why me?

"Yes, I am a man, now among gods. Without truly understanding why, yet feeling it is right, I have made a pipe of peace. I have carved the pipestone under the watchful eyes of Stone Smith. I have hunted buffalo in the old way with the spirits of hunters from many tribes and ages, with the help of Buffalo Woman. With Thunderbird, I have found the spirit feather of an eagle. I have made this pipe and now bring it to you. I bring this pipe to you. Where would you have me go from here?"

As Luke finished, it seemed that all the gods spoke at once amongst themselves, debating. When they finished, three gods stepped forward to face Luke. Neon bolts of blue electricity crackled and popped about them as they moved. They were identical in appearance, each dressed in black loincloths and moccasins, with black hair and iridescent black skin. Each had vivid yellow lightning bolts on their chest, arms, and cheeks. Each god held a shield, also black, decorated with lightning, and spears with heads, as far as Luke could tell, fashioned from lightning stabilized into razor points.

"These are the Thunder Beings," whispered Teacher.

When they spoke, the sky echoed with thunder. "It is good you have fashioned the pipe and brought it to Us. We know the root cause of your actions is to get back what you think Manitou has taken from you. But you have also accepted the weight of bringing our worlds back together. Divine quests ask much of those who accept them."

The pantheon shouted affirmation. The ground shuddered with the strength of their voices.

The beings thundered, "You wish to know more. The pipe is the first symbol of what we hope will come, what all gods the world over need to come. The bowl of the pipe is of sacred stone, the strength and stability of the earth. The stem of the pipe is of a bison's leg, a symbol of all that lives on the face of the land. The eagle's feather is of the sky and all that dwells there. And the carvings are a prayer to unite them all together, earth, life, and sky, into one life. This must be the shape of the world to come, if any of us, man or god, are to survive. One life."

"Ah," said Luke. This was what his father had tried to teach him so many years before. He heard the chanting of the boy at Wounded Knee. He also heard and smiled at the memory of Pierce and him in the helicopter head-nodding to Bob Marley. The beats overlaid like harmonious twins.

"I see now. Unity. One life. One love."

The old man filled the pipe and handed it to him with a small, burning branch to light it.

"You have done well," the Thunders said. "We have a gift for you. In your most desperate hour, say a sacred word, and you will receive this help."

Luke looked in the direction the Thunders pointed and saw what they wished him to see. He watched it unfold across the night sky. It was a gift he could understand.

Luke bowed his head as the Thunder Beings whispered the sacred word. Luke committed it to memory, knowing that he would soon have a use for it.

"I thank you deeply," he said. "I am unworthy."

"Yet you continue to prove your worth. Smoke with us now, for one life, or as you said, one love."

Luke said, "Yes. To one love," and lit the pipe.

He puffed three times, raising the pipe to the sky, then passed it to his right. The tobacco was strong and harsh, yet full of memories: woodsmoke and autumn, golden, ripe fields of harvest, the rich lives of man and god integrally connected. Memories of eons of mankind following mammoths and buffalo across the plains, warring, loving, living, and dying. He watched the pipe pass from hand to hand to claw and other godly appendages.

As the pipe made its way around the far-flung circle, Luke became light-headed. He felt his spirit separate from his body and hover, held to the Spirit World by a small thread of being.

The voices of the pantheon united in a singing chant that moved in time with his heartbeat. Each beat pushed him farther from his body out into the star-brushed blackness of the night.

"Dream," they sang.

And Luke walked along a dry, dusty ridge top. To the north and east were low mountains covered in pine and fir. Behind him were the snow-capped peaks of a larger range. It was pleasantly warm, and the wind carried high desert scents of rock, grass, and sage. He felt that he was much farther west than he had started—maybe Idaho, Oregon, or Washington.

To his right was a wiry old man with gray hair pulled back into a ponytail. He was dressed in old faded jeans, a denim shirt, and good, sturdy boots. Though gray and wrinkled, his back was straight, and he walked with strength.

"Who are you?" Luke asked him.

The old man had a strong, slightly hoarse voice heavily accented by his native tongue. "I am Joseph Three Clouds. Among my people, the Nez Percé, I am simply Old Joe. In this dream, I am your teacher. But also, I hope to be your friend. I will show you what I have to show you, and perhaps you will see me again."

As Joseph spoke, the earth around them changed. Luke recognized the low, snow-covered area bisected by a stream and lightly covered with thin groups of trees.

"This is Wounded Knee Creek. The date is December twenty-ninth, 1890. You have been here twice now."

An Indian camp sat by the creek. Luke saw hundreds of cavalry soldiers on the hills in and around the camp. The tension was intense. Soldiers were disarming a crowd of Indians. A large pile of rifles lay at the soldiers' feet.

Joseph spoke. "This is the band of Big Foot. They are one of the many tribes who have gathered to dance the Ghost Dance. The Indian nation is in despair. They see everything they know fading like smoke in the wind and gather to dance to save their way of life, or what is left of it. They have nothing but a small promise of hope. You are about to see that hope extinguished."

A cavalry officer tried to disarm an Indian wearing a white sheet over his head, in imitation of the white man's ghost. The warrior refused to let go of the rifle, and they struggled.

"The man in the sheet is Yellow Bird. Without his rifle, he cannot defend his family or hunt for them. He will not give up this fundamental right. Would you?"

Luke said, "Never. "

"The soldiers are here because the white people are afraid of the Ghost Dance. They believe it could bring war or something even more frightening, a return to the way of life before the white man came. A time when Native Americans fought and warred across the plains in ways that were brutal and savage to the minds of white men. The whites hope the soldiers will make this threat to their Christian, civilized way of life . . . go away."

There was a muffled shot, and the captain fell back, clutching his chest. There were confused shouts . . . and then the soldiers opened fire.

Luke watched in horror as the soldiers raked the camp with cannons and gunfire. Bullets stitched across the teepees, mowing down fleeing men, women, and children alike. Campfires were scattered, and teepees broke into flame. A group of Indian warriors fought the soldiers, hands against guns, as they struggled to get their rifles back. A few managed to make short stands before withering hails of lead brought them down.

The soldiers chased them all down through thick drifts of gun smoke, slaughtering women, children, and warriors with brutal efficiency. They left behind shattered dreams and victims, women and children whose only crime had been to hope.

"The Wounded Knee Massacre broke the Sioux nation's back, but because of that one special young boy, the dream did not die. It crossed time to find you. The Ghost Dance was the vision of a world where the bad white people and all of their civilization were rolled up and removed from the land, leaving only good people and the way of life that ruled before the colonialization of North America began. How will Luke Kimball bring back the land as it once was and restore the Hoop of all people?"

The terrible vision faded, to be replaced with a large clearing. In the center stood a gray, weathered tree, as great in circumference as a giant redwood, but with the bonsai, windswept flow of a broadleaf tree, branches bare and lifeless. A red band had been painted around its circumference. Dancers circled the tree. Their cheeks and foreheads had been painted with brilliant red. The dancers were of many peoples, of many times: young and old, men, women, and children. Luke could feel the joyous power of their hope. The steps they danced were familiar to him now.

"The Ghost Dance," he whispered.

"Yes. The vision for the Ghost Dance first came to Wovoka, a Paiute shaman. He was the first indigo man, one who sees across boundaries of race and religion to the full potential of mankind. He evangelized his vision across tribal boundaries. In the ideology of the Ghost Dance, all who treated all men as equals would remain in the land. The Indians would have welcomed them with an eagle feather for their hair, marking them as brothers."

"All men living together as one, in harmony with the land. Unity. One love."

"Yes. The vision was exceptionally strong in one Sioux, a man named Black Elk. He was truly a visionary who only wanted for his people —and all peoples—an end to war and to live in harmony. Behold his vision."

One of the dancers became more noticeable. He was a strong-faced young medicine man with flowing black hair. He wore a hide shirt covered with intricate designs—a medicine shirt. Luke became one with Black Elk and felt the power of his vision.

Overwhelmed with the power of the Ghost Dance, Black Elk fell to the ground, and they sped off across the hills, following a golden eagle to a beautiful green land. There were six villages in the land, and Black Elk/Luke landed at the edge of the sixth one. They were met by twelve men. They took him to the center of the villages, where the great tree Luke had just seen was alive and in full bloom. Its thrumming song powered the earth.

Under the tree was a man with his arms held wide in front of him. Black Elk could not tell what people he came from. But Luke, seeing with Black Elk's eyes, realized with a shock that the man was himself. His hair was long and hanging loose. On the left side of his head, an eagle feather had been tied to his hair. His body was ridged with muscle and painted red.

As they watched, the man with Luke's face began to change and soften, multicolored lights giving him a powerful aura. Intricate designs whirled across his face and body.

The Luke in front of the tree spoke. "My life is such that all earthly beings and growing things belong with me. Your father, the Great Spirit, has said this. You too must say this."

The man leaned back and became one with the tree. Luke, abruptly in his own body again, blinked and found himself again in the forest clearing with the great tree. Around him were tall, snow-covered mountains. A small group of tents and teepees were at the northern edge of the clearing.

Joseph spoke. "This is the Tree of Life that has lived forever. The synergy of man and gods gave it life, and the Tree unified our worlds. It became lost from this world when mankind stopped believing in their gods. Life needs a connection to the balance to perpetuate. The balance must be restored. It is here where the balance is centered. This is where you must bring the Key of Seven.

"Tell me, Luke, can you make this Tree breathe the world again? Can you start life on a new turn of the Hoop?"

Luke felt the rock beneath his knees, the harshness of wilderness tobacco still in his lungs. He raised his eye to the dawn of a new day. The Hoop was high and thin in the sky. Joseph was gone; his dream was done.

Only then did he face the rising sun and say, "For the hope of all men, I will, Old Joe. I will."

TRAPPED

Oppressive heat blanketed the Sevier desert in west central Utah, softening the asphalt of the road beneath and making the gun-barrel-straight highway flicker into infinity. Mindy screamed down the highway at over ninety miles an hour. Her leather jacket and helmet kept the dust and bugs off her, but did nothing to cool down the oppressive heat.

She traveled by day, both for the sake of speed and to see any ambush she might miss in the night. The motorcycle Mindy rode had already saved her from one death with a simple burst of speed. Bullets had hailed on the pavement around her. Mindy had slammed the throttle, lifting the front wheel as she hugged the bike's low-slung saddle. "Fuck you!" she had screamed as she roared away from the ambush, laughing at the danger, giddy with the power of her own life.

On either side of the highway, the ground was littered with large boulders and volcanic rock. The barren, gray peaks of the Confusion

Range ran jagged across the horizon. The land was arid and lifeless, except for snakes, spiders, and scorpions. There was no place for an ambush as far as she could see.

In their nightly communiqués, Mike and Mindy had agreed that it was best for her to avoid trouble, and fight only to save her life. That was fine, because her overwhelming desire was only to be with Mike. And she had driven herself relentlessly to get to him.

Originally, Mindy had thought to drive through Salt Lake City and connect with Mike and the others in Oregon. But he had warned her away from northern Utah, at the advice of Kimball. The entire eastern edge of the Great Salt Lake was still a radioactive pile of rubble that would probably glow into the next century. So, here she was, skirting some of the most radioactive real estate in the nation to get to Winnemucca, Nevada; from there, only a short drive to the Oregon state line.

Mike and the others had traveled the same route a few days earlier. As they grew closer, they spent more and more time "talking" each night, the decreasing distance adding strength to their telepathy. They were waiting for her in the high desert a few miles north of the Oregon/Nevada border.

Tony, the green-eyed boy, had called wild horses into their camp the night before. She had watched through Mike's eyes. Billy was teaching

Mike how to fight with a knife. Although Mike wondered if he could ever like the Indian, he had accepted him—how could he not?—and respected the warrior's skills. She would be one of them soon, the last of the Key of Seven. Mindy did not know exactly what the Key was, but she felt Mike's urgency, and it took all she had not to let the motorcycle go hurtling down the road even faster.

With her mind on Mike, Mindy missed the scavs coming from behind until they had her bracketed. She saw their shadows first, black and stretching in front of them on the highway. It was enough to make her gasp and almost lose control of the motorcycle. There were two, both on café bikes like hers, wearing helmets and a variety of faded battle gear. As they drew abreast of her, Mindy took her hand off the throttle, reached inside her jacket for the .38 Airweight, and blasted the one on her right off his motorcycle. The bike flipped end over end into the desert.

Mindy switched the revolver into her left hand and pointed it at the other rider. She could not see his face through the smoked glass of his visor. He lifted one hand off the handlebars in a gesture of surrender, then pointed at his helmet. Mindy saw with dismay the thin gleam of an antenna.

Looking in the small side-view mirror, she saw a motorcade of trucks and motorcycles filling the highway behind her. The scav dropped back until he was lost in their midst. Mindy eased off as military humvees pulled onto the road a mile ahead, completely blocking all escape. The ground on either side of her was so rocky that the Yamaha would never make it. They had her trapped.

She stopped the motorcycle a hundred yards from the roadblock. The motorcade behind gave her the same amount of space. Armed men and women rose from behind piles of volcanic rock on either side of the road. Mindy counted well over a hundred. She gunned the throttle desperately, spinning the Yamaha in a smoking circle, looking for any way out. There was none. She let the cycle back down to idle, feeling fear replace the steel of her strength.

"Michael, help me!" she prayed. "I'm in big trouble! Mike! Hear me!"

Mike rolled up from the ground and wiped dirt from his face. He picked up his knife, point down, and angled it along his arm. It was actually a piece of wood carved to look like a knife. He darted in high and dropped at the last moment to make his attack. Billy blocked it, but staggered back at the force of it.

"Strong bugger, aren't you! That was good. But you have to turn the knife sooner. Block and cut at the same time." Billy pantomimed the technique. "See what I mean? Try it again."

Mike nodded and readied himself for a new approach. It was their second day in Oregon. They had stopped at a road station between Blue Mountain Pass and Basque on Highway 95, in the heart of the Alvord Desert. It was some of the lightest country Mike had ever seen, uniform shades of beige and pale reds, and hot like a furnace during the day.

A Quonset hut hid the MOC from the highway. They slept inside the coolness of the building, grateful for the space after the cramped, close quarters of the motor home. They had stopped to rest and wait for Mindy. Mike had assured Luke she was only a few days away. The reality of her coming had given everyone butterflies in their stomachs, especially Mike. She was the last of the Seven. None of them knew what would happen when they were all together.

They all used their waiting time differently. Ellie was teaching Tony to read and write, with occasional guidance from Cal. Mike had asked Billy to teach him how to fight better. Luke worked on the MOC, making minor repairs and adjustments, while the image of the Tree of Life stayed prominent in his mind.

Mike backed off, wiping grimy sweat from his face. Billy dropped into a new stance and motioned Mike to come at him again. Mike began to crab in sideways, then stopped, face strangely slack. Billy wrinkled his brow as the wooden knife fell from Mike's fingers.

"You okay, bro?" he asked.

Mike didn't answer. He fell to his knees, face ashen, mind in another place. "Get Luke," he whispered.

Billy ran.

Mike shared Mindy's fears from two states away. He saw flashes through her eyes, the trap, the size of their force. He gave her his strength and told her what to do.

"Survive, no matter the cost."

But he kept behind walls in his mind the queasy fear that the price for survival would be greater than she—or he—could pay.

Luke, Billy, and the others came at a dead run.

Luke asked, "What's wrong?" But he already knew the answer.

Mike held his eyes, and Luke saw his hopeless fury. "They have Mindy. Pierce and the preacher have Mindy."

They had her pinned in the center of the highway, broiling under the white-hot sun. She unzipped her leather jacket and put the revolver in her waistband. There was enough firepower out there to shred her. But she would disarm herself only when they told her to. Then she felt Mike in her mind. He touched her long enough to look through her eyes, to realize how grave her danger was. When a British voice boomed out over the ambush, they knew who it was.

"Mindy Barsky," the voice said. "Put down your firearms. You will not be harmed unless you attempt to retaliate."

She tossed the revolver to the ditch beside the highway, then pulled the rifle over her shoulder and let it clatter to the pavement. She took off her helmet and shook out her hair, damp from the enclosure of the hot, padded shell.

"It *is* her!" cried an excited voice. "I told you it would be her!"

Mindy dropped the kickstand on the cycle and dismounted, stretching the muscles in her legs. The air was filled with hundreds of little clicks as the army readied their weapons. She held her arms in the air, hands open.

"Chill out," she called, laughing. "All this firepower against an unarmed girl? What a bunch of losers."

She hoped the laughter masked her fear; she felt on the verge of peeing her pants.

The tension was momentarily thick, then eased as a large, feral man with a mustache stepped around the roadblock and approached her. His hands were empty. The man moved like a jungle cat, and with just as much menace. His eyes were stony and lifeless. Mindy felt a chill come over her despite the desert heat.

He stopped just outside arm's reach. Then there was a muffled argument behind the roadblock, and another man stepped onto the road. He wore a dirty monk's robe and combat boots. The robe was cinched with an olive-drab web belt, from which hung a pistol. His face was badly sunburned and had the sagging jowls of someone who had recently carried much fat on his body. In his hands was a staff. Mindy looked him in the eye and turned away just as quickly, repulsed by what she saw. He gave her a smile that made her hair stand up.

"It *is* her," the robed one whispered. "The negro woman. I told you. I told you!"

Mindy looked at the big man, clearly the leader, and nodded her head at the lunatic. Struggling to keep her voice casual, she asked, "Who's the asshole?"

The leader laughed. "Ms. Barsky, I am Mr. Pierce. My colleague," he accented the word with some distaste, "is Brother Jed, a man of God."

Jed joined them. Perversion oozed from him like slick sweat. He thumped his staff on the pavement with a wooden ringing sound that had the same effect as fingernails on a chalkboard. "God has led us to you," he proclaimed. "You seek to join the devil, Kimball. Now you belong to us!"

"Jed, you will be silent!" Pierce commanded.

The preacher recoiled as if he had been slapped. Mindy saw a look of pure hatred flash across his face. She realized that these men were as much antagonists as allies, and she filed the information away as something she might use to help her escape.

"You know who I am," she said to Pierce. "But what do you want with me?"

"Luke Kimball has something we want. We are holding you until we get it. Come out of the sun and I will explain."

Pierce turned, and Mindy followed, Jed just behind her. She could feel his hot stare wandering over her ass. Others came forward to take her motorcycle. She almost spoke up about the LightForm panels she had hidden in the lining of her pack, but decided against it. If she was lucky, they would think it was part of the built-in frame.

As they passed the roadblock, she asked, "Will I be able to get my pack back after your people search it? There are . . . feminine things . . . inside that I need."

"Of course. We will also give you private quarters—under guard, of course. These are brutal times, but we are not savages, Ms. Barsky."

The camp beyond the roadblock was much larger than she would have imagined. As they approached a large tent that was Pierce's, Mindy wondered just how far from the truth his statement was. Armed guards ringed Pierce's tent. Two held the flap aside as they entered. Mindy slipped off her sunglasses and blinked her eyes rapidly to adjust to the gloom.

The tent was spartan and neat, filled with furniture that could be easily collapsed and moved. A guard moved in behind her and ordered Mindy to hold up her arms. She felt the touch of cold steel on her back and obeyed. The guard frisked her, functionally and thoroughly, making sure that no crevice of her body held a weapon. Pierce averted his eyes.

"Just a formality," he said. "But this is war, and you are the enemy."

Mindy saw Jed watch hungrily as the guard's hands moved over her breasts. He was dangerously creepy. The guard felt her slight motion and increased the pressure of his hands.

"Are you going to lick them next?" she asked, and Pierce's eyes narrowed.

He motioned his head to the guard, and the man moved away. Pierce's hands blurred, and suddenly a knife was lodged in the guard's throat. The man dropped to his knees, then fell on his face, choking on his blood.

"I told you that you would not be harmed," Pierce said as he retrieved the knife. He wiped it clean on the dead guard's clothing and slipped it back into a sheath on his wrist. "Remove this rubbish from my tent. You," he motioned to another guard, "search her pack."

The other guard rummaged through her pack with rapid, clinical precision. He removed a nail file and a small folding knife she hoped he would miss. When he opened a package of tampons and held one up for inspection, she almost laughed. Satisfied, he put her things away, having missed the solar panels completely.

"Please sit, Ms. Barsky, and we shall get down to business."

Mindy sat in the offered chair and was given a glass of water. After the heat in the desert and the hot, plastic-tasting water from her canteen, the glass was pleasingly wet and cool.

Mindy said, "I don't know what kind of game you've got going with this Kimball. A friend of mine is with him. I'm going to join my friend. I don't see how I fit into your business. And how did you know who I was, anyway?"

Pierce braced his chin on his hand, staring off into the dark corners of the tent ceiling. "There are things afoot beyond my understanding. Jed knew where you would be, just as he knows where Luke Kimball is. How, I do not know. But here you are. And Kimball is not all that far away."

In the darkness of the tent, Jed could have been a shadow. But when he spoke, his eyes gleamed with manic intensity, even though his voice was barely louder than a whisper.

"Luke Kimball is Satan. He has come to romp on the ashes of a once-proud world. Even now, he calls the last of his imps to him. You are the seventh imp. Drop your posturing and pretenses. All you are and all you try to do is known to me!"

Pierce fixed his gaze on Mindy. "Jed is tuned into a wavelength I don't want access to. You might say he's psychic. We know Luke has searched for seven people. You are the last. Whatever he's trying to accomplish, he cannot do it without you. But now we have you, and he has something I want."

So, they knew, Mindy thought—and felt hope take one giant step away from her.

"What do you want from him?" she asked.

"Kimball has the MOC," Pierce said briskly. "It is a mobile home with the electronic sophistication and firepower to be a noble command post. I need it to ensure the survival and growth of my team." Pierce's voice grew ugly. "I also want him. We were friends, once upon a time. He owes me a life. If Luke will not face me in combat, your life will be forfeit, and I will take the MOC by whatever force is necessary."

"What does *he* want?" Mindy nodded at Jed.

"Luke's head to take back to his 'kingdom.' If Kimball will not bargain with us, then Jed will gain a consolation prize. I will give him . . . you."

Pierce spoke with such brutal, simple honesty that Mindy had no doubt he told the truth. Jed's confirming grin left nothing to suspicion. Whatever he had planned for her would be worse than the most frightening nightmare she had ever dreamed of.

"Where is Luke Kimball now?" Pierce demanded.

Mindy felt the barest whisper of Michael

in her mind. It was like new strength, just enough to restore hope. She was reassured.

"Right now, they're in Oregon, a little over two days' hard ride from here. He monitors the radio every evening on this frequency. . ." Mindy recited it while Pierce wrote the numbers down. "Call him in three hours. He will be listening."

Pierce appeared skeptical. "How do you know this? You didn't have a radio."

Mindy smiled without warmth. "How did Jed know who I am? Strange things are happening in the world that you know nothing about."

Their eyes locked. Mindy held his steely gaze, melting with fright inside. She thought she saw the barest hint of doubt flicker across his face before he smiled.

"We shall see," he said. "Guards, take Ms. Barsky to her tent, please."

They walked out under armed escort. Jed was at her side. Mindy refused to make eye contact with him, feeling his gaze wander over her body like a slimy worm. When he spoke, his putrid breath washed over her.

"You will be mine very shortly, Blood of the Lamb. You shall pay for your sins with a sacrifice. It will be most special. It may not be to your tastes, but it will certainly be to mine."

Mindy could hear the anticipation in his voice. Then he touched her arm. It was all she could do not to scream.

"All these people here will soon be mine . . . an army of God to march across the world. More and more shall join me. Yours shall be the bones upon which the foundation is laid, with Kimball's head on a stake to mark the way!"

Her tent was as heavily guarded as Pierce's. Once she was inside, her composure fell. Mindy lay on the cot and bit her fingers hard to keep her sobs from being heard.

"Oh, Michael," she whispered, "help me to be strong. Help me to survive. I'm caught between Pierce and Jed. They're spiky walls, and they're closing fast. Don't let me be caught!"

". . . and Pierce will be on the frequency tonight," Mike finished. "What are we going to do?"

Luke heard the anguish in his voice. It was an emotion that, in this proximity to each other, the group shared with him. "I will talk with Pierce tonight. He can have the MOC; I don't care about that. He can even try to have me. If we have to go to war to get Mindy . . . then we will go to war."

Billy said, "But there are over two hundred of them, and only six of us, man. Odds are in their favor."

"I just may have a surprise or two for them, if it comes down to it. What we're pursuing is too important to let go of. All our hopes and dreams are focused at this point. Will you abandon them now?"

The group shook their heads no. Even Tony was grave, in full realization of the seriousness of the matter.

"Let me talk to Pierce. Then we will hold our council of war. Mike, come with me, please."

They went to the MOC. Inside the Quonset garage, the armored vehicle was dark and cool. He turned on the radio bank. Red and blue graphs flickered as the receiver locked onto the contact frequency.

"What are we going to do?" Mike asked.

"I need you to get into Mindy's head and tell me how Pierce's camp is laid out, the surrounding terrain, and any other pertinent details."

Mike linked with Mindy. Tears streamed down his cheeks as he felt what she felt. When he had what Luke had asked of him, Mike began to talk. Luke listened very carefully. Then he was ready for Pierce.

"Luke Kimball, do you copy?" The voice on the radio was Britishly crisp and clear.

"Matthew Pierce. I read you loud and clear. It's been a long time, Matt."

"Too long. Our friendship died in radioactive dust."

"Or your hatred was born. I'm sorry we have come to this. Is there no hope of reconciliation?"

"None," said Pierce. "You owe me a life. And we each have something the other wants."

Here was the heart of the matter.

"Yes. But some things are better discussed face-to-face. There is a high mound of rock about a mile northwest of your camp. Can you be there in forty-five minutes, alone?"

"What kind of trick are you playing, Luke? Are you going to drop a guided missile on me?"

"No tricks. There are none I can profit from. Remember, I know your skills as well as you know mine. And if our friendship is gone, we are both still men of honor. I give you my word that I will be at that mound in forty-five minutes, alone and unarmed. Deal?"

Static crackled on the airwaves as Pierce considered. "Deal. Bring your terms."

Luke keyed the microphone twice in acknowledgment, then turned off the radio. Mike looked at him in astonishment. His voice rose to hysteria.

"What are you doing? You just promised him that you would be there in a few minutes, when it will take days to get there! Are you crazy?!"

Luke leveled his eye at Mike. "I will see Pierce in a few minutes. Nothing is what it seems anymore, Mike. In this, you must trust me. If you choose not to believe me, then ask Ellie. She will tell you. Have some faith, and share it with Mindy. I need you both to be strong."

Mike stumbled from the MOC.

The sun was dipping into the west,

painting the grassy high desert red. It was easy to disappear in the sage, tumbleweed, and rocky ground beyond the Quonset hut. In moments, Luke was out of sight of the highway station.

Bushes rattled to his left, and Samson's head appeared. Luke regarded the wolf for a few moments and said, "Well, come then."

The wolf followed him as he ran. Luke stopped when the sun touched the western rim of the world. He pulled off his shirt and used it to dust a circle on a high rock. Samson climbed up with him and lay down, panting, facing the setting sun. Luke sat in the clean circle. He drew several deep breaths to calm himself, then brought his mind back to when he had first become an eagle. The way of it lay before him, a form he could reach himself into. Luke followed it and felt his arms grow wing feathers, his feet becoming talons.

In moments, the transformation was complete. He launched into the sky, winging to the cloud tops. With every beat of his wings, he heard the pounding of a drum. Without conscious thought, he synchronized his wings to the drumming and soon became the rhythm, the focus. He climbed until the sky turned light and the Spirit Hoop flamed brightly.

His wings fanned the Hoop. The flames in turn tugged the winds to gale force. Luke was hurled across the sky faster than any jet had ever flown. In the vortex made by his passing, thunderstorms were born. They gave birth to rain that soaked earth laid to waste by the war. The rain had been born in the Spirit World and was a cleansing rain. The places it touched were made free of radiation. Even before the rain had ceased, green shoots inched from the damp soil. In a year, these would be the first forests to live in the deserts since the ice ages had scoured the earth. The world was indeed changing.

Of all this, Luke was unaware. He saw only the large, ordered camp of Pierce's commandos. His old friend was standing on the mound as promised. Luke circled twice, searching with keen eagle eyes for any deception. As he had anticipated, there was none. He winged onto the mound, landing ten feet from Pierce. His former friend took a step back and reached for a knife on his belt.

Luke transformed before Pierce had time to draw it. Pierce cursed, astonishment clear on his face. "What kind of devilment is this?"

Luke smiled and held his hands out from his sides. "Hello, Matthew. Nice to see you too. As you can see, I'm not armed."

Pierce put the knife away. "I don't know if I should believe what I just saw."

Luke sat on the mound. "Believe it. I have always been straight with you. A lot of water has passed under the bridge since you and I last saw each other, the day before the war. The world is not the same. I am not the same as you have seen.

Nor are you."

"What happened to your eye?"

"I lost it in a fight. You've some new scars as well."

Pierce sat heavily on the mound, keeping his distance from Luke. The last three years had weighed even more on Pierce than on him. Where Matthew had once been lean and fit, he was now gaunt and savage. Beneath the deep tan, Luke saw the pallor in Pierce's skin that came from too many sleepless nights, from being constantly in command of wild forces, and from leading with a combination of charisma and brute force.

Luke took a handful of red dust and let it trickle from his fingers, much as he had more than three years ago in the Nevada desert. "In my way, I am now as strange as Jed. I think we represent two sides of a greater issue: good and evil. I know you have used him to get to me. But at what price? How much of your power has he taken?"

"Enough," Pierce answered. "But he is nothing that a bullet or a blade can't fix. I will be able to rid myself of him and his religious vermin as soon as I have dealt with you."

"Why do you carry such hate for me, Matthew? We were good friends, battle brothers. I always trusted my life in your hands at any time without a thought. When the war came, I mourned you most of all. And I would rejoice in your being alive now, if I were not what I have become.

"I am a pawn in a game played by gods. I can do things I never imagined possible. I am on a quest to accomplish something that is still beyond my complete understanding. Now I have lost everything I treasured most—including your friendship."

Pierce cradled his head in his hands, then looked to where the sun had passed below the rim of the world. "I envied you, Luke. You had a strength and singularity of purpose that I could only dream of. I often wished I could be more like you. SCI was my life as much as it was your creation. If only you would have come to Las Vegas with me that night, instead of hiding in your little cave, none of this would be happening now." He pounded his hands into the dirt, barely controlling his anger.

"I had just arrived when the first warheads struck," Pierce continued. "Indian Springs and Nellis Airforce Base went simultaneously. I was standing in the lobby of the Bellagio and saw it all. The twin concussions blasted Vegas, turning the strip into stripped skeletons of broken glass. Half of the lobby of the Bellagio fell on me. That was the only reason I survived the heat blast. I came to with the whole town burning around me. I crawled from the wreckage and ran, cut and bleeding, all night long. Thousands ran with me. I was in shock, Luke. I knew what had happened, but it did not seem real.

"As I fled, I wished that you were with me, so we could back each other up, so we could survive like the team we had been. But I imagined you safe and snug in your cave in the wilderness . . . almost as if you had known and let me go anyway. And I began to hate you.

"The wind moved faster than I did, running on the road. Fine dust drifted from the sky. Then the flakes became larger. I left the highway, trying to quarter out of the wind. I found a small ranch. The husband and wife who lived there refused to let me in. I shot them . . . used their water and soap to wash the radioactive dust from my body. I washed again and again, but almost died anyway. The radiation had poisoned me, and I grew deathly ill. I lost my hair and shat blood. For a time, I wished desperately that I might die. But I lived—and hated you more.

"It took half a year for me to recover. The fallout was gone, so I worked my way southeast, away from most of the targeted military installations. At first, there were many living people. But the plagues decimated them. I killed many times to survive, to take what I needed. The winter was cold, even in the southern states. I was forced to head to Florida to stay warm.

"In central Florida, I found a small National Guard armory. It was completely stocked with weapons, clothing, and rations. And I grew to hate you even more because I was alone. I realized how dependent I had been on our camaraderie, and it took that hate to free me of those bonds. I buried you in that armory . . . and set off back into the world with a Stryker loaded with gear. I found men and women willing to fight for survival. My best soldier came from New Orleans."

"Yes. Billy. He's with me now."

Pierce shook his head. "I'm not surprised, though I can't understand why he left. He was closest to me."

Luke answered, "He needed something no army can give. The reason he came to me is partially how I have come to be here now."

Pierce balled his fists. "I cannot understand it! I struggled to build a band of survivors out of the ashes of this country. We are strong. Unstoppable! But now, after making it work, it's coming apart at the seams. What is happening in this world, this ruined, ugly world, to destroy the one dream I had left?"

Luke's voice was gentle. "Matthew, the world is waking up. Think of the war as a giant eraser that has swept the blackboard of our world clean. There was a time, not too long ago in the history of the world, when all things—man, animals, the earth, and the gods—lived in balance with each other. But then the world became civilized, and the beliefs that made balance possible were forgotten.

"You and I helped perpetuate those beliefs with the work we did at SCI. Now a balance is once again possible. Everything is possible. Matt, I've seen gods dance across the sky. I have spoken with them. We are nearing a point in time where mankind's future will either be ensured . . . or committed to a slow, dark death."

"Gods? While I cannot deny how you came here tonight, I'll not believe gods are tromping on the Earth. You've gone bonkers."

Luke shook his head. "You don't realize how close to the truth you are. I went insane at the beginning of the war. Even before. I had to live with myself . . . with what I had become. I was my own personal Hell. I am not the same man I was three years ago. I've seen unicorns in the Dakota Badlands. Magic is alive in the world now. We can be a part of it. If you can put aside your hatred of me for even a little while, I can show you a future where you will be needed and can build any dream you have. It could be like before, but with a better purpose."

Pierce laughed. It was the saddest sound Luke had ever heard. "In all the time we worked together, you always led, and I always followed. We're too far apart now. It took your death to let me build something that was all mine: this army. Now, three years into the grave, you return and offer me a back seat in a future filled with myths. I'll see you dead first, and hammer the nails into your coffin myself!"

Luke sighed. "I held the hope that our friendship would count when it mattered. I am sorry you hate me, Matt. I had a dream and pursued it selfishly. I will say that you were always my equal, and what we built at Secon, we built together.

"Now I am pursuing a new dream more relentlessly than anything I have ever tried to do. My life depends on it . . . as well as the lives of the future. If you are not with me, then you stand against something as big as the world. Give me Mindy. I need her. I'll give you the MOC, and we can go our separate ways."

Pierce shook his head. "No deal. I want something more. We sparred and shot against each other hundreds of times over the years. Sometimes you were better. Sometimes it was I. But now I have to know who the best is. If I win, I take the MOC, and Mindy goes free. If you win, you take Mindy and go save the world. You have my word that Jed will not pursue you. These are my terms. I will accept no others."

"Will you not back down just a little and let each of us go our separate ways? For old friendship's sake?"

"I cannot. I have to know."

Luke felt the Spirit Hoop move slightly and click into a new future. He sighed again. "As you wish. Where and when?"

Pierce pulled a map from inside his shirt

and laid it on the ground. Luke heard the map paper crinkle in the darkness. A small flashlight illuminated the colored paper. Luke sat across the map from Pierce.

"What about here?" Pierce asked, indicating their present position.

"No," Luke said. "Too far for me to backtrack. Here." He put his finger on the map.

"What's the terrain?"

"Gently hilly," Luke answered, "with some rock, but open enough so that any kind of ambush would be difficult. It is honest land. There is nothing for me to hide. I have six people. You have hundreds. I'd say you have us outnumbered. There will be no treachery."

"Done. In two days at, say, dawn?"

"Dawn it is, north of Winnemucca, Nevada."

"At the foot of Bloody Run Peak. How appropriate. And Luke, it will be knives. To the death."

Luke nodded, and they both stood. "To the death. Goodbye, Matthew, I wish you well."

Pierce faded into the night. Luke let the transformation take place and then soared low over the desert away from Pierce's army, seeing night creatures eating and being eaten, killing and being killed, procreating to ensure the survival of their species.

Never before had Luke felt the emptiness within himself as he did now. He had relied

JOHN SAUER

on Matthew as much as he had counted on his almost blind friendship and trust. Pierce had idolized him, Luke realized now, and he had subconsciously, selfishly used that idolization to his benefit. Luke had directed him like a general led his officers. Friendship had always come second. It was what they had both learned in the military, but that did not make it right. And now, time, the war, and the gods had conspired to drive an irrevocable wedge between them, once friends, now bitter enemies.

One or the other would die in two days, and there was nothing Luke could do to alter this destiny. Either way, Bloody Run Peak was a nexus point. What happened there would bring them closer to waking the Tree of Life, or seeing the world slide into darkness.

Locked deeply into his thoughts as he was, Luke barely noticed his landing and transformation until he felt the gaze of Samson upon him. In the light of the half moon, the wolf's eyes were brilliant amber and full of wisdom. Samson's ears were perked forward, tuned to Luke's movements and, he suspected, his thoughts.

"What do you see, Samson? Often I watch you with Tony, and I wonder what kind of thoughts you share. How do you fit into this? Will you talk to me now?"

Samson tilted his head and lolled out his tongue, panting in a very doggy way.

"Or maybe you're just a loyal, dedicated canine friend. And since you're here, maybe you will listen to my dilemma."

Luke told Samson about his friendship with Pierce, the happy and not-so-happy memories they had shared during the birth of SCI and the successful years, and the upcoming battle.

"What do you think, Samson? Where will all this lead?"

Samson looked at him for a long moment, then tilted his muzzle at the sky and howled. It was a long, mournful sound, filled with sadness and lost friendships. A lone coyote picked up the howl, then more. Soon the high desert night was filled with sorrowed songs of the brothers of the wolf. The wails pitched high and low, and in their chorus, Luke heard the story of his friendship with Pierce, of how the Hoop had turned so that friends became enemies.

The pack songs rang with love, hatred, and the inevitability of death, and Luke threw back his head and joined his voice with theirs in the only outlet he could find for the emptiness inside him. The brothers of the wolf accepted his song, making it their own, and he felt the Hoop of All Life swing wide and far, touching for him what he could not touch, feeling what he could not feel. He howled with them long into the night, until the moon had fallen and his voice was a hoarse whisper. Then he fell into sleep on the rock, Samson by his side for warmth, keeping watch.

ONE THOUSAND AND ONE PAPER CRANES

The Tree of Life stood like a tall, wave-formed skeleton of a giant in a large clearing at the far southern end of the snow-capped Kettle Range in northern Washington state. The tall, ancient pine and fir trees surrounding the clearing were emerald green in the morning sun, the long grass at their bases lush and sparkling with dew. The air was cool and pure, fresh with the morning. But the thick branches of the Tree of Life were bare and lifeless.

The Tree of Life had been almost barren when Old Joe was born in the late eighteen hundreds, and it had gone completely dormant as he became an adult. Now, after so much time, looking up into the starkness of its branches, Joseph felt the potential for the Tree to grow new green leaves. It was a promise of life, of another turn of the Sacred Hoop, of being young again. If the Tree would blossom, it would be a sign that mankind had survived the long night and could live in harmony with the world once again.

Joseph sighed and looked down at the work in his hands. He sat at the base of the Tree, folding tiny squares of colored paper into interlocking, delicate origami cranes. His fine, brilliant white hair hung free almost to his shoulders. The complex bronze map of his face held clear brown eyes that burned with life. A red checkered shirt and blue jeans hung baggy on his skinny frame. His hands were wrinkled, but strong and sure, covered with the calluses that more than a hundred years of labor had provided. The delicate rice paper he folded stayed smooth and unwrinkled.

He completed another crane, this one blue, and slipped its neck into the body of the one he had folded before, locking them together. The chain he was making was just under three feet long.

It had been the idea of Setsuko, the seven-year-old daughter of the Japanese blacksmith who had joined the People a month ago. Setsuko had told him the story of a young girl burned horribly by the atomic blast at Hiroshima. The girl had dreamed that if she made a chain of one thousand paper cranes, her life would be saved. The girl had died just a few cranes short of her goal. The people of Japan had been so taken by her courage that many chains of a thousand cranes had been made and placed on her grave. She had been a symbol of desperate hope.

"If we make a chain of a thousand cranes, maybe we can all be saved," Setsuko had told him.

The idea was so poignant and full of hope that he had been taken with it, as had many of the others who had joined the People over the last few months. Johnny, a young architect who was designing simple, environmentally friendly housing for the People, had gone all the way to Seattle, risking the dangers of the road and radiation to find a warehouse full of colored rice paper. Now people all over the camp were learning the art of origami, under the tutelage of young Setsuko.

It was one small example of the social and educational exchanges taking place in the cultural stewpot of the Village of the People. Many becoming one, such a diverse group of men, women, and children. Joseph already thought of them as the People, a group three hundred strong: Amerindians, blacks, whites, Asians, and Latinos, all the races of man, from all backgrounds and with all manner of skills. They had come to this beautiful valley somewhere in the northeast corner of the Colville Indian Reservation, following their dreams.

Many had seen the Tree blossoming in their visions. They were eager to provide, to help each other, to forget differences in race and creed, and to believe in the one love. If Kimball, the one-eyed man, could bring the Key of Seven here, these few special People would become the nucleus for the rebirth of the world. The Tree of Life would blossom again . . . if.

It would be the culmination of a dream that had survived through generations of his family. Joseph was his tribe's last medicine man and the last guardian of the Tree of Life. His responsibility was to observe and protect, to make sure that no one, in his or her ignorance, would cut down or deface the Tree. His father had passed the knowledge of the Tree to him when Joseph was a young man. Though versed in the lore of his people, the Chief Joseph band of the Nez Percé, the secret of the Tree surprised and frightened him.

The Tree of Life was a powerful secret to keep from the rest of the world . . . especially when it was right underfoot and virtually ignored by all! But his tribe had known legends of the Tree, not knowing how true they were. Once, long before his people had been Nez Percé, they had known the Tree of Life and had danced with many other tribes under its boughs, heavy with sweet green foliage.

When the first white men, the Vikings, had touched the eastern shores, the Tree had begun to wither. There had been sadness among his people and all peoples of the Tree, for they knew these strange men with yellow and red hair and strong weapons walked on the earth, not with it. They had strength, like a good enemy, and powerful gods of their own, but no balance with the earth. Never before had they encountered men like this, and it made them sad. As the Tree slowly withered, the memories of its greatness, of the true meaning of its life, also faded.

Even then, the gods had been losing their foothold in the mortal world. Where all tribes had sent men and women, those with the strongest dreams, to become a member of the tribe who watched the Tree, now no one came, and only his family held the secret. It was passed down from father to son or daughter, to son or daughter, to son or daughter. But he had fathered no children.

His father had passed the secret on to him: "Watch the Tree. Protect it from the perils of the civilized world. Watch, for one day the Tree will live again."

After the war, the first people had shown up here. He was alone in this corner of the reservation and very surprised to see them. But when they told him they had dreamed of the Tree, he felt there was nothing to hide anymore. They had dreamed of the Tree of Life and him. So, he showed them the Tree, and they decided to stay. And more came, and he told them, and they stayed. And thus the village was born. Soon thereafter came his first Spirit vision, and he had come to know the gods again.

In return for protecting the Tree of Life, the gods had given his ancestors a gift, to be passed on from generation to generation of Watchers. It was a gift Joseph exercised often for the sheer joy of it, for the kinship it gave him with the world. Those who had been made Watchers also became Speakers with Animals. Each creature on the land and in the sea had its language, its thoughts and wishes. Joseph and those who had come before him had been granted the ability to understand and communicate with them, from earthworms to eagles and everything in between.

In the service of the United States Army during World War II, Joseph had traveled over much of the world and had spoken with the creatures of every country he had visited. Animals knew no boundaries of state or nationality. They had little sense of time and lived fully in the now. Their tongues were universal, as people had once been and hopefully would be again.

Animals spoke of things that concerned them. Songbirds trilled of the warmth of the sun and the wind, of the tasty insects they had caught. Their single-minded chatter never failed to cheer him. Only the cetaceans of the great seas, the greater simians, and the wolves dwelled on matters greater than their own lives.

Joseph had not been to the sea in over

a decade and had not spoken with cetaceans in twice as long. But wolves were everywhere in this part of the country. They had been dramatically affected by the war. Many had eaten carrion tainted by radiation and died. Others had lived to pass altered genes on to their cubs. Some were born hopelessly defective. Others appeared normal . . . but had evolved to be far more intelligent.

Joseph had played with these cubs at twilight at the base of the Tree, playful, loving creatures full of questions and crackerjack intellect. As he rolled and tickled the happily growling balls of fur under his gentle hands, Joseph felt the bond that could develop between this species and man. Whatever evolutionary tract the wolves were taking shared the same hoop as mankind . . . if man survived the coming events. If Kimball could bring the Key of Seven here. All rested on Kimball's shoulders.

Luke had already been fractured by a lifetime of fighting against demons, both real and imagined. He had made a stew of his soul. The Manitou had left him isolated from his emotions. The gifts the gods had given him— the ability to move faster and hear better than any man, plus transformation and access to the Spirit World—had not changed the essence of what Luke Kimball was, only given him the tools to grow if he used them.

After meeting this dream savior in the

Spirit World, Joseph felt pity for Luke Kimball and no small amount of awe. If Kimball delivered the Key and fought the Manitou, he would be in for a surprise greater than anything he could ever imagine.

Joseph's thoughts were broken by the beat of shuffling feet on the ground, boots walking in a rhythm Joseph had come to know well. It was Antonio, a young Apache in his mid-twenties who acted as the People's wrangler, caring for the fifty or so horses the village held in common. Antonio was a cowboy to the core, with faded blue jeans, chaps, spurs, and a white T-shirt under a denim jacket. A battered black Stetson sat atop his closely shaved head. The friendly youth was a contradiction of rock 'n' roll, a music form Joseph had never cared for, and horse lore—something he and the boy shared deeply.

"Old Joe," Antonio called. "Wake up, Grandfather!"

"I am awake, man," Joseph answered in mock crankiness. "Why do you pester me on such a fine morning?"

Antonio flopped down on the ground beside him, the wide grin on his face showing even white teeth and the essence of the young man's good nature. Antonio snatched up a piece of paper and folded a crane with almost blinding speed. He handed it to Joseph and immediately began another.

"That's not fair," Joseph retorted. "You

have the advantage of youth."

"Yes, Grandfather, but you have the advantage of, of . . . let me think. . ." Antonio ducked as Joseph took a playful swipe at his head. "Wisdom! Yes, that's it. You have the advantage of wisdom."

Joseph chuckled, thinking how much like a son this young man was to him. In a way, all the People were his children. But though he tried to love them all equally, Antonio was special. "What is so important to bring you racing away from your horses?"

"Another group just arrived. One of them is a woman. She's pregnant."

"Truly? That's wonderful! Is she healthy?"

Antonio shrugged. "She seems to be. But I'm no doctor. They all dreamed of the Tree and would like to see it."

"So, let them see it. It's not mine," Joseph said gently. "The Tree of Life belongs to all People."

Antonio blushed. "Yeah, well, you are the Watcher. And you were sitting here and looked like you were asleep or meditating or something. We just didn't want a bunch of noobs coming up and disturbing you."

Joseph smiled. "Thank you for your kindness. I'll take a walk so our new people can see the Tree in the light of their own emotions. There will be time enough to talk. Show them around and let them share with us."

Antonio left, and Joseph carefully stored the origami chain and squares of colored paper in a niche made by one of the Tree's great roots. Let the newcomers wonder about the cranes. Setsuko would tell them soon enough. It would be a good way to bring them into the community.

He left the clearing on legs still sturdy after a century of walking. The forest here was rich with a tapestry of life: deer, wolves, bears, moose, and hundreds of species of birds and ground-dwelling animals. As Joseph walked, he listened to their songs and calls, hearing their messages, the symphony of their voices.

A whitetail fawn crossed his path and stopped, long white tail raised in a flag of alarm.

"Good morning, little friend," Joseph said. "I will not hurt you. Go to your mother."

The fawn whistled and stamped its hooves in a show of bravery. *"You are bear?"* the fawn asked.

"I am man," Joseph answered. "Know my scent and shape."

The fawn rolled its eyes in alarm and bolted, tail bobbing. Its mother had told it about man.

As Joseph moved farther from the clearing, the sounds of the forest quieted. He knelt on the trail and saw why: fresh wolf tracks on the moist, dark ground. He stood and kept walking, alert for sounds and movement. They came to him a short time later, circling him silently. He could not hear them. He saw only a flash of gray fur out of the corner of his eye.

Joseph kept hiking until he found a stump. He sat on it and called out, "Enough of games, my brothers. Come speak with me."

They came in ones and twos, the youngest first, quiet-eyed and somber. They were troubled and transmitted enough of their emotion to make Joseph uneasy. The wolves were a pack of twelve. The alpha male came last, a long, lean wolf with silky black-and-gray fur and massive shoulders. Joseph went to his knees and bared his neck. The alpha bit Joseph so gently that he barely felt the sharp fangs on his skin. Then the wolf raised its head, and Joseph did the same in return.

"My brother," he said.

"*My brother,*" the alpha answered.

"What is afoot to bring you into the forest in the full light of day?"

"*We are troubled by the songs of our brothers sung to us by other wolf brothers from far away. We are troubled and sad and frightened by the disharmony of the song.*"

"Sing me the song," Joseph asked.

The wolves began to howl, their voices twining into the melody of the song. A friend forced to battle a friend . . . to the death. The hopes of all put on the line to satisfy the desires of one. A man ruined to give another creature pleasure. Honor reinforced by treachery. A day from now, Luke Kimball and the man Pierce would fight to the death. It was a sad thing when a friend fought a friend, part of what the turning of the Hoop had wrought. It was a part of the terrible price Luke had to pay for the unification of the Seven.

This was the lesson of the wolf: the life of one for the life of many. But regardless of the outcome of their fight, the Wendigo had managed to manipulate events against Luke. Either way, he would lose, by the hand of fate or by treachery.

"What will happen now, brother?" the alpha asked.

"What will be, will be. The Hoop will turn. We can only wait and see," answered Joseph. "Thank you for coming to me, brothers. But now I must seek higher council. My spirit will be with you. Hunt well!"

Joseph touched each of the wolves in farewell. They returned to the forest as silently as they had come. Joseph sat quietly, letting the gentle wind blow their scent out of the clearing, the subtle thoughts and flavors of their speech flowing from his mind. He sat cross-legged on the ground, palms open in his lap, feeling the warmth of the sun, the lightness of his being.

Here, near the Tree of Life, the Spirit World was very close. And as close to death as he was, from age and natural causes, the Spirit World was exceptionally clear. Joseph opened his mind to it, and the path from this world to the other became clear to his spiritual eyes. He felt himself come free, then looked down to see his mortal body seated on the ground.

Unencumbered by flesh and blood, Joseph was strong and fast. He raced into the clear blue of the sky, feeling the current tugs of the high, wispy clouds and the winds that jetted across the top of the world. The Spirit Hoop first appeared as a thread-fine red arc in the sky. The higher Joseph ran, the closer it became. When he could hear it crackle and spin, Joseph looked down. The ground was an eerie frozen ocean of red sandstone waves, towering over the sandy floor of the Spirit World. Joseph suspected that not even the gods knew exactly what all dwelled in their world.

He touched the ground between two towering arches and followed the path between them to the Council Fire. The Council was deserted in the light of day, and the charred, smoky remains of the fire lay ringed with large sooty stones. No one was here to help him. For a moment, Joseph wondered if, by coming here, he was being too audacious. Gods demanded respect as well as worship. But he was here on a mission of their survival. Only, what would he do now? He could not go trekking through the Spirit World. Not every creature here was kind to humans. Joseph sat next to the fire and stirred its ashes with a stick, searching the gray embers for answers.

A puff of smoke hissed from the coals. It rose into the sky as a small, perfect circle, and then dissipated. Not long after, he heard feet in the sand behind him. He turned to see who was coming.

"Teacher," Joseph cried, "old friend!"

The aged Santa-Claus-like academician sat next to Joseph, beard flowing like new, gleaming wool and bare feet sticking out from ragged khakis. The eyes behind the small, round glasses were kindly blue and full of wisdom.

"Hello, Joseph. Welcome back to the Spirit World."

Joseph reached out and smacked him on the arm. "Is it you? I have not seen you for over thirty years! I imagined you had been killed along with so many others."

Joseph was beside himself. He had first met Teacher when he was fifty years old and Teacher was a scholar fresh from the university. He had been a student of Amerindian mysticism, working on a thesis on the ongoing discord between the Native Americans' and the white man's world. Teacher had been thin then, with graying hair and a desire to learn which was most compelling. Joseph had liked him immediately. He had taught Teacher much about the Nez Percé way, and in turn, had learned much about the world from the young man—so much so that he had taken to calling the boy Teacher.

The name had stuck.

They had been friends ever since, writing or visiting often. But eventually, Teacher had married and raised a family. He accepted a position with a major university, and they had communicated less and less. Distant, yet good friends still. Now, to meet here, in the Spirit world. . . Was this in fact Teacher, or a god wearing a familiar guise?

Joseph asked again, "Are you truly Teacher, or a god wearing a friend's image?"

Teacher smiled. "My good friend, it is truly me. I am here under circumstances that are the culmination of my life's dreams. All my life, I believed in the Spirit World. We talked about it many times over the years. Yet it was always closed to me. I know now it was closed to all men—until the war opened the doorway. The gods pulled me from the ashes, close to death, and gave me life. They let me touch my inner spirit and past lives. I found my true inner self and became more than just Teacher; I am now Teacher Oldman. I was given the task of guiding Luke Kimball in his first encounter with the Spirit World. The others have sent me here to talk with you, old friend, because of your friendship and because they know what has transpired."

Joseph nodded. "Aye. But do they know of the treachery guiding Kimball's and Pierce's battle?"

"Yes," Teacher replied. "And there is more to it than even you know. If Kimball loses to Pierce, the Key of Seven can never be united, and mankind will be doomed. If Kimball wins, the Wendigo will use treachery to try to kill him, Mindy, or both. And if Luke survives the Wendigo's ploy, there is a third element to the Wendigo's machinations."

Teacher told Joseph the last detail. Joseph's spirits plummeted. "Then there is no hope left for us. Mankind will die a slow death."

"It appears that way," Teacher said morosely, "unless Kimball can find the strength to defeat his true worst enemy."

Joseph put his head in his hands. "Yes. But is Luke Kimball strong enough to face him?"

"That," Teacher replied, "is a question only Luke Kimball will be able to answer. And I pray he can. He is our only hope."

A GOOD PLACE
TO DIE

Winnemucca, Nevada, had once been a rollicking cowboy gambling town in the Oregon/Nevada borderlands of the high desert. It had been an oasis of cheer and good times in a silent country of wind, rock, and desolate, vast expanses where gray peaks broke up every horizon. The place Luke and Pierce had chosen for their battle was twenty miles north of Winnemucca in Desert Valley, at the foot of the Santa Rosa range.

The jagged peaks surrounding the valley were particularly foreboding and covered with scrub pine, sage, and tumbleweed. Few signs of life were visible, even to Luke's trained eye. At the northern edge of the valley, near the foot of Bloody Run Peak, was a low plateau almost a half-mile across.

It was a good place to die.

Luke had parked the MOC on one side of the plateau, facing the way Pierce would arrive. They had driven through the night to get here. The ride had been filled with their apprehensions.

"Do you believe that those scavs will let you just walk away with Mindy if you take Pierce?" Mike asked.

"I don't know. Pierce has always been a man of honor. He will not break his word, just as I would not break mine."

"That's true," Billy pointed out, "but you can't forget about Jed. That bastard is too twisty. You don't know what he has done with the army. If they're under his control now, then nothing Pierce does or says will have any effect. If Jed has the power to turn the army against us, we're dead meat."

Cal had been sitting on one of the bunks, listening to the exchange of words. "Do not forget what we are destined to accomplish. We've all felt the bond. If even one of us is killed during the upcoming foray, we're all doomed. So much depends on us all being together. Is there not another way we can win Mindy back and just disappear into the desert, to do what we must do?"

"I agree with Cal," Ellie joined in. "Can't we just give Pierce the motor home, take Mindy, and go? We can find other transportation. There's enough of it just lying around. That's what Pierce wants, isn't it? Give him the MOC."

Luke answered, "If only it were that easy. Pierce doesn't really want the MOC. It's the hook

Jed used to involve Pierce. What Pierce wants is my blood—that, and nothing else. Think about how the war has changed each of you. It has given you a strength that, when combined, will rebuild the world. The war has changed Pierce as well. He is a deadly and bitter man driven by demons of his own creation, and some that have been set on him. I do not wish to fight him, but I must. By fate's decree, there is no other way."

He sat with the others in front of the motor home, waiting. The barrel of the .50 swung slowly on its axis, searching for a target.

"This is one measure of safety we have," Luke said. "No one but us can come within the perimeter. Of course, it won't stop a rocket, but we should be safe."

"A lot of good that will do us when they start shooting," Ellie said, with no small measure of scorn.

"If Pierce doesn't see all of us when he arrives, he will suspect some sort of trap . . . and we'll be in deep shit!" Billy replied.

"There is only one way we can play this," Luke stated calmly. "I will fight Pierce. If something goes wrong, the door of the MOC is open. Get inside as fast as you can and get the hell out of here. You know where in Washington state to go."

"What if Pierce kills you?" Cal asked.

"Same plan: get in and go. There is an old man named Joseph Three Clouds, Old Joe. Find him. Maybe there will be something he can do. If I die, forget about me . . . and Mindy. We will both be no more. Mike, I hope you will find the strength to leave with the others. You and Billy will be the guardians of all we share."

Mike raised his eyes from the ground and pointed a finger at Luke. His voice was low and void of emotion. "Don't lose."

"What about Jed?" Billy asked, to break the tension.

"If I defeat Pierce and Jed tries anything, I have something I can use that may save us. Call it a gift."

"Look!" Tony shouted.

A cloud of dust boiled on the horizon. They watched it grow larger until the sounds of engines could be heard.

"It's showtime," Luke said, getting to his feet. "Remember, if this works out, we're home free. If we don't make it . . . I'll see you in another place and another time."

If we don't make it, Luke thought, *then all I have ever loved will have died—the curse of my life. This is the one chance I have left to save something worth loving, to save the world. But why must it be at the cost of my truest friend? Do I have the strength to take the life of Matthew Pierce? I must! Or nothing else will ever matter.*

The army stopped at the far edge of the plateau, as agreed. Pierce pulled onto the low rise of ground in a camouflaged MRAP. Jed rode on top, manning a .30 machine gun. He aimed the barrel at Luke for a long moment, then pointed the weapon at the sky, a triumphant grin on his face.

"Today you will meet your maker!" he called out as the truck came to a halt.

Luke said nothing, but came forward until he was halfway between the two vehicles. The day was already hot enough to raise sweat on Luke's back under the black T-shirt he wore. Pierce climbed down. Two armed guards brought Mindy from the rear of the truck. She looked frightened, but otherwise all right.

"Get my backpack. I want my damn stuff!" she called out angrily. Pierce nodded his head without turning away from Luke. With her pack, Mindy was held to the side, a prize of war. Pierce came forward until only a few feet separated them.

"Going to be hot today," Luke said.

"Yes," answered Pierce. "A good day to die."

Luke bounced the keys to the MOC in his hand. "Can't we just let this thing go? Here are the keys. Leave us to what we have to do. You will never see me again; I promise you that. But there is no need for one of us to die."

Pierce shook his head. "No. It's too late. It was too late when I first learned you were still alive. I am stronger now than I've ever been. Faster! I like what I have become. I lead now, not follow. There's no room for both of us in this world, alive. One of us dies today."

"Then let's be done with it," Luke said, and unclipped his gun belt.

Both men shed weapons and other gear until they stood with knives only under the sun. Cast from the same mold, forged in the same fires. Afghanistan. Croatia and countless operations. The final war. Their faces were lean and intent. Each was packed with hard, fast muscle. Scars, old and new, mapped roads of pain on their chests and arms.

Pierce wore leather pants and knee-high motorcycle boots. Luke wore OCP combat fatigues and standard-issue, coyote-colored combat boots. He drew the Japanese tanto knife, twelve inches of gleaming, razor-edged steel, folded and refolded until the metal had been doubled a hundred times. Its length glittered with rainbow colors. The knife was hundreds of years old, forged by one of Japan's last master swordsmiths, with a sharkskin leather grip, wrapped and rewrapped with a tang solid enough to take the blow of a sword.

Pierce smiled. "I remember that blade well. It suits you. And it is fitting we fight the last fight with exotic steel." He pulled free a large knife with a blade bent almost to the shape of a boomerang: an Indian kukri, a knife designed to behead men. The heavy blade was hand-forged and gleamed in the sun. It was slightly longer than Luke's blade. The strange design gave the user extra speed and an attack that was dangerously difficult to block. Luke knew it would be as sharp as his own. It hissed as Pierce spun the blade in his hand.

"Shall we dance?"

Luke and Pierce bowed, eyes locked. Each dropped fluidly into a crouch, a mirror image of the other. Luke spun the tanto in his right hand so that the blade pointed down. He had greater reach. But any solid slash he received from the kukri would cause serious damage, and in the past, Pierce had had an edge in speed.

The two men paused, feeling the aura-like strengths and weaknesses of the other. Their stillness was eerie. Pierce edged slightly to the left, and Luke knew he would try to take advantage of his blind side. Pierce could attack him where he could not see. Or he might try to take out Luke's other eye, leaving him blinded, in pain, and without defense. But what was Pierce's weakness?

They had fought in mock combat hundreds of times, until each was intimately familiar with the style and tactics of the other. Weaken the enemy, make him bleed. If Pierce had a weakness Luke could exploit now, it had to be something that had happened since the war.

Pierce slashed at him twice. Luke blocked each blow with the tanto, surprised at how fast Pierce had become.

"Let it go, Matthew," he said quietly.

But Pierce would not listen. He came at Luke like a steel whirlwind, attacking almost faster than Luke could parry. Suddenly Pierce reversed the kukri, brushing the back of it against Luke's chest, opening a razor-fine cut.

"First blood, Luke," Pierce said. "I always drew first blood!"

He came in again, knife flashing in the sun. Luke absorbed the force of the attacks, stopping the kukri just shy of cutting, drawing Pierce forward into motion. Pierce slashed, and Luke leaned back from the swinging arm, uncoiling with a short, sharp kick to Pierce's solar plexus. Pierce grunted in pain and rolled with the force of the blow, coming to his knees fast enough to block Luke's next attack.

"Very good," Pierce said, voice only slightly labored, "but you're losing blood. How long until you get weak and slow?"

Luke could feel the blood running down his chest, soaking the beltline of his fatigues. He had a scant handful of minutes—maybe less —before he would begin to lose strength. Pierce seemed to have limitless energy. He kept pushing Luke, making him work, bleed. Luke defended himself, searching for the will to end his old friend and failing to find it.

Steel rang on steel. The sun climbed higher, shortening their shadows on the gray, dusty plateau, the heat oppressive, covering them both with slick sweat. The only sounds were their grunts and the clash of steel as they circled. Luke felt tiredness creeping into his muscles and heard a high C-pitched ringing in his ears, the first sign of blood loss. Unless he did something soon, he—and all he was fighting for —would be done for. And that was what this was about.

The war had changed Pierce into a hateful man. Therein was his weakness. He would continue to attack Luke until one of them was dead, for no other reason than because it was what he had set out to do, manipulated first by a shattered self-image and then by whatever drove Jed. Luke knew he had the strength to defeat that demon.

He reached into the calm, dark well of himself and brought to the surface the abilities he had developed. In this void, Luke heard nothing but the beating of his heart. Time became fluid, a force for him to manipulate. His vision became ultra-clear. The potential for heightened speed and strength, for unnaturally quick reflexes, flowed through his tired limbs.

With Pierce isolated from the essence of himself, Luke saw that the Pierce who had been his friend had died in Las Vegas on the first night of the war. Who he fought now was someone else.

When Luke defeated that flesh, a part of him would die as well. This was only another sacrifice in a seemingly never-ending string. The gods demanded much for mankind's survival. The Manitou had demanded much too much. And here was where Luke chose to stop it.

He concentrated first on the slice across his chest, closing the veins and capillaries, stopping the flow of blood. He breathed deeply, making his blood sing with oxygen.

Pierce crabbed in sideways and attacked with a series of slashes. Luke parried each one. On the last attack, he held the tanto along Pierce's forearm as the man pulled back his arm. It cut deeply. Pierce hissed in anger, trailing ribbons of blood. Luke closed on him before he could recover and feinted a slash at Pierce's stomach, then hammered him in the face with two rapid, heavy blows. Pierce went to the ground, and Luke was out of his reach before the man knew what had hit him. He was off the ground in a flash, astonishment on his face.

"You were never that fast before," Pierce said in surprise.

They circled, Pierce low in a crouch to make it more difficult for Luke to attack.

"Neither of us is who we used to be," Luke replied. "You have become stronger and faster. But at least you have retained your humanity. What I have become is not quite human. You know this; you have seen it. You cannot beat me, Matthew. You only have your life to lose. I have the lives of all people at stake, and if it takes your death to save them, then it will be done. Give it up, for the last time. I do not want you to become another sacrifice. But if I have to choose your death over the death of all mankind, I will. Do not force that choice."

Pierce shook his head. "It's too late. I can't. Not now, Luke. Kill me, or I kill you. It's all the same."

Luke smiled with a sadness he could not feel and sheathed the tanto. He held his hands open, palms out, then brought them parallel to the ground as he dropped into a fighting stance. Slowly he and Pierce circled, moving closer with each tense revolution. Pierce struck as they closed within arm's reach, cutting upwards to rip open Luke's belly. Luke stopped the blow, then the others that followed. Pierce kicked and Luke blocked, then shattered Pierce's left kneecap with a blinding arc of his foot. The man lurched, and Luke caught him by his empty hand, immobilizing it.

Screaming at the pain, full of rage, Pierce hacked at Luke with the curved kukri. The knife grazed Luke's cheek. He grabbed the wrist holding the blade. Pierce struggled to free himself, but Luke was much stronger, squeezing until the bones in Pierce's wrist creaked and threatened to shatter.

Pierce put all his weight on his good leg and pulled at Luke until the cords stood quivering in his neck, trying to bring Luke close for a head butt. Luke held him immobile until the man's strength began to fade.

He took Pierce's knife hand in both of his and looked his old friend in the eye. Pierce saw what he intended to do. "No!" he shouted, unable to move.

Luke saw rage cross Pierce's face, followed by a fleeting glimpse of . . . release from his self-imposed Hell? He bent the hand holding the kukri until the knife was resting against Pierce's belly. Pierce struggled, and Luke saw in his eyes the faintest outline of twisted antlers.

"Goodbye, old friend," he whispered, and put all his strength behind the kukri, driving it deep.

The image faded from Pierce's eyes. A strange look came over his face, as if for a moment, Pierce was not sure where he was . . . who he was. He looked down at Luke's hand around his own on the knife in his belly, and he went limp. Luke released Pierce's free hand, and Pierce placed it over Luke's and his own on the knife. Blood dribbled over his lips.

"All right, lad," he whispered, "finish me good. Let's do this right."

They both pushed on the blade at the same instant. Their combined strength drove the kukri deep into his chest. He collapsed to the ground. Luke knelt beside him, holding his old friend's head on his knees.

"I'm sorry, Matthew," he said.

Pierce's eyes were glassy. His voice was a bloody whisper. "And I am dying a fool. If only we could go back. . ." Pierce coughed and shuddered with pain. He grabbed Luke's arm. "But you can't go back. Go forward. Save all that you can, now. Beware of Jed. I think he can control my commandos with me gone. He will not let you leave here alive."

Pierce's body began to relax. "I . . . wish," he whispered. "There is nothing to be afraid of. . . You've always been your own worst enemy."

Luke waited until Pierce no longer breathed, then gently closed his friend's eyes. He laid Matthew down on the ground under the hot sun, blood soaking into the soil.

All watched in stunned silence as Luke strode to where the guards held Mindy, his boots ringing on the hard, rocky ground. He shouldered one guard aside. The other moved back automatically. Luke took her by the hand and immediately turned around, back towards the MOC.

Mindy bent down to grab her pack, and Luke almost jerked her off her feet. She bit her lip to keep from crying out, feeling the tension build. Jed watched in shocked silence from the truck bed, seeing all his dreams melting away in the footsteps of Luke Kimball. All the time he had spent voicing to Pierce's (that weak coward!) soldiers had been in preparation for this moment. Now was supposed to be the hour of his triumph! His unholy rage built to a head, and he released it in the most powerful Voice he had ever used.

"No!" he called out in the Voice, the sound of it ringing out like no earthly bell ever had.

Mindy stumbled, dazed by the power of the Voice, and Luke pulled her along. She tried to regain her footing, feeling as if she had been stunned.

"No!" Jed called out again.

Luke heard the army rustle as the Voice took control. He could feel Jed's eyes on his back and wished now that he had shot the preacher in Minneapolis when he had had the chance.

"Kimball is evil. He is Satan! He has killed your leader by treachery and deceit. You all know the story. Once, they were friends. Kimball used their friendship to trick Pierce into his death!"

The soldiers raised their voices in anger. Luke pulled Mindy faster, breaking into a run, passing Pierce's body. If they could get into the MOC before the army attacked, they had a chance —a small chance. Right now, they were trapped out in the open.

"Did you love Pierce?" Jed cried out.

"Yes!" the commandos shouted.

"Did he bring you honor and victory in combat?"

"Yes!"

"Does his memory live on in you?"

"Yes!" they shouted again, in thrall with

Jed's Voice.

"Jesus," Mindy whispered numbly.

"It gets worse," Luke said between ragged breaths.

"Will you avenge his death?"

"Yes!" the army thundered. "Yes, yes, YES!"

"Oh, shit," Mindy said.

"Shit is right. Faster!"

They began to run hard, fleeing to the shelter of the MOC. Every step took them closer, but it was still so far.

Jed screamed, "Then Luke Kimball is your enemy. Kill him! Kill all who are with him. Let the memory of your leader stand for all eternity. This I command you! This is the Voice of God!"

The commandos roared, a sound to make the ground tremble. Luke heard a thousand metallic clicks as weapons were armed and readied. The others were only steps away. He shoved Mindy forward, yelling, "Get in the MOC!"

Then he turned to face the army. Jed saw him turn. Madness raised the veins in Jed's forehead. He scrambled to the top of the cab of the truck.

"There is your enemy," he cried, pointing a rigid arm at Luke. "Destroy him now! NOW! NOW! NOW!"

His words were whips, goading the army on. They surged forward in a line, hundreds of men and women armed with combat rifles, heavy machine guns, and other weapons of war.

Their snarl was the call of a beast more savage than any that had ever walked the earth. The first shots rang out, spattering the dust at his feet. Luke heard the MOC door close as Mindy and the others made it inside.

Now was the time. He raised his arms to the sky and uttered the word he had been given in the Spirit World, calling forth the gift. His words made the ground tremble.

The shaking grew with the force of an earthquake, bringing Pierce's commandos to their knees. The ground around Luke began to crack open in long lines that stretched like claws towards them.

Luke, standing unmoving, unaffected, heard the war cries of warriors long dead. Their calls were carried by the thunder of horse hooves. The cracks opened wider, and the first warriors emerged, grim skeletons riding skeletal horses. Their horse blankets and headdresses were scraps of worn and faded cloth and hide, their hair long and dusty from the beyond. But their lances and weapons were stone and steel, bright and sharp. They leaped from the bowels of the earth as fast as the wind, a hundred at a time, until more than a thousand raced across Bloody Run.

One stopped in front of Luke and raised its lance in salute, jaw hanging open in a deathly smile, skeletal horse hooves raking the air, before joining the foray. Their war calls and the screams of their mounts chilled the air. Clouds of dust rose from their hooves. Luke watched as the commandos, transfixed with terror, forgot about him and opened fire on the warriors. It did no good; bullets could not harm those already dead.

The skeletal warriors fought with courage and spirit remembered from flesh long gone. The soldier's bullets cut through them, shattering bone. But the dead ones felt no pain. They charged into the first ranks, spears lowered, to impale their enemies.

Somewhere in the confusion of combat, Luke heard Jed's cry of terror. He waited as the warriors circled the army, raising more dust until the battle could longer be seen. The sounds were enough. He went into the MOC and sat with the others, letting Ellie bandage his chest, waiting silently until the battle was over.

The last war cry came in the late afternoon. The setting sun colored the sky red, bathing the battlefield in bloody light. Trucks and jeeps smoldered, frames charred and burning tires pouring black smoke into the sky. Bodies were scattered everywhere, but not a bone of the warriors was to be found. The Seven walked among them, shocked by the savagery the warriors had delivered. Pierce's army had been hacked and speared. Many had broken lances sticking out from their sides. Luke saw that they had been scalped—trophies of war.

There were no survivors. Luke threaded

his way to the truck on which Jed had stood. It was in flames. Luke searched carefully, but Jed's body was nowhere to be seen. He walked slowly, not answering the questions of the others until he had seen every body on the battlefield. Jed was not among them.

Then Billy called him over to the smoldering hulk of a jeep. "I think what you're looking for is here."

The corpse in the driver's seat and was crisped black. Luke could not make out any features. Even as he observed the smoking, human wreckage, the charred remains of its robe disintegrated into piles of ash. White bones gleamed through the blackened flesh. The corpse's feet were covered in the burnt remains of combat boots. Jed. Something gave way in the skull, and the jaw fell into Jed's lap, making a crunching sound.

In the mid-ground between the MOC and the slaughter, Pierce was gone, swallowed into the earth with the retreat of the warriors. Luke only hoped that his friend could join them and realize a better beginning if he made it to the Spirit World.

"Let's go," Luke said and turned his back. "This battle is over."

They followed him to the MOC, afraid of what was going to happen. They stood in a circle next to the vehicle. Luke held out his arms.

"Take them," he said softly. "This is the

moment we were all born for. This is what we have become through our losses and sacrifices. Everything the future is begins now."

"I'm afraid of what I'll feel," Billy whispered, looking small despite his size.

"We all are," said Cal. "But there's nothing to lose . . . that we have not already lost. Would you have it be for naught?"

Ellie stood next to Luke. "I love you," she said.

It was a quiet declaration that touched them all. She closed her hand around Luke's, then reached to Mindy on her left.

"I love you," she said.

"I love you," Mindy answered, and took Ellie's hand.

Mindy reached out to Michael, who said the words and gave his hand to Cal.

"I love you," the black man said to Tony and took the wild boy's hand.

Tony said the words and held his pale hand out to Billy. The big man took it gently, then held his hand out to Luke. Hope touched his fear.

"I love you," Billy said.

Luke clasped Billy's hand and closed the circle. He looked at each in turn, feeling the strengths of their souls, feeling the moment hinge on his next words. Their faces were so full of fear, so full of hope, so aware of their weaknesses, so unaware of their power.

"I love you," he said—and the sky opened.

They were flies trapped in the amber of eternity. The Spirit Hoop crossed over them with the tidal roar of a tsunami. Each could see the complex, colorful soul lights of the others leaping from their bodies to join the Hoop. They lived the lives of the others and felt their loves and losses, joys, sorrows, and hate. They saw how each had changed to develop a strength that bridged worlds.

The Hoop called in a multitude of voices, and they could see, bonded as they were, that the Hoop was of many colors and many soul lights . . . the lights of all the peoples of the world throughout time. The light in which the gods lived was the Light of Man.

Tony's green light found a center between them. Billy's blue joined it. Then orange for Cal, golden for Mike, green for Mindy, and silver for Ellie. And for Luke, nothing.

They touched him, and as they lived his life, shared the tragedies of his past, his battle with the Manitou and ventures into the Spirit World, they saw what he lacked.

"You are not yet whole," the six spoke to him with one voice. "The iron in you is still to be tempered. "

He felt their love and compassion, their strength and support. He saw into his soulless life with their eyes.

He answered, "I thought that bringing us all together would complete the Key. Now I don't know what we must do. Where have I gone wrong?" He felt supported on the web of their minds. "I have no answers. I don't know what to do, and so much is riding on the decision."

"The touch of the Manitou is in you," Tony said. "For this, none of us has the answers. We must go to the Tree. Joseph will know how to help us. He is the Keeper."

"We will follow you," said Cal. "We have faith in you."

"But everyone close to me has died," Luke said. "Even Pierce. I don't want you all to follow me to that same fate."

Ellie gripped his hand tightly. "Then we will die knowing that we all lived as truly and purely as we could. We have a purpose worth dying for."

"Thank you," he said to them all. "Then, to the Tree of Life! It will be done."

The conviction of his words made the Spirit Wheel ripple. Reluctantly, they let go of each other's hands, but the bond between them remained. Mike and Mindy had their arms around each other as if they would never let go. Mike grinned at Billy, and the big man punched him lightly on the arm.

They knew how Luke felt . . . or could not feel . . . and continued to hold him in their thoughts. So strong yet so fragile, not yet the man he wished he could be, yet these people accepted and loved him as he was. Knowing that they could die, they loved him still, without condition. It was amazing. It was . . . like being home.

THE TREE
OF LIFE

Once, this heavily forested north central part of Washington state had been known as the Colville Indian Reservation. Bordered by the Columbia and Spokane rivers to the south and the Kettle River Mountains to the north, the reservation land was a transition from the high, rocky desert of the Grand Coulee dam area to the heavily forested slopes in the north. It was the burial site of Chief Joseph of the Nez Percé, the famous warrior leader who had said, "I will fight no more forever."

Even in the best of times, the reservation had been sparsely populated. Old Joe's people had lived in the northeast corner, in a valley north of Twin Lakes at the foot of the mountains. One of the many plagues sweeping the country during the war had hit the reservation, taking so many lives that the few survivors had dug mass graves for the victims. This had gone against custom and had left the survivors saddened that the old ways were truly gone. Joseph had stayed in his valley, keeping the essence of the old ways alive in his heart, watching over the Tree of Life and hoping for an awakening.

The first people to come to the Tree of Life had not been Native Americans. They had dreamed of the Tree and followed their visions, seeking a unity that transcended race or religion. He had welcomed all and had seen them in turn welcome newcomers with the same spirit. And now there was such a diversity of mankind here in this small but growing community. Red, black, white, yellow, Eastern and Western, Christian, Muslim, Jewish . . . and more.

Conversations around dinnertime fires were always rich with a wealth of opinions shared and debated with much passion, but little heat. He had known these people would come, had known the minute the gods returned to the world. And now the Seven were near. The People knew it. Joseph could feel their excitement as they prepared.

Hunting parties had brought back deer, elk, and grouse. Others had caught fish from the lakes in the area. Foragers had combed the reservation lands for berries and apples in the near-fallow orchards scattered around the territory. The children had made paper lanterns to hang from the trees and the newly built homes going up in a nicely planned fashion. The knowledge of the Seven was as universal here as the dreams of the Tree, and the People were ready to love them with a unity that could not have existed, Joseph believed, before the war. Let them believe. Let them hope. They did not know what the Wendigo had wrought. By now, Luke Kimball suspected, but he still had much to learn.

The windows to Joseph's cabin were open, letting in the warm air and mid-morning sunshine. He heard the happy calls of the children as they ran among the buildings and central plaza. His house was one of the first built by Johnny, the young architect who had grown up in Kenya. Simple and small, but so well-planned as to feel spacious, with windows all around to catch the sun and a wide, low roof to support the heavy snows of winter. Each house had a simple outhouse arrangement with chamber pots that were dumped on a "honey wagon" each morning. The slop was composted at the edge of a farther clearing to make fertilizer for fields that would be plowed this fall and planted next spring.

Water came from the Kettle River. Someday soon, they would have sewer systems and running water. He had dreamed of solar energy powering and heating houses. There were many tools and materials to scavenge from the ruins now, to incorporate into a new way of living, as long as they did not forget how to invent and create in harmony.

Joseph took a red flannel shirt from the

closet, buttoned it on, and left the house. The village of the People had been laid around a central plaza, a great circle where the people carried out common tasks and visited in the evenings. Each row of houses was being built in a ring, one in back of the other. Three rings had been completed so far. His was on the inside ring, as were the houses awaiting the Seven. The plaza was full of activity.

Spitted meat roasted over half a dozen large fires. He could smell the scents from many different cultures. Joseph caught the tangy odor of Chinese hot and sour soup, and the wonderful smell of salt-rubbed meat roasting Gaucho style over wood fires. It made his mouth water. Multi-colored paper lanterns and cranes were strung everywhere. Today would truly be a festive day.

People greeted him as he walked through the community. Joseph answered all with a smile and a wave, or a kind word. He loved these people. They were the future.

Antonio called to him as he passed the stables. "Old Joe! Look!" He paraded a chestnut roan around the paddock. The horse's coat had been brushed until it shone as bright as a copper penny.

Joseph said, "He is beautiful."

Antonio smiled. He was wearing black-and-white cowhide chaps and a new black Stetson hat. "Today, they will all be beautiful!"

Joseph laughed and continued, past the

stables and down the path to the clearing that held the Tree of Life. It was quiet here. Setsuko's chain of one thousand cranes hung from the lowest branches of the Tree. It was the only spot of color on the gray branches. The cranes were a prayer for the living, for life. They belonged on the Tree. Joseph felt a sudden, panicky urge to tell the People that their hopes of the future were in jeopardy, that the Wendigo had placed an obstacle in Luke Kimball's way that was seemingly impossible to overcome.

Instead, he clenched his hands tightly and sat down with his back against the Tree. He could not; they needed to dream, to have hope. Today was a special day. There would be a celebration. Laughing, dancing, and when night came, loving under the stars. A celebration for the Seven, but more—for themselves, for the gods, a candle to hold against the darkness, for each other to see, saying, "Here! Come to me; we are alive."

Yes, there would be a celebration. But also, he and Luke Kimball would talk. Joseph leaned his head back against the rough bark of the Tree and shut his eyes. Soon they would be here. All too soon.

The people were waiting when the Seven arrived. They lined the rutted road into the community, waving and cheering. Luke picked them up on the scanners and dropped the .50 into its compartment, disabling the weapon. Its usefulness was done—hopefully forever.

"Showtime," Luke called to the others. "We're almost there."

He had stopped at a roadside stream a few hours earlier so they could wash and change. Ellie had trimmed the blond, ragged thatch of his hair, and then gave him a new black eye patch she had sewn. He wore a pair of old, faded jeans, civilian clothing, for the first time since he had left the retreat. They felt strange, but good. Luke had a clean hide shirt he had found in the provisions left by Buffalo Woman. He put it on and locked his weapons in the back of the MOC. He asked the others to do the same. The place they were going to would be a place of peace.

Ellie and Mindy both wore skirts and were radiant. Mindy kept rubbing a red, raw spot on her chin. She had made Mike shave twice, so Luke could guess where it had come from: new loves. Ellie looked like she belonged with the people, brave and free. Even now he could feel her in his mind, loving him, waiting and hoping for the moment he could touch her soul and love her back.

Ellie had given Tony a much-needed bath. The boy had even allowed her to trim his hair. He wore an X-Men T-shirt, new jeans, and sneakers with heels that flashed with light when he ran. He looked so much like any normal child . . . except for the large wolf standing by his side.

Calvin was the same, inside and out:

clean, calm, and confident. He had found a light-colored flannel shirt and new, clean khakis in one of the towns they had passed through.

Mike and Billy seemed the most uncomfortable. Without their weapons, each felt naked and vulnerable. Billy had bound his hair into a loose ponytail, with a single feather hanging from the knot. He wore a sweatshirt with the sleeves and neck cut out. His jeans were pulled over a pair of low-heeled riding boots.

Mike had shaved both his face and his head, per Mindy's request. Without the mohawk, he looked completely different, younger, and more innocent. His leathers were stored away, and he now wore jeans and a navy sweater Mindy had pulled out of the store where Cal had found his clothing. Mike had even taken off his riding boots and consented to wear a pair of white, high-top basketball shoes.

"How do they feel?" Billy joked.

Mike pantomimed a kick at Billy's head. "Not bad, man. Really, not bad."

Even Samson had received a bath. Ellie and Tony had curried his coat until it was glossy. Now they were vibrating with excitement. Luke wheeled the MOC down the road at little more than an idle, windows down, so the others could see their welcome.

Ellie saw the people first. "Look at all of them!"

The others crowded forward. Ellie

suddenly had to deal with a boy and a wolf in her lap. Tony began to hoot and yell, too excited to speak. The cheers of the people grew louder until the Seven were waving and shouting back their greetings. The crowd began to throw wildflowers at the slowly moving vehicle. A small girl ran up to his window with a bouquet. She held them out to Luke, a hopeful smile on her face.

"Thank you, little one," he said. "You are very kind."

She ran away happy. Luke handed the flowers back to Mindy, who gave one to each of the Seven. He cast his mind over the crowd, sensing their happiness, their hope, the trust they had in him, a total stranger. He had come too far, survived too much to fail now. They knew with all their hearts that the Seven could make the Tree of Life bloom. No one had told them this; it was something they just knew. It was communal knowledge, sacred, larger than the whole of their sum. This was the seed of what the future might be. It was worth fighting for . . . worth dying for.

They rounded a corner and saw the community for the first time. Immediately Luke recognized their building plan: hoops within hoops, interspersed with trees and other greenery so that the sense of the forest and open, sunny glades remained. The road led to the central plaza. Luke could feel a presence waiting for them: Joseph. The man he needed to see.

Luke stopped in front of the flannel-shirted old man. They piled out of the motor home, happy to be in the sun. Joseph greeted each of them by name, making them feel welcome. Luke was the last. He could feel the power of the old man's spirit. It was a gentle spirit as well, tempered by time and wisdom . . . balance . . . a spirit of unity. Luke held out his hand.

"Old Joe, it's good to meet you face-to-face."

Joseph clasped Luke's hand with both of his. "Greetings, my son. Your being here brings me much happiness. You have lived through much to come this far."

He raised his voice. "Welcome to the People!"

The crowd joined his welcome, hundreds of voices together in spirit.

"We have much to talk about," Joseph said in a voice for Luke's ears alone, "and little time to accomplish many things. Today, we will all feast. Tonight also, we prepare you for the rest of your journey."

Luke nodded his head. "Then you already know?"

Joseph nodded his head once. "Yes. "

"I am ready. But I still need to find this crystal mask."

Joseph looked at him carefully. "Yes, you need the mask. But you may not want it. But don't think on it now. For the next hours, at least, have no cares."

The day was a whirlwind of activity. The houses chosen for them were part of the central circle. None of the Seven had many possessions, so moving in was easy. Each retreated to their new homes for a short time, desiring a moment of peace and solitude, so that they could assimilate being among so many people again. Luke sat on the bed and stared at the simply decorated walls, feeling very strange, trapped between his past and the uncertainty of his future. He wished . . . for many things, but did not know what he wanted first.

There was a knock on his door.

"It's open," he called.

Ellie came in, hands in the pockets of her jeans. She stood in the center of the home, examining the simple, rustic furnishings. "Looks nice," she said, "just like mine. They've given me a house a few doors down. We're neighbors now."

"Do you like it?" Luke asked, not knowing what to say.

Ellie looked down at the floor and shrugged. "It's okay, I guess. But it feels lonely. I suppose I'll get used to it again."

"I know what you mean. I've always been alone."

Ellie tilted her head to look at him. "Do you like it?"

Luke shook his head. "Not anymore. Once,

I thought that it was the only safe way to live. But I'm learning that the only thing you get from being alone is loneliness. If you don't like your house, you could . . . come stay with me."

Ellie sat on the bed next to him. "Do you want me to?"

Luke gently caressed her cheek. "Yes, I do. Only I worry that the past will repeat itself. And then I worry that you won't like me when you see what I'm like."

She smiled. "I'll take both chances. I wish you could see yourself as I see you. You are a good and strong man, Luke. You seem cold and aloof, sometimes, but you have been hurt so many times. You still grieve for all the people you've lost." Ellie cradled his face with her hands. "You can't cry for them, yet. I think someday soon, you will. But until then, can I cry for you? Please?"

Luke put his arms around her. He felt her tears wet his shoulder. He stroked the dark silkiness of her long hair, feeling her tremble in his arms.

"You're not alone now, not anymore," he whispered. "Go ahead. Cry for both of us."

He held her until Ellie stopped, then continued to hold her, feeling her warmth, her comfort.

"Where are your things?" Luke asked.

Ellie laughed and wiped her face. "Sitting outside your door."

"Well, bring them in. We'll just make the

best of what we have."

As Ellie disengaged from Luke's arms, the door burst open. Luke leaped up with inhuman quickness. But only Tony sprang into the room, followed by a frolicking Samson. Both boy and wolf were vibrant with excitement. Tony danced around the small house, his breathing as loud as the wolf's panting.

"I'm gonna stay here!" he exclaimed loudly enough to make Ellie wince.

Luke regarded Ellie solemnly, waiting for her to say something.

"I told him he could stay with me. He does need someone to watch over him," she explained. "A mother and a father figure. He identifies with us because we were the first to care for him. Please?"

Luke nodded assent.

"And Samson too?"

Luke replied, "The wolf is his best friend. Though I think he will soon be making more human friends."

He pointed at the open door. Half a dozen childish heads peeked around the frame.

"Okay, Tony. You stay here. But where will you sleep?"

Tony's face broke into a huge grin. "With Samson!" he said happily.

"Okay," said Luke. "Come here."

The boy came. Luke took the knife from Tony's belt before the boy had a chance to protest. Luke stopped him with an open palm and bent down to his level.

"Two things to remember. First: you are among people now. You will not wear a weapon until you have proven that you will not use it in anger. And second. . ." Luke put his open hand against Tony's chest. "You will not use your 'special abilities' against these people. They are all your family now. They will love you if you only love them back. Make them your friends. I know boys will be boys and you might get into fights, but use fists, not powers. Can you do these things?"

To Luke's surprise, Tony smiled, nodded, and then gave him a fierce, swift hug. He was gone out the door in a flash, yelling and screaming with the other children. Luke turned to Ellie and smiled.

"Now I have a woman, a child, and a dog. I will like being a family man."

Ellie brought her things inside and placed them on the bed. "I hope so. Soon your family will be a little larger," she said, indicating the people outside. "Shall we join them?"

"Yes," Luke answered, and they walked out the door hand in hand.

It was a feast, a celebration of the human spirit. People danced and sang all over the plaza. The Seven sat with Joseph in the center of it all, meeting the people who shyly came to greet them. Ellie marveled at the way the people seemed to work together in a coordinated effort, without anyone visibly leading them.

"They know," Joseph told her. "They feel the one love."

When the sun began to cast long shadows on the ground, Joseph stood. The people fell silent. In the medicine man's voice, Luke heard the same bell-like quality that had made Jed's voice so compelling. Yet Joseph's voice held none of that evil power—only love.

"We followed our dreams here to seek hope, to find life. We have survived much, clinging to our hopes like small candles on the darkest of nights. We are of all races, and yet we are one People. We have many histories, which we shall weave to make one future. We have one land, with which we shall become one heart. Let each be welcome here, in the unity we all share. Let each of our gifts enrich us all. Let us be of one mind, one heart, one love. This is the way of the People."

His words echoed among them. Then someone called out, "Yeah! Let's eat!", and everybody laughed, carrying the feelings forward.

The food was delicious, and there was plenty. They ate until they were full, overjoyed at both the taste of home-cooked food and the celebration surrounding their arrival. At dusk, five old Native American men began to beat a rhythm on a large drum. One began to chant. The others supplied the refrain. More people joined them as they picked up the chant, and some began to dance, following the beat with steps from all countries and styles. Luke reclined on a blanket next to Ellie, very full, listening to the chanting, hearing the happy tale it told, feeling it move him away from the center of his self. In the chant was magic that thinned the veil between here and the Spirit World. Luke could almost see the words rising like smoke, a force wonderful and powerful that he could touch if he desired.

The thought brought him back to center. As Luke watched, a black man joined the native dancers. His moves were clumsy. They laughed, and he laughed with them. They slowed their steps, showing him, until he caught the rhythm. Soon they moved as one. More joined in with shouts of laughter and joy.

The dancing slowed, and one younger woman started to teach a particular move. Step to the right, the right, the right: the Ghost Dance. Others picked it up quickly, shaking hips and shoulders, so that the dance was itself and something more, growing, encompassing, becoming. This is what he had come here for.

Luke looked around the darkening plaza for Joseph and was not surprised to find the old man hunkered down next to him.

"I want to learn how you do that," Luke said.

Joseph chuckled. "An old man's trick. It's

time we talked."

"Yes," Luke agreed and got up.

He followed Joseph away from the festivities, down the path that led to the Tree. This was the first time he had seen it in reality. Luke reached out to touch it, then slammed his fist into its rough, wrinkled bark. The Tree did not shake or quiver, or offer any sign that his blow had been felt.

Joseph asked, "Did that make you feel better?"

Luke put his split knuckles to his lips. "Not really. I just felt that I owed it something."

Joseph handed him a clean bandanna. Luke wrapped it around his hand.

"So much has happened. So many people have died, just so this tree can grow leaves again." Joseph patted the rough trunk. "It is a strong old tree, with roots that stretch to the beginnings of mankind and every place that can be conceived. It ties the spirit world, and all that is beyond it, to our realm of earth, to the underworld and all that lies beyond it. Yin and yang. Light and dark. It is the great unifier. And for some, it is a road that leads everywhere.

"What we see here is but a small shoot of the whole, the tiniest leaf. It has been known by many names in many cultures. The Tree of Knowledge. The Tree of Life. Yggdrasil and Jianmu. In the myths, the Tree connects the earth to the heavens and the underworld.

It is boundless and immensely powerful, yet so fragile."

Luke looked up at the field-side spread of its gray branches. "If this is so giant, I still do not understand why I matter to it—to any of all this. Why am I worthy, after all I have done?"

Joseph sat down with his back against the trunk. "I don't have any answers that will give you the reassurance you want. All I can say is, have faith and trust in what you have seen so far. Fate chose you. Forces so much greater than us chose you. This is what I believe.   If you complete your quest, the Tree of Life will blossom and connect everything as it should be. The Hoop of Life, of all existence, will again be round and whole. If you want to shake the Tree, Luke, complete your quest. You will move it, and the universe. No pressure."

Joseph smiled, and Luke sat down next to him under the heavy chain of paper cranes. A glint of colored paper caught his eye in the gathering twilight. Luke touched it, a single origami crane that had not been put into the chain. He twirled it in his fingers.

"My quest. The first part should be complete now. I have found the Key of Seven and brought them here. Yet something is wrong."

Joseph said, "Luke, take heart. You have overcome so much to bring the Seven here. This is a great accomplishment. But now you must prepare for the rest of your journey. Your hardest tasks still await you. Each of Seven is important because they have survived their trials to become something much, much greater. They have completed their hoop. Your hoop, though, still turns and is not yet complete."

"Me? How?"

"Because of your encounter with the Manitou, there is a void in your spirit, something I know you are very aware of. Of the Seven, you alone are not yet whole. The iron of your soul has yet to be tempered, the voids filled with new metal. There is only one way for you to do this."

"I must defeat the Manitou," finished Luke. "This is the battle it prophesied."

"Defeat? Hmm. Not all problems are nails, and not all solutions are hammers. "

"What does that mean?"

"Luke, you have always been a problem-solver, a fixer, a righter of wrongs. While your solutions have been effective, you have the single-mindedness of a hammer or a sword. "

Luke did not know what to say, so he said nothing, and the silence echoed around them.

Joseph sighed. "If you can overcome the Manitou, you will get back what you feel is missing. But before you can do that, you first have to find the crystal mask. If you hope to move beyond where you are now, the mask is the next journey on your quest."

"What will the mask give me?" Luke's words hung in the air. It was a while before

Joseph answered him.

"A clarity of vision. You will see the truth of things."

"And will the truth be a powerful weapon against the Manitou?"

"Luke, the truth is so powerful that it might destroy you," Joseph replied. "If you can get the mask and survive, you will have a chance —only a chance—of defeating a god in mortal combat. This is what will complete your hoop."

In the falling night, the air was crisply cool. Luke leaned his head against the Tree, accepting the inevitability of his fate, his trip around the Hoop.

"You must seek the crystal mask tomorrow night. Tonight, rest and gather your strength. You will need it. Remember, all that you have done in your life is leading up to what you have the potential to become. But you must seek it. And try to keep an open mind."

Luke stood and ran his fingers over the chain of origami birds. "The Hiroshima chain."

"You know the legend?" Joseph asked.

"Yes. Very well." Luke added the paper crane in his hand to the end of the origami chain.

"Why did you do that?" Joseph asked.

Luke could barely see the chain in the darkness. "For luck. A thousand origami cranes for hope. A thousand and one for luck. I need all the help I can get."

"Luke, we will help you all we can."

"I know you will. But I just hope that I have the strength it takes to do what must be done: to kill a god. I dreamt of this before and failed. Look at what happened. Am I strong enough now, Joseph?"

The old man laid a hand on Luke's shoulder. "Did you really fail? Remember, hammer and nails. I place my faith in you, Luke. I believe you are strong enough. If you have any hope of success, you need to have that same faith. Believe, Luke, in yourself."

THEATER OF THE NOH

Ellie expected the worst. Luke could feel her fear for him. They lay on the bed in their new home, hearing the shouts of children as they played in the plaza in the late afternoon. The early evening air was cool, full of the promise of winter. This morning there had been a thin, hair-like coat of frost on the roofs. The forest and tall grasses of the valley were cast in silver. The sun had warmed into a beautiful Indian summer day, but the portents of winter were there.

They had spent the day wandering the community, meeting their neighbors, and seeing the industries that were springing up around the plaza and at the edge of town. Mindy had shown her solar panel to the engineers and architects in the community. Already, they were planning scavenging trips into Seattle and Spokane to get the materials needed so that every home could have environmentally safe hot water and electricity. There were weavers and woodcarvers, shoemakers, a blacksmith, and even a gentleman named Kunimasi who was a Japanese swordsmith.

Luke and Kunimasi had shared tea, discussing sword forging and swordcraft. They both shared knowledge of kendo, Japanese fencing, and agreed to spar soon. Around midday, Luke retired to their house to rest and center his mind.

"Don't worry, Ellie. I'll be okay," he said again.

She ran her hand over the scarred, hard musculature of his chest. "I'm sorry. I can't help but worry. I have the feeling that something bad is going to happen to you."

"I've made it this far. We have made it here. And we'll see it through."

Luke gently slid from next to her and began to dress. He put on black fatigue pants, combat boots, and a loose, dark shirt; clothing he could move in. His weapons were stored in a chest at the foot of the bed. They would not be needed tonight. He splashed water on his face from the basin and sat back on the bed, waiting for dusk. Ellie sat up and pulled on her clothes. The smell of food came in through the window. Meals here were prepared in a community fashion.

"Do you want something to eat before you go?"

"Yes," Luke answered, "that would be

good."

She left, and Luke leaned back on the bed, letting his mind relax, concentrating only on the image of the mask from his dream. It was clear as air itself, but what kind of truth would it reveal? He reached deeper into himself, bringing his heightened senses forward. He slowed his heartbeat, taking deep breaths. Calm. The void. Centered. Ready.

Ellie came back with two plates. Luke was so quiet that she did not immediately notice him. When he moved on the bed, she gasped and almost dropped the food.

"Don't do that! You startled me. How can you sit so silently?"

Luke took one of the plates from her. "Practice. To sit silently, you have to make your mind quiet too. I'll show you, sometime."

"Hmm." She sat next to him. They ate in silence. "When are you leaving?" she asked.

Luke glanced out the window, at the shadows in the plaza. They were growing long. "In a few minutes. I will meet Joseph by the Tree. I don't know how long I will be gone. You and Tony might want to stay with Mike and Mindy."

"No. We'll wait for you. We all will wait for you, here. Just make sure you come home to us."

Luke smiled at her. "I'll be back."

He mopped up the last of the food from his plate. Ellie suddenly leaned over the table, grabbed his head, and kissed Luke hard. "You'd better come back," she said breathlessly.

Luke put his hands over hers. "Count on it."

He kissed her again and was gone. Ellie cleaned up their dishes, then sat down, waiting for the others, waiting for Luke to come home.

The old man was waiting by the Tree of Life. He was dressed as always in a flannel shirt and jeans. He examined Luke. "You are ready, then?"

Luke nodded once, tersely. "Yes. I am ready."

Joseph turned and led him down the path into the forest.

Luke asked, "Aren't we going into the Spirit World?"

"Yes and no," Joseph replied over his shoulder. "We are going to a place you have been before."

Luke was too puzzled by this answer to ask any more questions. He followed the old man deeper into the forest as the sky darkened. They hiked for hours. The forest, already black with night, became even more indistinct as a cold fog rose from the ground. It became difficult for him to make out the outline of Joseph as he led them.

"We are almost there." Joseph's voice was muffled by the fog.

The ground became harder under Luke's feet—smooth rock. He felt a strange vibration that was familiar, something he had once known well but could not now place.

Joseph said, "Here we are. Good luck. I hope you find what you are looking for."

The old man's voice was fading as he finished. Luke realized he was now alone.

He crouched in the fog, feeling the vibrations grow stronger through the soles of his boots. He heard a rumbling, and then two large, gleaming eyes rushed at him from the darkness. Luke leaped out of the way. He heard an angry stream of Japanese as the taxi rolled off into the night, tires noisy on the pavement.

The air had a peculiar smell, familiar. Fish and diesel, sesame oil, garlic, and steaming rice. He could make out the shapes of buildings, now visible through the heavy veil of fog, lit with neon kanji symbols: Tokyo.

Luke looked at himself. He was wearing a black suit and an overcoat. In his hand were two white slips of paper. Tickets. Reiko grabbed his arm.

"Haven't you ever seen a taxi before? Come, Luke-san," she said, "we'll be late for the show."

He allowed her to pull him down the crowded street, numb, thinking that Reiko was long dead and that this was not happening. Or was it? Yesterday he had arrived in the community of the People (gone hiking with Reiko in the mountains outside of Tokyo). Luke touched his face and found . . . an eye patch. He almost pulled his arm from Reiko's.

She stopped and touched his forehead. "Are you sure you're alright? You've had a lot on your mind lately and need to relax, my love."

Her hand was cool and wonderful on his head. She brushed his temple, and Luke could have wept, wishing that this were not a dream. The Noh Theater was two doors down. They joined the line waiting outside. Luke knew what would happen after.

He had a wild thought of just continuing down the street with her, arm in arm. He knew that he could keep this fantasy if he so wished. They would have children, grow old and die together. Nothing would ever go wrong, for him. The rest of the world would die, but if he made that sacrifice, he would have happiness. Left or right, live or die. The choice was his, but there was no choice at all. If the world would live, he had to let Reiko die all over again. The gods had taken everything from him now, even this, again.

He took several deep breaths, quelling the tears that threatened to rise from the depths of his heart, and patted her hand. "I'm alright," he said with a smile. "Let's see the play. And Reiko-chan? I love you."

She kissed him on the mouth—a bold thing in such a public place, and his love for her, his terror at was about to happen, almost brought him crashing down. But he maintained an appearance of calm as they entered the theater and took their seats, at the foot of the stage, as they had so many years before.

The stage had been set to have a dark, foreboding, urban look. A city, perhaps, vague, indistinct, menacing. Wisps of fog drifted across the stage.

"The Noh is one of Japan's most treasured art forms," whispered Reiko. "Behind the costumes and masks, the actors carry the soul of our country. These artists are melding the traditional with the contemporary. This should be fascinating!"

Musicians began to play in the dark corner off to the side of the stage. The audience around them faded until only he and Reiko were in the theater. Fog billowed at the rear of the stage. In the dark, the stage seemed to have grown larger. Luke saw a figure press itself up against the side of a building, moving with stealth, coming closer with careful, silent steps. The drums beat in time with his movements. It was night. The actor wore a long black leather trench coat—the coat Luke had just checked.

"This is not the play we saw," Luke whispered to Reiko.

She nodded, and Luke saw sadness in her eyes. Luke could see the mask the actor wore now. He was not too surprised.

"Must I watch this?" he asked.

The ghost of Reiko shook her head. "No,

lover; you must live it. Again."

The actor stopped only a few paces away from Luke. They were a part of the stage now. The air was cold and dank, wet with fog. Luke could smell the fish and sewage tang of the warehouse district.

The actor took off the mask bearing Luke's features. Its face was a black, eyeless blur. Luke stood, stepped onto the stage, and took the mask. As soon as it touched his hand, the mask turned to ice-clear crystal. Dreading what was to come next, Luke put it on.

"Now you shall see the truth of things," Reiko said from the audience. "This is what the mask does. It will show you what is, not what you think or hope or wish to believe."

The mist swirled up around her, hiding her from view.

"Face what is with an open heart, Luke. An open heart."

"Reiko?" Luke called to her.

The fog swallowed his voice. He called again, louder, more anxious. He screamed her name, sweat beading his face, knowing she was gone into the night.

Luke leaned against the cold, clammy wall of the warehouse, catching his breath. The echoes of his shouts were short and muffled. He looked around wildly, for a moment not sure where he was, or why. Then he remembered.

This was happening. Or had it already

happened, so many years before? He opened the leather trench coat and reached inside, gripping what he had hidden beneath. He no longer wore a suit and pulled the collar of his black turtleneck shirt away from his body, letting the steam of his sweat rise into the cold air. It was all in front of him now. Damn Trinkla—damn him to Hell! Luke thought he had killed the Russian in the desolate, rocky war zone of Afghanistan. But the bastard had survived.

Two nights ago (or was it longer?), Reiko had disappeared from the theater, where they had gone to see the Noh. Yesterday, Luke had received a package via courier. In it was a set of instructions . . . and the smallest finger from Reiko's left hand. Now Luke was here, tracking them to a conclusion that would only end in tragedy.

There were no streetlights in this industrial district. The bright neon and glitter of downtown Tokyo were distant, hidden by the fog and smog. Here the buildings were dark and silent, dingy in the moist night air. Luke heard rats scurrying in the alleys, and once, distant voices. He moved down one side of the narrow street, combat senses in overdrive, ready to attack, feeling the large, solid forms of the dark structures looming over him. He had expected Trinkla to make a move against him before he reached his destination: an old warehouse described in the note that had come with Reiko's finger. But all was quiet. This part of the city was asleep, unaware of the deadly drama about to play out.

He turned a corner. The warehouses here were separated by narrow, claustrophobic alleys. Luke hesitated before each, feeling for the presence of an enemy. But nobody was waiting for him. He felt beneath his coat again, keeping a hand on the sword. It was another reminder of Reiko. She had bought it for him. She had arranged for his training in its use and had turned out to be a formidable student herself, along with another traditional Japanese weapon, the naginata. Tonight, he would use the sword to save her . . . if he could. If he survived whatever trap Trinkla had set for him. Right now, Reiko was bait, Trinkla the hunter, and Luke the prey and hunter as well.

The tuna warehouse was at the end of the street, backed against the harbor. The air smelled heavily of fish. In a few hours, this district would come alive with tuna vendors preparing the day's offerings for sushi restaurants across the world. The first arrivals here would find quite a surprise. The drive-in doors of the warehouse were locked tight. A sign in English and Japanese, just visible in the night, read, Happy Mountain Fish Co.

Luke loosened his overcoat and pushed on the smaller pedestrian door. It was open. A dim light came from within. Luke could feel Trinkla waiting and knew the Russian could sense him as well. He hoped Trinkla could also feel his rage. He had seen the fear in Trinkla's eyes, in Afghanistan, before shooting him in the face. He wanted Trinkla to feel that terror again.

The warehouse was cold and deathly silent. Luke waited outside the door, listening, trying to feel the presence of any trap waiting for him. He ran his fingers inside the doorjamb from bottom to top. No wires. He pushed the door open wider and quickly stepped in, then away along the wall, to avoid being silhouetted against the doorway. He pressed himself against the wall and waited, examining the interior of the warehouse. Inside, it was much larger than it had seemed, empty save for stacks of wooden pallets awaiting giant carcasses of bluefin and bigeye tuna. The pallets were neatly arranged at regular intervals. Steel beams supported a grid of rafters from which the lighting hung. Most of the fixtures were dark. Every sixth light had been left on. The low ceiling above the rafters was pitch black. There was no sign of Reiko or Trinkla. At any other time, Luke would have suspected that he had been led to a dead end. But he could feel the presence of his enemy.

The Russian's menace was an echo of his hate. It made Luke want to kill him even more, for his brother Thomas and Reiko; for every bad thing that had ever happened to him. Luke moved into the warehouse, ready to drop and roll at the first sign of movement. It would be too easy for Trinkla to take him with a bullet, but he suspected that Trinkla would try to kill him by means more personal. That was how he would have done it.

A distinct click drove Luke up against the nearest pile of pallets. But the sound was from a door being opened at the far end of the warehouse. The room beyond was brightly lit and spilled a corridor of light on the concrete floor. He took the invitation and walked briskly to it. What he saw inside stopped him dead. This was exactly what Trinkla wanted. It was too much for Luke to handle. He dropped his guard . . . and Trinkla attacked.

There was a metallic whisper and a quick glint of steel as the wire dropped over his neck. The wire was sharp enough to cut to the bone. Trinkla jerked it tight, pulling upwards with all his might. Luke came to his toes, choking and flailing his arms for balance. He reached blindly with his left arm, trying to find the wire, moving his arm up until he had a tight wrap. The leather of his overcoat gave him a small measure of padding. He put all his weight on the wire and pulled back against Trinkla, ignoring the blinding pain in his throat.

Trinkla's arm came out from the darkness of the rafters into the light. Luke jerked hard, gritting his teeth at the sharp pain of the razor wire slicing into his arm. He felt the Russian slip, and Trinkla's face was caught in a cone of light. It was hideous. In their previous battle, Luke's last shot had blown away the man's lower jaw. The Russian's once rugged face was now a twisted mass of scar tissue. His mouth was an ugly wound. Pure hate, horror, and madness glared in the Russian's pale blue eyes. The strength of that hate shocked him, surpassing even his own. For a moment, Luke felt guilt at what he had done to Trinkla. But then he remembered Thomas and Reiko and found purpose in his hate. He ripped at the wire.

The wire cut deeply, giving Luke a scar he would have for the rest of his life. Trinkla fell from the rafters, screaming his hate in words as twisted as his face.

"Look what you have made me!" he screamed. "I will kill you. I have killed her!"

Luke could not talk; the wire cut off all speech. He reached under his coat and grasped the weapon he carried, pulling it free in a gleaming arc of blue-hued silver. The katana hissed as Luke brought it upright, humming as he spun it in his hand. Trinkla's face had just begun to show surprise when Luke swung. The steel severed Trinkla's head from his body. It bounced across the warehouse floor and stared at Luke with surprise and hatred before the life drained away and the pale blue eyes glazed over.

Luke dug the wire from his arm. Blood welled from the long, spiral cut, making the sleeve of his coat shiny and slick. Struggling for every breath and fighting black spots in his vision, Luke reached trembling fingers to his neck, loosened the wire, and pulled it over his head. He reached inside the collar of his turtleneck and removed an armored collar made from plates he had taken from a flak vest. The wire had cut them deeply, but not enough to hurt him.   Trinkla's blood spread in a black pool surrounding his body. He felt no elation at his enemy's death. He only wanted Reiko to leave this place and for this chapter of his life to end. Luke hoped he had not seen what was in the room before Trinkla attacked him. The door was open, waiting. He entered . . . and saw what his vengeance had wrought.

Reiko was still alive. Trinkla had kept her that way. But what he had done to her echoed the madness Luke had seen in his eyes. Reiko was tied to a door laid across a set of trestles. Trinkla had peeled the skin from parts of her body like rind from fruit. His work had been done with surgical precision. It was a wonder she still lived. Her pain had to be immense. Reiko's once beautiful face was now a raw, slick mask of muscle and bone. Her eyelids were gone, leaving her unable to close her eyes. Her nose and lips had been peeled back and her tongue removed, so she could utter no word.

The Russian had performed similar tortures on other sensitive parts of her body. The bloody horror was enough to turn his stomach. Reiko watched him, and the hope that had been in her eyes as he entered the room turned to despair. She tried to turn her eyes away from his in shame, but she could not. A tear spilled from the corner of one mutilated eye. Luke had come too late.

"Oh, Reiko," he moaned, "what have I done?"

There was nothing she could say. Her eyes beseeched him. He began to cry.

"Trinkla's dead. He'll never hurt us again," Luke rambled on, frozen in place, trying to get his mind to work, to find the best way out of this situation. Finally, he said, "I'm taking you to a hospital. They can fix you, make it right again. "

He knew it was a lie even as he spoke. He saw the lie mirrored in her eyes. Reiko looked at the sword, then back at him, and whimpered. The sound wrenched a sob from deep within him.

"I can stop the pain, Reiko. I can make you sleep."

Luke used the sword to cut a strip of cloth from his shirt. He placed it over her eyes. That done, he kissed her on the forehead, the only place untouched by Trinkla, and whispered, "Goodbye, Reiko. I will always love you. "

She lay unmoving, waiting. Luke lifted the sword, but could not carry it through.

"Please, Reiko, I can't," he pleaded. But he

knew it had to be done. Luke stepped to the table and raised the sword. He felt her gratitude and thought, "She is thanking me for taking her life, when I am to blame. I am not worthy. This happened to her because of me. "

Luke held the sword high, then dug deep into his soul to find the strength to take the life of the only person in the world he loved. And in finding that strength, he discovered a void in his soul where he could be, indeed, where he had been during his father's and brother's deaths, isolated from all the pain and emotions that threatened to shatter what remained of his life. In this void, he had no emotion or feeling. He could not hurt or be moved by the love or hate or feelings of another. Here he could be safe. As the void surrounded him, he squeezed the tears from his eyes and brought the sword gently down.

The blade dissolved in his hands. The horrible scene before his eyes faded into the fog, and Luke found himself standing in the center of the stage, hands clasped in front of him. The mask was a stifling weight on his face, and he ripped it off, gasping for air. The face of the mask was smooth and unrevealing, giving no hint of what he had just done. Luke turned to the audience. He could see their outlines veiled in fog. The void left him, and the weight of everything he had suppressed, the feelings he had run from, fell on him like a mountain.

His voice was a ragged cry. "This is the

truth of it. I was to blame for this tragedy, yet Reiko did not blame me for her death. She loved me without condition and accepted what that love brought her, without hate. In her was a strength I was never able to attain. Instead of learning, I chose to run away and create a place inside myself where I could hide. I turned away from the responsibilities of what I had wrought.
"

Reiko's voice answered from the audience. "Understand how your actions affected the turning of the Hoop of Life. Things you do today have a bearing on events that occur much farther along the Hoop. The mask has opened you to how you felt at this moment in time. It also brought you to the void that the Manitou called forth in you when he took your ability to emote. This void has always been in you. So you understand the irony: the Manitou did not take anything away from you. It only led you to that which you had opened in yourself. Every action we take is a pebble in the possibilities of life. The ripples, the echoes, spread through time. Now experience the rest of what your vengeance wrought."

Luke pulled the heavy crystal mask over his face again and felt the features flow and shift. Strange, frightening thoughts filled his mind. His name was Nicolai Trinkla.

He lay in the rafters above the doorway, waiting to spring the trap he had set for Luke

JOHN SAUER

Kimball. It was so hard to think straight, to concentrate on what he had to do. Every time his mind seemed to clear, the inflamed muscles of his face contorted in blinding agony. The doctors had told him this would never go away. He could remember a time, not long ago, when he had been handsome, when his face did not hurt, when he was a career officer in the *Spetznaz*, the Russian Special Forces. He had been a good soldier, loyal to his country, on assignment in Afghanistan to support the rebels and help them with covert operations against a bigger, better-equipped United States. He had had no political inclinations; he was a soldier and followed orders. Outside of Leningrad, he had a wife and two strong, young, handsome sons. But try as he might, he could not remember their faces!

Now he was a monster, made that way by this Luke Kimball. He could never go home to his family. What would his wife think when she saw the monster he had become? And what about his sons? He could imagine the look of horror and fear on their faces the first time they saw him like this. *Spetznaz* command would report him as killed in action to his family, so they would never know.

Every time he looked in a mirror, Trinkla saw the icy Hell in Kimball's eyes as he had pulled the trigger. Those eyes haunted him and made him weak with fear. They dominated his waking hours and chased him unrelentingly through his sleep.

Who was this Kimball? Some crazed American who was out for revenge for the death of his brother, a casualty in a strike Trinkla had led against American forces deep in rebel territory. He had not known Kimball's brother or any of the enemies that had died. This was war, and he was a soldier... He was doing his duty. But Kimball had made it personal and ruined his life. The only way he could end this pain was to hurt him—to kill Kimball. If he could darken those eyes forever, maybe he could have his revenge. An eye for an eye. That was all he had left. Then he could die with some kind of peace.

His plan was perfect. Kimball was in love. Trinkla had followed them day and night, face hidden beneath a scarf. It had been too easy to take her to the women's bathroom of the Noh Theater. His face had shocked her into immobility. He had covered her face with a rag soaked in chloroform, then dragged her limp body through the window. Trinkla had tied her to the table in the warehouse and cut off one of her fingers to send to Kimball. Then he sat and watched, waiting for her to awaken.

Reiko Mackland knew who he was. She was not shocked. She regarded him with a calm that touched the last shreds of his sanity. She knew what had happened in Afghanistan. Though he felt tremendous guilt at what he was about to do, he was too far along his path of vengeance to stop. The knife he used was thin and razor-sharp. She screamed as he sliced away —screamed for hours. Trinkla ignored her pain, telling himself that it was punishment for Luke Kimball.

Even before he was done, he could feel Kimball approaching. He left the bloody nightmare that had been Reiko Mackland and climbed into the rafters, holding the wire leash ready. Trinkla waited in the darkness, closed around himself, concentrating on the frightening memory of Kimball's eyes, on the moment when he would separate Kimball's head from his body with a sharp jerk of the wire. Only then would his fear end, and he could put the woman out of her misery and go to sleep forever.

Trinkla stirred when Kimball entered the warehouse. He could feel his enemy examine every dark corner. But he knew Kimball would not look up. The ceiling was too dark, too creative a hiding place. As Kimball moved deeper into the trap, Trinkla pulled a string attached to a latch on the door below. It opened slightly, letting a bright sliver of light fall on the floor. Bait.

Minutes seemed like hours. He almost screamed with tension when Kimball came to the door. As his enemy stared in at the havoc he had caused, Trinkla felt a moment of sharp victory. "Now you feel what I feel!" he thought and spun the wire over Luke Kimball's head.

THE DIVIDED MAN BOOK TWO

The thin, silver wire hissed through the air. Trinkla jerked it tight before Kimball could respond. He tugged at it with all his strength, trying to bury the thin filament in Kimball's neck. He pulled Kimball to his toes—then watched in shock as his enemy reached up to wrap his arm around the wire!

Kimball pulled against Trinkla so sharply that he could see the wire bite into his arm. He was too strong! Trinkla hung onto the rafters with all his strength. But fear of what lay below made him lose his grasp.

Hate further contorted his face as he fell to the floor. "Look what you have made me!" he screamed in rage and fear. "I will kill you! I killed her!"

He babbled on, a torrent of screams and curses, as his mind slipped away. He barely registered surprise as Kimball pulled the gleaming sword free from under his coat . . . and welcomed the blade as it arced towards his throat, for it meant an end to his fear. There was a moment of jarring pain, then no sensation at all. He floated, watched Kimball watch him as his vision darkened. Now he could sleep in peace. And sleep he did.

Luke screamed and tried to claw the mask from his face. But it was sealed to his skin and would not come off. His body convulsed with the remembered agonies of Trinkla's pain, sadness, and madness. He was jerked inside out, tortured by the madness he had brought to his old enemy's mind.

"He was evil," Luke sobbed. "He deserved to die!"

Trinkla's voice answered him from the audience. "Is that the truth, or the way of it that you have manufactured to justify the outcome?"

"I was right to kill you! You mutilated Reiko. You killed my brother!"

"We are not here to debate right or wrong; only to see the truth," Trinkla answered. The mist over the audience parted, and Trinkla came forward. He was whole and unmarred, like Luke had first seen him in the jungles of Vietnam. His face held no malice or evil intent.

"Here is the truth. I was a soldier, same as you. I had a family and a job to do. All I wanted was to do my work so I could go back home and be with them. I did not want to be in the desert any more than you did. And I did not know your brother. He was the enemy that day—nothing more, nothing less. In the service, you planned forays in which many men's brothers died. Yet they never came after you for revenge. You were the only one. You set this wheel in motion. "

"No," Luke whispered. Yet he knew it was true. The mask did not lie.

"If I would have died in the desert, none of this would have happened. But I did not, and I went mad. You were the only man I had ever feared, and it drove me over the edge. Every time

I looked in a mirror, I saw the twisted horror I had become. I went mad and struck back at you the only way I knew how: karma, a turn of the Hoop, both of our hoops spinning into tragedy. Three lives ending in regret. "

Luke collapsed in the center of the stage, crushed by the weight of this new knowledge. A sob wracked him.

"Stand, Luke," Trinkla said, "there is one more life you must live. "

"No," Luke whispered again.

"Yes," Trinkla replied. "It must be. This time we will see if you are truly worthy enough to bear the truth."

Trinkla faded back into the fog. Luke stood and tried to touch the mask. But he could not; he was flat on his back . . . full of the worst pain she had ever known. The mad Russian had done things to her that went beyond horror, beyond pain. Yet she had kept her sanity, centered in the void of clarity she had learned from decades of martial arts practice, clinging to it through the torture, finding a way through the seemingly endless agony, for the void was all she had left. It was her way, the calm at her center. Reiko almost wished she were insane now, so she would not feel the maelstrom of emotions that raged beyond her calm center. Overwhelming physical agony. Anger. Despair. Most of all, shame, for she knew she was bait in a trap for Luke, and that he would see her like this, disgraced and shed of her beauty.

Reiko had seen what she looked like. Trinkla had shown her in a mirror. She looked like some animal strapped to a table and vivisected, alive and screaming, unable to close her eyes because she had no eyelids. She could not speak; he had taken her tongue. Now she no longer screamed. She had done that until her voice was gone. She could not die; he had not taken her that far, not yet. All she could do was wait for Luke, so she could find some way to beg his forgiveness and die with dignity.

In waiting, she remembered her life. Happy memories of her father, Major Mackland, and her mother, daughter of a wealthy Japanese industrialist. Growing up in Tokyo and London, East and West. Meeting Luke Kimball, so hard and dangerous and kind and thrilling, a warrior and gentleman who touched her soul. Her love.

The years of practice with sensei from the East and West. Aikido. Kenjutsu. The naginata. Walking under the full blossoms of cherry trees in spring with Luke.

Tears welled in her lidless eyes, for the life and children they would never have, for herself and the dreams she would never be able to live. Most of all for Luke, because she could not soothe the scars war had already left on his soul, and that this night would leave upon him. He would have sadness for the rest of his days, for she had failed to protect him from his enemy, and she knew that he would blame himself.

Reiko heard a click as the door to her torture room was opened. Reiko heard Luke gasp, then the sounds of fighting. Trinkla screamed at Luke, words full of inarticulate rage, then silence. She saw the bloody sword in Luke's hands and knew Trinkla was dead. But her soul was shattered by the look in Luke's eyes as he saw how she had been disfigured. She turned her eyes away. But there was nowhere she could hide her shame. She was *onna-bugeisha*, a trained warrior. The Russian should never have been able to surprise her. She had brought this to Luke.

"Oh, Reiko," he mourned, "what have I done?"

Reiko's wounds gaped wetly in the yellowish light of the ceiling lamps.

"I'm taking you to a hospital. They can fix you, make it right again. "

They both knew the words were lies; there was nobody in the world that could heal her. She tried to speak, but Trinkla had taken her tongue. There was so much she wanted to say to him, mostly, to beg forgiveness for the pain she had caused him. And one request to make. She snapped her eyes at the sword in his hands. He saw her plea.

"I can stop the pain, Reiko. I can make you sleep."

"Yes," Reiko thought, "please, make me sleep. My love, end my pain."

Luke used the sword to cut a strip of cloth from his shirt. He placed it over her eyes, so she, mercifully, had darkness and a place to hide her shame, not realizing that Luke had done it so he would not have to look in her eyes. He kissed her on the forehead, the only spot on her face untouched by Trinkla's cruel knife, and whispered, "Goodbye, Reiko. I will always love you."

She felt the heat of his tears. Reiko could see him, in her mind's eye, standing over her, sword raised. She thanked him silently for giving her an end to the pain, and then heard Luke say, "Please Reiko, I can't. "

"Please, Luke," she wanted to cry, "I want this!"

But then the blade touched her neck, seeming light as a feather to her, and Reiko was safe in the void, free from pain and shame. The world fell away from her, and she began her next journey.

Luke's cry was a soul-rending sound that split the night, shattering the dream-gauze of the Noh Theater. He felt the cold, rocky footing of a mountain beneath him. A frigid wind buffeted him into a fetal ball. The mask held the truth before his eyes like letters burned across the sky. Reiko had blamed herself! Not him. Her love, her pure devotion, had been so strong that it touched him, with all its power, now, across the span of decades. Her death had been a consequence of his actions, the price he had paid for his blind, selfish revenge. She had seen this, yet had taken the blame for herself so that he might find some absolution. Now, in the truth of the mask, he finally understood just how much his revenge had cost him . . . how much he had lost, and how much damage he had done to the lives intertwined with his.

On his face, the mask glowed. All his life, he had pushed this hoop, pursuing his selfish desires. Now he had a chance to make life, to atone for the lives he had ruined, to complete himself and the Key of Seven, to give life back to mankind. He had pursued his dream path to get back his soul, but in his selfishness, had missed the true importance of the act. This was not something he could do only for himself.

And in seeing the necessity for defeating the Manitou, Luke saw the truth behind the god. The Manitou had drawn on Luke's soul to enter the world. Therein lay his greatest liability and hope for defeating the god. There were no two opponents in the world that could be more evenly matched. Yet, there was something he was missing, some vital truth that stayed just outside his grasp.

The mask shone with brilliant light. Luke accepted the inevitability of truth he had learned with an open heart, of his past and the void he —not the Manitou—had created in himself. Then the crystal mask sank into his skin, into the bones of his face, until no sign of it was visible. Now the full force of truth was before him. Never again would he turn the Hoop of Life without being aware of the consequences spinning from every action.

He was completely self-aware and woven into the fabric of existence. He was clear-headed and calm. He could not change the past, but he could work to change the future.

He uncurled and rose from the ground, unmindful of the cold. It had begun to snow. The wind whipped the white flakes in curtains, almost obscuring the bulk of the mountain before him. Luke roared a challenge, and the mountain quivered with the Manitou's answer: five days from now, at the top of the mountain. Joseph was gone. Luke began the long hike back to the People. Dawn would be here soon, and he had little time to prepare for what lay ahead.

JUDGMENT

The first gray light of dawn brushed the sky behind the black height of the mountain. Snow from the previous night had turned the thick stands of pine at its base into white, impenetrable walls closing in on the old mountain pass highway. The wind whipped bitter ice crystals into rolling clouds and sent them billowing down the road. Above them, the mountain towered, its snow-swept reaches grim and foreboding in the face of dawn. Here the future of mankind would be decided. None of them wanted to be here. But none had any choice.

The MOC was parked across both lanes of the road. Luke sat hunkered down on the snow-drifted tarmac a short distance from the others, facing the mountain, wrapped in the hide of the white buffalo. Underneath the hide, he wore moccasins and leggings, also of white buffalo hide. Even though the paint covering him from his forehead to his ankles had fused into his skin like a tattoo, he could feel it, tight, like a second skin. A long bundle lay on the ground between his feet, also wrapped in decorated hide. Luke was as ready as he would ever be. Today he would battle a god.

The other six sat and stood next to the MOC behind him, afraid and silent, bundled in heavy clothes against the cold. Luke inhaled the icy air deep into his lungs, steadying his racing mind and concentrating on what lay ahead. The last four days had been a blur of ceremony and ritual, of the arcane and animistic, as he was prepared to battle the Manitou.

Returning with the mask of truth embedded in his soul, Luke had found Joseph waiting for him under the Tree of Life. The snow was falling heavily by then, in windless, white curtains that seemed to muffle out the world. Joseph had stood so still that snow had accumulated on him, transforming him into a white statue. When he shook himself, the snow fell away, destroying the effect. Joseph regarded Luke for several long moments. When he spoke, there was sorrow in his voice.

"You have survived, but you are changed. "

Luke answered, "Yes. I ride the Hoop of Life, the cause and effect, from moment to moment. The past and future have become very small. It is . . . strange."

Joseph asked, "What comes now?"

"I battle the Manitou in five days. Will you help me prepare? There is much that I still do not know. "

Joseph nodded. "You still don't see, but yes. If you survived, this was anticipated. We have been waiting. We must begin in the morning. Tonight, you will rest. We have a special place for you. "

Luke said, "I can't stay with Ellie tonight?"

"No. It is better that you be alone. You will see her before you climb the mountain."

Joseph brought him to a clearing many miles from the village. A low hut had been prepared for him. Luke crawled in and was asleep as soon as he could pull up the blankets. He awoke in the morning to the sound of a drum softly beaten. Joseph's voice carried over the beats. Luke crawled out of the hut and found a large group of young and old Native American men and women assembled in the clearing, with Joseph at their head. They were from many tribes and knew the old ways, Joseph explained, and together could help him make powerful medicine. As Luke studied the assembly, he could feel their collective focus and resolve. Someone handed him a sandwich of venison and thick, crusty bread and a cup of strong black coffee. Luke ate quickly, anxious to begin.

They built a sweat lodge, a temporary domed structure of boughs and hide just large enough to hold a few men. Next to it, a fire roared. At its center was a pile of smooth, fist-sized stones heating to a bright red. Joseph led

Luke to a stream. The water ran fast and dark. It looked very cold.

"First you must bathe," Joseph said. "It will awaken your blood. "

Luke stripped and stepped into the stream. The icy waters made him gasp. He ducked his head under the surface, then took handfuls of sand from the bottom and scrubbed until his skin tingled. He stayed until he began to feel numb. Joseph handed him a towel.

"I think my blood is awake now," Luke said as his teeth chattered.

Joseph laughed and clapped him on the shoulder. "You are young! A little cold water is good for the heart. Now we sweat."

Back in the clearing, Luke and Joseph changed to loincloths and crawled into the steamy hut. The inside was dark, lit only by a small fire of fir and sagebrush. The fragrant smoke filled the hide structure. Joseph gave him a handful of the pungent leaves.

"Rub yourself with the sacred sage. It will help to cleanse and purify you."

Luke briskly rubbed himself with the leaves.

"This is the sweat lodge," Joseph continued. "It has been used by the people for many centuries to purify their spirits and open their minds to the divine. You must be pure for what lies ahead. In the sacred steam, the gods will find you worthy . . . or not. Repeat after me this prayer."

Joseph opened his medicine bag and took out a smaller pouch. He sprinkled a small pinch of its contents on the fire, and it flared bright and green. The acrid smoke made Luke slightly lightheaded.

"On a sacred path we are walking," Joseph chanted, "on a sacred path we are walking, in a sacred way. In a sacred way we are speaking; hear us! Hear us, Thunder Beings! Hear us, Talking God! Hear us, White Buffalo Woman! Hear us, Stone Smith!"

Joseph called upon many gods—the supernatural beings Luke had sat with at the Sacred Council, the beings that had been worshipped by Native Americans across time and the ages. Luke joined him, repeating each name after Joseph chanted. The air seemed to tremble with the strength of the prayer. As they prayed Luke, felt something . . . a power . . . coalescing around and inside him in the smoky gloom. The force tightened in his stomach like a gyroscope moving closer to a point of center.

A torch was handed through the opening of the hut. Joseph leaned forward, blew out the fire in the pit with the smallest of breaths, and said, "The Gods who support you now gather their strength to lend if you pass their final judgment."

He scraped the ashes out of the fire pit and lined it with a deer hide to form a basin. Buckets of water were handed in, and Luke poured them into the depression.

"The Gods will find you in the sacred steam," Joseph instructed. "Let them see you as you have become, bound with truth, ready for battle. Ride the words of our prayer as you would the wind. I pray for you. We all pray for you. "

Luke jumped as the first red-hot rock was tossed into the pit. It landed with a sharp explosion of steam. More followed, cutting the darkness like tracer bullets. Steam boiled through the small hut, searing Luke's body. He gasped, unable to breathe, as the flap was closed.

Now the hut was lit only by the rapidly fading red glow of the stones bubbling in the water. Luke managed to hiss air between his teeth. He shut his eye tightly against the heat, momentarily thankful for the patch covering his empty left socket.

Joseph's voice rang out, potent with power, rocking the earth. Luke caught the prayer and felt his spirit soar to the top of the hut, seemingly miles above the bubbling stones. He sensed vast movement around him. The steam lost its volume, and the gods appeared before him, one at a time, each presenting its strange, inhuman form as their eyes cut to the very depths of his soul. Their scrutiny was intense, peeling away the layers of his self as if he were an onion, seeing every transgression, every wrong and right he had committed in his life.

Before the Manitou had set him on this journey, Luke would have hung his head in shame at such a spotlighted examination of his life. He had done many things in which no pride could be taken, even though he had tried to be a good man, or at least an honorable man.

Now he was no longer the same Luke. With the coming of truth, he had accepted his past—all of it—and the consequences of his actions, meeting these gods eye to eye with no shame or no fear. Certainly no pride. If the gods were to accept him and find him worthy of their powers, Luke must first accept himself. When the gods did grace him, the sheer magnitude rocked Luke's soul. He drifted in a void, stunned by what now filled him, not fully understanding the gifts as the cooling steam drew him back to earth and his tired body.

He did not stir until Joseph drew back the flap of the hut, letting in sunlight and cold winter air. Luke rubbed his eyes open and raised himself on an elbow. Joseph helped Luke up and out of the steam hut. He was handed a mug of broth. Luke wrapped his hands around it.

"How do you feel?"

He stood on shaky legs, squinting against the light. Someone put a warm blanket around his shoulders. Luke drew it tight, grateful for the warmth.

"Feeble. Yet, full of . . . potential . . . I can't begin to understand."

Joseph appraised him with a look of wonderment and pride. "Never before in all the histories of the People has there been one like you. You have the favor of many gods. Now you must learn how to use these abilities. There is a way to call the powers out of yourself, to bring them to your fingertips. This we can help you with."

"Where do we begin?"

"Once, you dreamed of being a painted man. The designs are the keys to your new strengths. If you are to gain mastery of yourself, you must recall your original dream on the plateau, and retell the colors and the shapes of the runes you wore. This is the design of your armor. Once we paint them on you, you will have their power."

Luke could remember the dream all too well; it had launched him on the journey that had led him here. The image of how he had looked, every color and line, was locked in his mind. "I remember," he said.

They painted him for days. Luke stood in the center of a small cave, walls heavily coated with soot from old fires and a thousand years of paintings that overlaid each other, telling the history of the many peoples and tribes that had inhabited the river valleys that flowed into the Columbia River. Joseph and a few others gathered around him, mixing bright pigments from ground minerals and plants. Luke described to them, body part by part, what he had looked like in the dream. The first component of the design was a spiraling sun in the center of his chest, marked with the cardinal directions.

As the design was finished, Luke felt his chest grow warm. The design became, for a moment, a living thing, and then sank into his skin like a glowing tattoo. There was no pain. The medicine men gasped with astonishment. But Luke relaxed, because he now knew how to use the gift the Sun God had given him.

He described the next part of the design. It was painted on him and likewise became part of his skin. At the end of three days, Luke gazed along his arms and body. The dream had turned its hoop. Running his hands over himself, he could feel no traces of the paint. Yet he glowed with color from his neck to his wrists and ankles. Each part of the design was a gift to be called upon. The total design was a representation of himself and all the hope that had been embodied in him. He could no longer feel the weight of responsibility that had hung on him throughout his journey. It too was in him.

The medicine men brought forth a cloak made from the white buffalo hide and ceremoniously draped it over Luke's shoulders, then departed, leaving only Luke and Joseph in the cave.

"It is done," the old man said. "You climb the mountain in a few hours."

Though he had been awake for days, Luke felt calm and rested. "I am ready. I know the others will come with me. Will you?"

Joseph shook his head. "No. My place is here, with the People and the Tree." He pulled the cloak tightly around Luke's shoulders. "Fight well, Luke, and know that the dreams of an old man go with you."

Luke blinked. His feet were becoming numb. It was light enough now to discern a black thread from a white, the Muslim definition of true sunrise. He stood and turned to face the other six of the Seven.

"Goodbye," he said. "I'll see you when I see you." There was nothing more he could say.

Ellie held his gaze for a long moment. Even in the dim light, he could see tears on her face. She shrugged deeper into her blanket, turned, and pressed her face against the MOC. As he left the roadway and began to climb the narrow, snow-covered path up the mountain, the notes of a lonely song floated to him from Mike's guitar.

The trees grew high and thick along both sides of the path, creating a tunnel through which the wind howled. The heavy snow on the branches had turned to ice, glazing the trees into impenetrable walls that were dangerous in their icy, glittering sharpness. The temperature plummeted well past the zero mark, threatening to coat his exposed skin with ice. Already, wind-born tears were freezing on his face. It grew even colder, unnaturally so, until Luke knew that no man, however clothed, could stand this extreme. His legs were numbing to stumps of wood.

Luke placed the palm of his hand over the sun in the center of his chest and spoke a sacred word. Heat enveloped him like a cloak. The ice on the path melted beneath his feet. He reached out to touch a frozen branch. The ice grew thin and then fell away, leaving cold, dead twigs. But under the power of the Sun God, the branch came to life and sprouted tiny green buds. Warmth. The branches became green all around him as he continued up the path.

He climbed until he broke the tree line. He was on the mountain proper now, with only a treacherous path to follow made by generations of bighorn sheep. The wind had pushed snow into the crevices, leaving the surrounding barren stone cold and darkly gray. It still gusted heavily, pulling at his cloak.

On the horizon, the sun seemed frozen at the rim of the world. It should have been higher in the sky. Wrapped in the powers of the gods, Luke felt that the Manitou had stopped the rising of the sun—had stopped time.

As Luke continued higher, another lethal obstacle was in his way. Winding his way up the treacherous mountain path, Luke came to a high, vertical wall he could not avoid. The only way up was to climb, using finger and toe holds. At times, his entire weight hung from two fingers jammed into a crack in the rocky face as he stretched high for any purchase. Hanging like this, he was completely vulnerable. Luke knew the Manitou would be aware of this opportunity and was not surprised when the wind began to gust along the rock wall. It was strong enough to swing him like a pendulum, hanging by one arm, stressing the muscles in his shoulder and back until Luke gritted his teeth from the pain. Bracing his legs against the mountain, Luke reached higher and felt a crack large enough to get his hand into. He gripped solidly and pulled himself up, balling his fist deeper into the crack so he could rest.

It was what the Manitou had been waiting for. Luke first felt the tremors, faint vibrations, through his hands. It seemed as if the stony skeleton of the mountain was shifting. The trembling rapidly grew stronger, until the mountain moved beneath him. Luke clenched his fist tighter into the crack, waiting for the tremors to subside. Instead, the mountain began to shake itself to pieces. Sensing danger, Luke looked up to see a large boulder falling toward him. He kicked himself to the right, straining with his hands and toes to hold himself nearly horizontal, and felt the rock skim his head as it fell past.

Luke dropped vertical, dodging again as more stones fell towards him. A brick-sized rock hit his left shoulder, numbing his free hand. Hanging by one arm, he had to twist and dodge the barrage of stones that now fell at him. The quakes continued to increase in strength. Luke found the crack his hand was shoved into becoming wider. He was losing his handhold. As he struggled to hold on, a stone glanced off of his temple, turning everything black.

His fist slackened, and Luke slipped from the rock face. He fell and was conscious of the wind hissing in his ears, of falling away from the bulk of the mountain. His thoughts, scattered like the wind, touched upon his first experience with transformation into an eagle. Even as he realized he was falling to his doom, Luke flapped his arms once, then again, trying to hold the shape in his mind. He willed the change, and the agony of transformation brought him back to full consciousness. For a moment, he gloried in the power of flight and the renewal of strength it brought him. The pain fell away like old skin. Luke screamed the eagle's war cry and soared in a great circle back to the mountain.

Luke landed on a ledge atop the vertical wall he had been climbing. Feeling the stone shake through his talons, Luke remembered another time when he had felt the earth shake. Stone Smith. Feeling the potential inside of him, the power, Luke extended the focus of his mind deep into the heart of the mountain. He could feel the plates shifting and grinding against their will, forced by godly power. Though it could meddle here, the backbone of the earth was not the Manitou's domain. Therefore, its powers were not supreme. Overriding that energy, Luke touched a design on his shoulder and used the stronger power Stone Smith had given him to quiet the heart of the mountain. The tremors ceased, leaving the mountain, for the moment, peaceful and silent.

Cloaked in the form of the eagle, Luke debated flying directly to the top of the mountain. But even as he thought it, his shape was involuntarily changed back to his human form. That was not to be allowed. But again, the Manitou would make this mountain shake no more. Luke surveyed the mountain, still cloaked in the cold shadows of dawn. He had reached the halfway point. He kept climbing.

Each step brought him closer to the summit. As he ascended, Luke kept himself focused on the calm center of his spiritual void. Images drifted from its dark depths. He noted them and let them go. Pierce, the way he had been before the holocaust warped him. The time he had spent with the sensei in Tokyo, learning the ways of the sword. The interwoven memories of Reiko and Trinkla. His father and his brother. The moonlit winter night long ago when he hunted the wolf. Ellie. No past. No future. Only the now.

The mountain gradually leveled out as

Luke neared the peak. There was weariness in his legs now, and he stopped to rest, sitting atop a boulder with his back to the frozen dawn. The cold in these heights had the feel of ice that never thawed, and the air had the thinness of high elevations. He brushed the hard callus on his palm across the gray-and-orange fibrous lichen covering the boulder. This was the only life that lived here.

As he examined the summit, looking for the best path, Luke felt a distinct change in the air. The pressure fell so rapidly that his ears hurt. At the same time, the air thickened so that he could push against it with his hands. Above the summit, a single black cloud rapidly billowed into an anvil-shaped thunderstorm. Red lightning boiled in its heart and arced downward to strike the mountain. The electrical charge raised small hairs on Luke's arms and the back of his neck. Growing, becoming even more menacing, the dark mass of cloud began to descend on the mountain, coming to Luke.

Thick bolts of glaring red lightning shot from its base like deadly legs, marching the storm downward. With each strike, thunder crashed and echoed across the mountain peaks with enough force to vibrate Luke's bones. He stood, not knowing if he should try to dodge the storm, duck below the boulder for shelter, or just be still.

The decision was made for him. Luke

felt an increase in the charge. His hair stood on end. Instinctively he leaped to the side and rolled, keeping his bundle from under his body so it would not be bent by his weight. Lightning followed close behind him, striking and shattering the boulder upon which he had sat. Luke ran and rolled again, bolts striking all around him, giving him no rest, no time to call forth the defenses he possessed to stop the storm.

At one point, dodging, Luke inadvertently held his bundle in the air. He felt the air quicken as a hail of lightning bolts rained down on him. They fell close enough to shock him. Luke stumbled, legs numb. The bundle! Being metal, it was guiding the lightning. But Luke could not put it down! It if were destroyed, he would have no chance at all of defeating the Manitou. Instinctively, Luke held the bundle closer—and a thick, sizzling bolt struck him in the chest.

The world went white. He flew across the rocky steppe like a ragdoll. His hand clenched around the hide-wrapped bundle, and his only thought was that he could not let it go. Lightning hit him again, square in the back. As if from a distance, Luke felt his body convulse. His teeth chattered like castanets. As his vision blacked out completely, Luke captured an image in his mind and held onto it tightly.

A great bird, a God Bird, rising into the sky. Along with it, multicolored beings riding cloud steeds and carrying lances of lightning. The Thunders and the Thunder Bird. As lightning struck him for the last time, Luke whispered a sacred word.

The bolt should have killed him. Instead, it filled him with warmth. Luke's arms and legs tingled pleasantly as the feeling returned. The trembling knots eased from his muscles, leaving him relaxed. Luke sighed with relief. His hand eased the death grip on the bundle. Booming through the thunder, Luke heard the triumphant laugh of the Manitou.

Luke smiled and reached out a hand. There was a moment's pause as the storm gathered itself again, then heavy lightning fell on him. Each bolt that struck him increased his well-being and gave him more energy. He sat up, rotating his hands in amazement, seeing blue and yellow auras crackle along his arms and fingers.

Gazing into the heart of the storm, Luke stood and raised his bundle high. As with a lightning rod, the bolts arced to the bundle in a steady stream. But it was not enough. Using the powers of the Thunder Gods, Luke used his mind to touch the heart of the storm and focus all its unnatural fury on the bundle. Now in his control, the storm responded, and the bolts of lightning became a river of light flowing down through the bundle into Luke.

Never before had he felt so strong, so full

of power! Luke increased his pull on the storm until the river of light weakened and the clouds lost their black, ugly pall. The storm began to shrink as rapidly as it had formed, until only high wispy cirrus clouds remained. Luke released them, and the clouds whisked away on the high winds.

Luke's voice boomed across the mountain. "I'm coming for you now."

Fog boiled and flowed down the summit like a waterfall, cloaking the higher reaches from Luke's view. But the path before him was clear. Luke resumed climbing.

At the edge of the fog, Luke dropped his white buffalo hide cloak. He was wearing only moccasins and a loincloth, and the brightly colored, vibrant designs etched in his skin gained a life of their own. Luke could feel the loops and whorls ripple under his skin. As he entered the fog, the designs glowed brighter, cutting through the opaque, diffused light. Luke paused, adjusting to the visual whiteout, shutting his eye and feeling the rock under his feet. Centered in the void of his soul, Luke could feel the presence of rounded boulders and other obstacles in his path. It was as if there were no fog at all.

Ahead, Luke heard a high-pitched growl, a scrabbling of claws on stone. Something the size of a small dog launched out of the white mists, heading straight for his throat. Before Luke could react, he felt a quick stirring on his right shoulder. Something, Luke could not tell what, was born from him, covered in fur, with wings and very sharp teeth. The guardian intercepted the creature inches from Luke's face. He had a fleeting impression of razor-sharp claws and fever-red eyes before his guardian carried the beast screaming into the fog.

More sounds came from ahead: cries, snarls, and growls made by nothing that had ever walked the earth. Some called his name. The Manitou's nightmare children. Luke kept walking, homing in on his enemy.

Creations horrible beyond comprehension came at him from all directions, too fast for Luke to avoid. But for each attack, a guardian emerged from the patterns to protect him. Luke gave his full trust to the magic and pushed forward. Soon the rock beneath his moccasins was flat. He could climb no farther. He had reached the summit.

The top of Gold Mountain was a small plain, not much more than a football field in size, littered with rocks and pebbles made slick from the fog. As the last of the Manitou's nightmares were destroyed by his guardians, Luke cast his awareness through the opaque whiteness, searching for the aura of the Manitou. The evil god was only a short distance away. Using the last of the voluntary power available to him, Luke lifted the fog.

The Manitou stood on a mound of rock

with its back to the dawn. Its heavy antlers were silhouetted against the red glare of the sun. Luke walked forward at a tangent to the Manitou's position, keeping the sun out of his eye.

The Manitou laughed. "A cautious man to the last. You have hunted me a long time. "

Luke stopped a short distance from his enemy. "I feel as if I have been hunting you for most of my life."

"Indeed. Perhaps you have. Or have you been running away?"

"Perhaps both."

"But don't you have what you originally wanted, to be free of the pain and sorrow that has haunted you most of your life? I have given that to you."

"I once thought that being without emotion, being the way I am now, would free me of pain. I was wrong. Just because you can't always feel pain does not mean it isn't there. I have missed so much since you set me on this journey . . . that could have made me feel alive again. By awakening my void, you did not help me. You only put me in a different kind of Hell. No more."

The Manitou shook its head. "You cannot win. Remember the prophecy. . . After this meeting, only one of us shall live. "

"The choice of weapons is mine," Luke replied.

The Manitou stepped down from the

THE DIVIDED MAN BOOK TWO

rock. They were left with the evenly matched strengths of their bodies, and the knowledge locked in their heads. Luke held his bundle before him and reverently unwrapped the hide.

The Manitou sighed. "Tachi," it said in a tone of respect. "A fitting way to die."

Luke let the hide slip to the ground. The red dawn gleamed like fire along the black lacquered sheath.

"A fitting way to die," he echoed.

The Manitou extended his right hand, and it held a sword identical in shape to Luke's, gripped parallel to the ground. Metal hissed like rain as they drew their blades. Luke placed his sheath on the ground and stepped away. The Manitou followed him, movements becoming longer and slightly exaggerated, mimicking Luke's movements, slipping into combat mode.

Luke kept the sun to their left, both hands on the sword, right hand forward, point level with his eyes. The beginning. The Manitou echoed his position, bringing his blade over to touch Luke's. As it did, the Manitou's shape shimmered and changed. Luke found himself staring at . . . himself . . . only blue. The designs covering the Manitou were the same as his, only white. Luke felt the Hoop complete a full turn, past and present converging, a prophecy about to be fulfilled.

"A better shape for combat," the Manitou said. "Isn't this what you came to fight?"

What did the Manitou mean? Luke lost the thought in the electric contact of their blades. The Manitou slowly stepped back, almost casually, then was a blur as it slid forward and attacked Luke's blind side. Luke parried, steel sparking against steel, feeling, not seeing, the deadly nearness of the Manitou's blade.

Images flashed quickly in his mind, memories, a morning far outside Tokyo in a field, lavender sky, Mount Fuji white-capped on the horizon. Luke was in a white *gi* and a black divided *hakama* skirt, the whisper and clash of steel ringing out as Sensei and he traded blows. The feel, the technique.

When he attacked, the heightened speed of his reflexes turned Luke into a whirlwind of death. Again and again, he lashed out, only to be met by the Manitou. Luke's battle cry, which would have paralyzed most mortal men, was answered by the Manitou in voice and timbre. As they traded blows, Luke slipped automatically into a defensive stance, parrying each strike as if he were reading the god's mind. But that was impossible—not one of the special powers he had been given! But blow for parry, parry for blow, they were evenly matched—so matched that neither could make any headway. Both Luke and the Manitou altered the pattern of their attacks many times, trying the unexpected, moving faster or more slowly, cutting high and low, mixing their attack with kicks and

THE DIVIDED MAN BOOK TWO

punches, blows to the shoulder. And each time Luke attacked, he found himself staring into the Manitou's eyes—his eyes. It was a hypnotic mirror. Luke had to tear his gaze away and concentrate on the battle.

Eventually, he stepped back and wiped heavy sweat from his forehead. "You cannot win," he said to the Manitou between breaths.

The Manitou seemed as winded as he. "I cannot lose," it answered. "In this, as with all things, we are equal."

The Manitou followed its statement with a lunge that Luke both expected and parried. He returned the attack, which was blocked by his enemy, as a disturbing thought blared in his head. It could not win. Luke could not win. If neither could win, one could not lose. He and the Manitou were equal . . . the same. *No!*

In denial of the thought, Luke attacked savagely. It could not be. The Manitou was evil, a destroyer, a corruption of good.

I am not evil, Luke told himself. *I have tried to be good, to be a protector, not a destroyer. This creature cannot be me!*

The Manitou fell back, blocking each of his blows, then it counterattacked just as fiercely, the bared-teeth grimace on its face a mirror of his own. Their blades locked, spitting sparks. With faces only inches apart, Luke could not tell whose breath washed over who.

"Who are you?" Luke gasped.

The Manitou strained against his sword. "I," it answered, voice trembling, "am you. Who are *you*?"

With a hoarse shout, Luke pushed the Manitou away, each breath rasping in his lungs. The Manitou struck the same pose. Their breathing, Luke noticed, was even on the same rhythm.

"You can't be me!" he shouted. "You are evil!"

The Manitou wiped the sweat from its eye. "I can't be anything else. It was your soul that called me back from the exile of the Spirit World. It took your soul to bring me here. Every emotion and desire that drives me now is fueled by the essence of you. I am all you denied in yourself. Am I not your selfish desire?"

Luke, stunned by the Manitou's words, almost failed to block the creature's flashing blade. The crystal mask locked beneath his skin pulsed with awesome power Luke could not deny. With the Manitou's statement standing like a monolith before him, Luke was forced to study the god again . . . the god and himself.

In the clear, objective light of truth, Luke was able to look back down the path of his life and project what would have happened if he had not killed the wolf and had not gone to war. He saw himself graduating from college with a degree in international business, ending up as the chairman of the board of a precious metals mining conglomeration, and living in the western US with a wife and children. It would have been a rewarding, successful life, free of the pain and troubles he had experienced. Then he and his family would have perished instantly when the first bombs hit Denver, all traces of his existence gone from the world.

Alternate realities spun away from each action of his life, some ending in the same place, some leading him to where he was not, some in between. Actions and reactions. Consequences spreading from each action, each decision, like endless ripples in an ocean of possibility.

But in the here and now, Luke had left his mark on the world. For better or worse, the mark of dedication and excellence he had forged in SCI still lived on in the survivors of his empire. Some, he was sure, would be like Pierce. Others would be more honorable, fighting to protect, laying down their lives to preserve whatever they felt was worth saving in this post-nuclear world.

So, his life had not been a total loss. He had done much good as well. SCI had held the promise of preservation, of protecting what was good and just in the world. Upon the cornerstones of his many faults, he had still managed to build something strong. Why? Because of the balance of his soul. It was not a mental imbalance that had driven him into manic depression; it was guilt.

What the Manitou had taken was the dark

side of him, the mirror image. It had taken what Luke had secretly wanted to be rid of. He believed, he saw now, that by losing that side of him, all that would be left was good. The Manitou had given him what he wanted. The Manitou had not taken away his ability to feel or emote; Luke had walled his emotions away from himself.

There it was. The Manitou had taken nothing. It had only given him a mirror. The Manitou *was* him. What Luke had been battling, truly, for the course of his whole life . . . was himself.

The knowledge was a weapon keener than any blade. Reaching deep, Luke let loose what he had walled off for so long. The upwelling of emotion filled him with an ache of sensations he had thought he would never feel again. Happiness, sadness, joy, pain . . . all combined to bring new clarity. Separated as they were, each was unbalanced, yin without yang, dark without light. So much hinging on such a small thing as his soul! Luke could see only one way to bring them together.

He pulled back from the Manitou and dropped into a crouch, right leg extended before him, sword held above his head almost parallel to the ground. The Manitou moved into the same pose a sword's length away. Once, long ago, Luke's sensei had shown him an attack that could only be blocked by the same attack. It left one completely vulnerable, but it was also virtually unstoppable. Luke had seen a terrible beauty in the maneuver, called the Fatal Mirror, because your enemy could use the attack as you used it against him. Mutually assured death.

Luke locked eyes with the god. In its gaze, he saw the same determination he was sure must be in his own.

Shifting his weight to his back leg, Luke thrust himself forward, blade humming as he brought it to bear on the Manitou. He felt the Manitou follow the pattern as his blade touched the Manitou's chest, a mirror image of himself. Then he felt the Manitou's blade against his own skin. He pushed the sword forward with all his might and felt the Manitou's blade pierce his chest. As one, he and the Manitou pushed on their blades, ripping through bone, burying the swords to their hilts. It was done.

Luke had never felt such pain. It glazed the eye of the Manitou as it must have glazed his own. The god coughed blood. Luke felt it warm on his face and lips.

"You have finished everything," the Manitou gasped. He began to sag.

Luke wrapped an arm around its neck, holding the god close to him. "No," he whispered, "I think it has just begun. "

He felt his blood rise in his throat. It mingled with the Manitou's blood, mixing and uniting. Somewhere in the heavens, drums began to beat. The rhythm of his heart—the Manitou's heart. Their knees gave way, bringing them to the ground. Luke unlocked his hand from his sword and gripped the Manitou's shoulders with the last of his strength.

He blinked, and they both stood on the mountain. The sun was a warm glow in the crisp blue sky. He still held his sword, but there was no sword buried in him. He touched his chest. No hole.

The Manitou looked at him and there was humor in his eyes. "Are you done yet?"

Luke began to raise the tachi.

"Seriously? Aren't you done yet? With punishing yourself?"

Luke stepped back and lowered the sword. "What do you mean?"

"Think about all that has happened. You needed an enemy greater than yourself to defeat, to atone for the things you thought you were directly responsible for in your past. I gave you one. And you overcame immense obstacles, most of which were in yourself. And you succeeded. You defeated me. You have won. You defeated yourself, but it's the same thing. Now, can you forgive yourself and be done?"

His thoughts roared. Luke realized many things at once. He could feel again—everything. He could look over his life objectively and see what he had done wrong, what he had done right, and what the consequences were—and accept them, all of it with peace. He looked at the Manitou, and where he had seen malice, he realized that it had been guidance. Hard truths and lessons. The Manitou had given him what he needed to grow beyond the limitations he had put on himself.

Luke found the sheath for the tachi and put the sword away. He noticed small, bright meadow flowers growing among the rocks. It was a beautiful day on this mountain, as peaceful as he felt inside.

"What are you?" he asked the Manitou.

"Now you're asking the right questions!" the Manitou exclaimed. "Mankind has always created its gods by the power of their will and thirst for knowledge of who they are and how they came to be. But the first people here did not evolve from apes, as many scientists believe. The first peoples—those that every human on earth evolved from—were travelers who found this realm while traveling the Tree of Life."

Manitou waved at the horizon in the general direction of the village, and Luke, with new insight, saw the Tree—all of it. Not just the great, windswept bonsai form he had touched, but the reach of the Tree across the dimensions of time and space. Its trunk expanded to fill the sky. Above it, Luke could see its branches as big as continents stretching into space and could sense the branches reaching into realms and dimensions beyond basic human understanding.

As above, so below. The great roots of the Tree stretched down into nether realms, full of despair and darkness. Between them both sat the Earth, a realm that was also a gateway, a check valve. Luke could feel the Tree. It was dim and silent from the trunk on up, but crawling with the darkness below the surface. The darkness pushed hungrily at the balance.

"There was a time when people traveled across dimensions on the Tree. They knew that the Tree connected light and dark realms. One world, this Earth, was the center point, the key to maintaining the balance between them. These travelers dreamed of the first gods, all but two: the Manitou and the Wendigo. Each of them was born of the tree, one to protect the realms of light, one to rule the realms of dark.

"Unlike most of the gods in these and other realms that have been created by yearning, the Manitou and the Wendigo are mantles passed from sentient being to sentient being. They are called forth by the resonance of great good or great evil. Darkness had pulled the life from the light realms. The Tree was unbalanced. You stood in the cusp of the moment and could have chosen the greater good or the greater evil. But you chose the light, and the darkness has chased you since. See the truth of this."

Luke was back into the winter forest, thigh-deep in snow, the bowstring drawn to his cheek. He saw again the two creatures facing him and felt the decision to slay the darkness. He let the arrow fly. He stood in the ruins of Minneapolis, hot sun beating down on him, watching Brother Jed across the river. There behind Jed stood the Wendigo, twisted horns and malevolence—the true source of menace.

"Jed felt the call of darkness and accepted the Wendigo. The darkness consumed him until nothing was left. He had become the beast and has chased you across the land. The darkness you always thought was you is the Wendigo."

The truth of this snapped everything to grid. Luke, for the first time, understood. Actions begat actions. Motion and consequences. The turning of life's Hoop. The need to own your actions and accept the consequences, to atone where necessary, but not martyr yourself over what you could not control. He accepted himself, and a hush rolled away from him and the Manitou, a wave of silent, gentle thunder that left calm in its wake.

Away from them, far to the east, a scream erupted that made the ground tremble: the angry, wounded, twisted call of the Wendigo.

Luke blinked, and in front of him stood the First Peoples warrior he had seen in the winter forest a lifetime ago: Gray Cloud. His face was the same, but he had changed. He now wore brown leather boots and some sort of tactical pants. His shirt was made of bleached white hide and covered with colorful designs that shifted and changed. His graying hair was flowing free, and an eagle feather was tied in it. A short, powerful bow and a quiver of multicolored arrows were strapped to his back. And in his hand was a tachi that looked similar to the one Luke held.

"You would not believe the things I have seen. Starships burning off the shoulder of Orion." Gray Cloud laughed. "Sorry, I love that movie! But you would not believe the things I have seen, the places I have been. When I made my choice and struck the Wendigo, I was no longer able to stay with my people. What I had become, what I could see . . . what followed me would have destroyed them. So, I left and fought the Wendigo. The balance was struck, and I traveled as only those of us who have touched this next level of existence can to maintain it, for the dark always pushes against the balance.

"My journeys took me to the Tree of Life and across the connected realms. The Tree called me to anywhere darkness threatened the balance. There are so many realms that it would take an infinite lifetime to see them all. I experienced and grew. I started out with stone and sinew as high technology, then learned how to operate starships. Words cannot explain how much this will change you!

"I have fought darkness in worlds that defy description. The beings I met, the places I traveled, the adventures and sights and smells! The loneliness, missing the closeness of my tribe, my woman and my son, so far in the past. Now my turn on this Hoop is done. It's time to pass this mantle on to you, for your battle against the darkness is about to begin. It is a heavy burden, but the Tree of Life has seen that you have the strength to carry it."

Gray Cloud reached out and placed a hand over Luke's heart. The presence that passed into him was warm and good. He placed it in the void. As his heart made its last beat, as the Manitou's heartbeat faded with his, Luke breathed his last and died . . . and was reborn a god.

The world paused, a wave of silence that touched every living thing. He stood in the moment between lightning and thunder, the hush of an angel passing. The fiery Spirit Hoop leaped from the sky and took him. In these hottest of fires, he was forged into a new being. He felt his connection to the dormant Tree, the axis between everything light and dark in the universe, unbalanced. As his awareness peaked into the god mind, Luke understood the role of the Manitou. He was the Tree, the man, the eagle. He was both a bridge and a balance between all that was good and all that was not, against a darkness that knew no boundaries. And that was the key, the difference between light and dark. Light knew that only balance allowed the universe to be complete. One life. One love. For the first time in his life, he was whole.

He wanted to ask Gray Cloud why he had not been there to stop the massacre at Wounded Knee, but the memories of the Manitou gave him the answer. As horrible as that tragedy had been, at the same time, in another realm, there was a greater tragedy unfolding that threatened more lives and would have had a greater impact on the balance. To go where the Tree called was the way of the Manitou. To follow the way meant making hard choices on a level he never could have conceived. Shortly after the massacre, the Earth had been sealed from the balance. Gray Cloud could not return . . . until the war. Until the Ghost Dance prayer. Until him.

Luke raised his antlered head to the sky and bugled. The call echoed crisp and clear across the land. From the east, there was an answering scream, faint but growing louder. The horizon boiled with black clouds, heavy with malevolent force.

Gray Cloud smiled and said, "It waits for you. This is the battle on which the next thousand years depend. This will help you. Here."

Gray Cloud untied the tachi from his belt and handed it over to Luke. It was a twin to his own in appearance, but vastly different in substance. Luke slid his sword into the belt around his waist and pulled the Manitou blade free of its sheath. The blade glowed with blue power, lines and whorls running its gleaming length—a pattern much like the growth rings of a tree. He raised his eyes to Gray Cloud.

"Yes. It is forged from the Tree of Life. It is both wood and steel. It will cut through anything and will become an extension of your will. Call it, and it will come. In times of peril, it will help guide you. It is a fitting weapon for a god. It has a name, Equilibrio, from the Latin for 'balance.'"

Luke extended his awareness to the blade and felt a connection to his soul. The blade was alive, aware, and meshed with him. He sheathed the sword and placed it in his belt alongside his other tachi.

The Spirit Hoop pulsed, and the quality of the air changed and grew thick with the portent of impending evil. It was time for both of them to leave.

"Where will you go now?" Luke asked.

Gray Cloud looked to the sky. "To find my woman and my son. Somewhere in the Hoop. Maybe I will see you there one day. "

With one last nod, Gray Cloud walked away. Then he stopped and turned.

"The evil you are about to face is the greatest, but it is only one facet that pushes against the light. This battle may decide the future, but it will not end the war. Remember that. The war is eternal. Enjoy the moments you can."

With a wave, Gray Cloud kept walking. A

smooth path of fire descended from the Spirit Hoop to the top of the mountain. Gray Cloud stepped onto the path, upward and away, no longer the Manitou, but still part of everything, a man who had become a god and lived to tell the tale. Luke watched him fade into the distance.

Luke turned in place, seeing the world through new eyes and new perceptions. Everything was the same, but expanded. He knelt and picked up a stone. It was smooth and dusty in his hand, cool as the earth on which it had rested. But holding it, Luke could sense the eons of time that had worn great boulders of granite down to smaller and smaller pieces than the one he held. Reaching further back, he could see the great cliffs of granite that had been pushed up by volcanic action, the grinding spread of ice ages across the planet. He could feel the footsteps of men and other creatures as they walked the land.

He gazed at the Tree of Life, out of his physical sight down the mountain towards the village, and all around him at the same time. Like a planet pressed against the Earth, he saw the great trunk and gray, sleeping branches covering half the sky. The Spirit Hoop, a series of realms in its own right, was but a small, glowing hoop on one small branch of the tree, one of the myriad glowing hoops that covered the Tree like fireflies flashing in the universal night. All separate, waiting to be connected by awakening the Tree.

Below the Tree, great roots sunk deep into other realms, dark and mysterious, but just as vast—places where darkness ruled, and the light was the enemy. As below, so above. The realms that lived on the root tips were dark bangles devoid of any brightness.

Thunder cracked across the sky. To the east, black clouds were boiling, building to ugly, dark anvils. The storm moved rapidly in his direction, walking on legs of malevolent green lightning.

Luke opened himself to the senses of the Manitou and felt his form change. He wondered, briefly, how having antlers would impact his ability to fight with a sword, but the memories of the Manitou gave him the answer. The antlers manifested in several planes of existence and would not hinder his ability to strike or move. They were weapons in their own right, able to project force or block strikes against him.

As he moved towards the nexus of the black storm, he explored the Manitou god-mind. It was like having a supercomputer added to his brain, giving him access to . . . everything. A barrage of data he could call up, with an almost infinite amount of ancillary data and memories. He pushed this data stream away and focused on the Wendigo and their past battles.

This coming battle was an iteration of a vast cycle. Approximately every thousand years, the Tree of Life went dormant. The balance

JOHN SAUER

between light and dark needed to be reset, and that meant a clash between the Manitou and the Wendigo.

The battle always took place on Earth, the key planet, the axis on which reality turned. A stray memory from Gray Cloud flashed through his head: "Why, yes, I am the center of the universe!" A joke from a conversation long ago. He filed it away. The light had not always won the battle. There had been times when darkness swept the Tree, and life everywhere suffered. Ages of tyranny and slavery. Plagues of disease and demons sweeping not only Earth, but all the realms of creation. Famine and war. Darkness flickered across the branches of the tree like a blight. Only the forces of good in these manifold realms kept their worlds from turning completely. Not all were successful.

And what happened when the Manitou lost the battle? It was, effectively, like being sent to solitary confinement for a thousand years, without the powers of a god. The mortal flesh grew old and died, leaving the spirit to drift until the next cycle drew near and a suitable being was found to take up the godhood.

As opposed to when the Manitou won and spent the next thousand years maintaining the balance, being some sort of universal policeman, going from realm to realm . . . to do what, exactly? Fight the evil he had just fought? And then pass the mantle of this god to the next worthy being? The Manitou maintained the balance, but the Wendigo could destroy it. How was that fair? A voice answered him from the vast store of Manitou memory, in a language that had not been spoken for thousands of years. The voice said something to the effect of "Drink the flower."

He chuckled, despite the gravity of it all. Translated into modern language, the message for him was, "Suck it up, buttercup."

He questioned how Gray Cloud could have defeated the Wendigo and yet seen the evil mankind had done to itself over the centuries. The answer was that though this might be the key world, it was not the only world in creation, and balance was formed of all worlds, each with its cycle, based on choices made by its inhabitants and forces beyond their control. It seemed like such an uphill fight with no hope of winning. No matter whether he defeated the Wendigo or not, in the future, innocent blood would be spilled, and there would be nothing he could do about it. Because there was no light without dark, no good without evil. Because a tree that reaches heaven must have its roots in Hell. Because balance was the way. As the Manitou, his duty was to enforce the balance. But what would happen if he swung the balance in favor of the light? He attempted to look down that path with his newfound insight, but all he saw was chaos.

Luke shook his head. That was the wrong thought, for now. He would have plenty of time to think about that, and maybe do something about it if he won—*when* he won. The weight of what the future held for those he loved, and those he was now responsible for, settled on him. The fate of billions of lives spread across the magnificence of creation.

He ran his hands across his belt. Equilibrio was in its sheath on his left hip. He closed his eyes and expanded his senses to cover the world. The Wendigo was a pulsing pillar of malevolent green light to his east. Luke Manitou started walking, his steps covering miles, leaving the earth, moving towards his enemy and the coming battle for . . . everything.

SACRIFICE

The fires had burnt him beyond recognition. His skin, where he could stand to touch himself, was blackened, cracked, and bubbling. His once white robe hung on his scorched frame in gray, charred tatters. Every breath wracked him with pain. Jed had never known such agony, such suffering.

He pulled himself down a small, dry riverbed, little more than a shallow ditch full of small, sharp rocks, away from the sounds of the battle. The rocks cut at his burnt and torn flesh, the agony making him moan and whimper. Twice he hugged the dirt as skeletal horse hooves leaped across the ditch, the war cries of the Indian demons loud in his ears. Soon enough, the sounds of the battle faded, and he thought he had escaped. But a presence stopped his crawling.

He felt it in front of him: heavy darkness, forcing him down. A clawed hand sunk talons into his shoulder, and he was dragged further down the riverbed. He screamed, pain whiting out his senses as muscles tore and blood leaked from him. Sometime later, he was dropped. The dusty alkaline dirt burned his ruined flesh. Through blurred eyes, he saw the swirling darkness before him and felt the presence of God.

"My Lord," he whimpered. "I have failed you."

God sighed. "Jed, what have you done? I have given you everything, and you have indeed failed me. What hope have you of redemption now?"

Jed pulled his face from the dirt and looked up at the misty black form towering over him. God was shaped like a man with glowing green splashes where his eyes should be. Long, twisting shapes flowed from his head. So powerful. So awesome. Everything Jed desired to be.

In the presence of God, Jed's pain slipped away. His awareness flitted across memories and visions of his power. The hunger and satisfaction of the holy sacrament. Warm blood ran over his hands. The coppery taste, the feelings of lust. How all-powerful he had felt. Then it was gone, and the pain flooded back into him. Dying in some dirty ditch in the middle of a desert, an utter failure to his God. All hope fled him.

Jed sobbed. His voice was cracked and dry. "God, how can I atone for you? What can I do?"

He felt God's presence come near. His voice whispered in Jed's ear, comforting, but also frightening. "There is only one chance left for you. Will you give yourself over to me completely? Body and soul?"

God gave him a vision: the soft flesh of a girl's neck crushed in his grip. Her sweet smell. Blood. The lust fueled him. "Yes, my God," he whispered. "Take me. I am yours. "

He collapsed into the dirt, shuddering.

And God took him.

The Wendigo reached out with a clawed, misty hand. As it touched Jed, the hand became solid, then the arm and the rest of the God. The Wendigo gently rolled Jed onto his back so the human could look up at him. Under his touch, Jed's site grew clear.

In his mind's eye, Jed had always seen God as a tall, strong white man with flowing white hair, a white beard, and a stern gaze on the failings of mankind. His mind screamed with the horror of what formed from the black mist: a powerful body covered in rotting flesh falling away from its ribs and bones. A skull of a face from some animal. Twisted antlers stretching from its head. And the eyes, baleful and all too human, glowing green with malice.

Oh no, what have I done? he thought, as he sunk into a maelstrom of despair.

The Wendigo's eyes twinkled. "Now the fun starts. "

His grip tightened on Jed's shoulder. Jed felt his soul begin to stretch from his body. He had a moment to see his burnt and battered form before the pain of his soul being slowly ripped from his body swept him away like a leaf in a hurricane.

Eternity opened before him, black and driven by evil. In the moments before it swallowed him, he saw what the Wendigo was and what he had given himself to: an endless night of pain and horror. This was what his desires had led him to. He saw the others that had given themselves to the same hunger, lived their lives, and felt their endless torment. The ultimate cruel twist of fate, terrible knowledge that all hope was gone. He was but a tool that had given itself to the great evil. Now he would pay.

The Wendigo consumed Jed's soul and was once again fully whole in the world of man. He closed his jaws around Jed's lifeless neck and bit deeply, gorging on charred flesh and blood, savoring the fading life force, the evil this human had delivered to the world. A most suitable vessel to bring him back into this key world.

Unlike the Manitou, which required seven to balance the tree, he needed only one soul to sacrifice itself to him. It gave him so much more power, and more opportunity. He stood, holding Jed's corpse like a ragdoll. He had merely to think it, and he was beside a burning jeep. He placed Jed's body in a flaming seat, so it could burn a bit more. It would be most convincing.

As he walked away, he cast his senses around him. The battle was over. The native warriors had returned to their afterlives in the Hoop. Luke Kimball and his six were gathered near their vehicle. He searched wider, but could not feel the tainted presence of the Manitou. Good. He had time.

The body of Pierce was farther out. From it, he could glean nothing of the rage or darkness that had driven him. Disappointing. The man had held such potential, but now his flesh was useless. With a wave of his claw, the corpse turned to dust and scattered away on the wind. The Wendigo did not think of him again.

He reached out with his presence and touched the Hoop. It recoiled from him, but he forced the contact, and because dark and light were both parts of all life, it yielded. He scanned forward in time and got a sense of what the near future held. He could not see all, but he could see enough that he could force Kimball to fail before he faced the Manitou.

He spun himself into a black storm cloud and drifted north. As he did, he called the spirits that always hovered near him and gave them commands. Go here. Be ready. Attack. The spirits obeyed because he was the darkness. If he could stop Kimball from sacrificing himself to the Manitou, darkness would win. If he defeated the Manitou, darkness would win. If he could shift the balance and push the darkness into this and many other realms. If. . .

All light wanted was balance, to keep

things where they should be. But the dark was more powerful. His battle across millennia was to dominate, to rule. It was not balance the universe needed, but dominion.

He had come so close over the ages, so very close! At the start of this cycle, he had felt Kimball's fear and self-loathing. If only he had chosen then. But he had not, and now they would battle. In this iteration of the cycle, he could not lose. He had the experience of ages. He had lived the battles and the spread of darkness and power over the universe. Kimball would only have access to memories, like being given a book of great knowledge that was useless without a lifetime of study and practice. He would not have that time.

As he drifted, he saw the few scattered tiny sparks of human life across the land. Here and there were acts of darkness. Rape and murder. Slavery. Cannibalism. They drew his attention. Some of the hands that held the whip were weak and pathetic. Their spirits guttered like dim candles. Wendigo did not bother with them. But some glowed like torches in the night. Brutish humans, yes, but smart animals with intelligence and the cruel strength to build their little kingdoms.

He came to them, whispering from the shadows, wrapping them in anger and wrath. He started with the abused, those beaten and raped, and gave them dreams.

"Be angry," he whispered to them. "Rise and take revenge. Be weak no longer, but be the hand that holds the whip."

In these dreams, they felt the fierce joy of their revenge, the satisfaction of making their enemies suffer. It was like a drug, and some embraced it. In return, they gave him their pain and suffering, their anger and wrath. He took it all because it was their energy on which he thrived. These people would take their pain and pass it on to others, small pockets of darkness that would spread like cancers across the land.

The abusers were special to the Wendigo. They had already embraced the dark and carried out his will, whether they knew it or not. He appeared before them the world over, in his many forms, as their god. He praised them for their strength and gave them different dreams. Blood-soaked conquest. The enslaved, cowering at their feet. Young and naked flesh, crying with fear and shame. Dark dreams, lust, and temptation festering in the darkest corners of their souls.

Some humans saw him as the Wendigo, some as the Leshy, and others as the frightening horned gods of their legends. It was all him, had always been him. They prayed to him, giving their souls and lives, their worship and energy. He took it all, feeding and growing stronger for the coming battle.

"Pray to me," he commanded them. "Grow

your empires, and I will reward you."

What he did, the light could not stop, only try to balance. Dark would spread farther, wider for the next cycle.

One human in particular caught his attention, near the ruins of a city that had been called Reno. He put two men in an arena and made them fight. The word came to him: gladiators. He came to this human in the dark and praised him. The human bowed before him, a well of darkness for him to consume. The dark seeds he planted here would grow far.

Days later, he felt the first of his creatures perish, its life force ended. Kimball had begun his climb to the Manitou. He ached to interfere directly, but the great pattern of the universe, the weave of it, would not allow it. He could only throw obstacles.

He left the humans to their little games and gathered his energy until the storm cloud raged destruction across his path. More of his demons met their end. He bided his time, thoughts spread across the past and future. To the present, he paid no more mind. It was what was to come that was important.

From the darkness, he called forth his weapon. It was a sword forged from the purest dark of the root of the Tree of Life, both wood and metal, soul-chilling to the touch. It had always been a sword, since the dawn of time when the Creator had made the Tree and dark and light. Sentient beings of all realms always dreamed up the sword, crafted from wood and stone or steel or glass. They used it to wage their wars and commit their murders, tools to hack and slash and bludgeon. It was so gloriously brutal.

His weapon was long and slightly curved. Dark upon dark patterns flowed along its length. The hilt and handle were also black as night and long enough for him to hold in both of his claws. It had no name. It was the dark.

He held the dark and thought back to the beginning, reliving every battle of every cycle since creation. He lived the times the dark had triumphed, and the times it fell to the light, and what he had done to both win and fail. He would not lose this cycle; there was no greater power in the universe under the Creator than he. And the Creator did not care what won. It had made this creation and . . . left. An uncaring Creator with no way to change the rules, to force imbalance, to let strength win. If the Wendigo hated anything, he hated the Creator for leaving this creation in this balance, this eternal struggle. He held that thought and let the rage build inside of him, waiting for Kimball to fail. He imagined how the seeds he had planted would grow here on this Earth, this time, and the evil thoughts he had seeded in other realms across the light over the last hundreds of years.

As he prepared himself, he felt the rest of

his minions perish. When the call of the Manitou shook the world, he knew the attempts to stop Kimball from taking the spirit of the Manitou had failed.

No matter. He was the greatest warrior god in creation. He would not lose this cycle. He screamed a response, thunder and terror shaking the land. Northwest of him was a high desert plain. A good place to kill a god. He went there, drew his sword, and waited.

TO KILL A GOD

The ground was flat and arid. Nothing grew here. The presence of two of the most powerful gods in creation warped reality. The sky darkened until the battlefield was lit by starlight. The Tree of Life, far to the west, stretched giant dark branches into galaxies. Luke felt the presence of many beings watching them—hundreds of thousands. Some the Manitou sensed and knew, and some were alien to him, from the farthest reaches of light and dark. They waited, some for war, some for peace.

He had never seen the Wendigo in the flesh before this. The god was truly hideous. Twisted antlers glowed with a sick green intensity that was mirrored in its eyes. Its bony, elk-skeletal face grinned. Glowing, moving things writhed within its exposed ribs and the bones of its powerful arms. It held a sword that gleamed black as the void of space and radiated the sense of the Tree.

The Manitou drew Equilibrio from its scabbard. He and the Wendigo stood a few sword lengths away from each other. There was no sound, no wind, only their slow, controlled breaths. A blue glow defused from the tachi and spread to cover him, a ghostly aura. He rolled the Manitou memories through his head (there had to be a better way to access this knowledge!), but could find no consistency in the flow of battle or what it would take to win, only thousands of memories dogpiled on top of each other. Too much to sort through in an instant. He would have to rely on his learned knowledge. In the end, he faced his opponent and bowed slightly, his eyes never leaving the cold, green eyes of the Wendigo.

Instead of bowing, the Wendigo struck. It moved in a blur, too fast for mortal eyes to follow, almost too fast for the Manitou to comprehend. But his instincts moved him, and he blocked. Black blade met blue, and the ground shook. The blades rang like a hammer had struck the world.

The Wendigo's onslaught was relentless, black blade slashing at him from all quarters. It was all he could do to block the strikes while he searched for an opening, but the Wendigo gave him none.

Help came from a completely unexpected source. There was a blur of motion, and a small creature appeared behind the Wendigo. It was the size of a small cat and covered in brown fur. Its back was hunched, but its eyes were bright and full of intelligence. It held two branched sticks to the sides of its head and mimicked jabbing forward with them. The creature whistled a flute-like tune, and in it, the Manitou heard, "Use your antlers!"

Kokopelli, his memory told him—and then it was gone.

The Wendigo came at him with a massive top-down strike. The Manitou blocked it and pushed the blade to the right as he dug his antlered head to the left. The antler raked the Wendigo, drawing green, glowing blood. The Wendigo leaped back, ignoring its wounds.

Green, glowing strings of worms poured from the gash. The Wendigo grabbed a handful and threw them at the Manitou. They bounced off him and fell to the dirt, and he ignored them, until they dug into the ground and wrapped around his legs. Suddenly he was immobile, fighting to keep his balance as the Wendigo hammered strikes at him and the worms tried to pull him down.

He caught the Wendigo's blade on his own, holding it in place. The friction between the blades warped the air around them. The Manitou slashed downward with an antler and severed enough of the worms holding his feet to pull one loose. He staggered back as the Wendigo broke contact and struck again. The Manitou caught it on the tip of the opposing antler. The Wendigo's black blade sliced through the antler as if it were air.

The pain was earth-shattering. He staggered, and it was the opening the Wendigo had worked for. The dark god kicked him in the chest. The blow hurled him across the desert through the starlit darkness. He hit the ground with the force of a meteor crashing. His ribs collapsed, but immediately knit themselves back together. He sensed his power to heal, but also that it was not limitless. The Wendigo could wear him down.

The Manitou rolled to his feet as the Wendigo streaked towards him, slashing from the top and sides, giving him no room to counter or do anything but defend. The Wendigo wore him down, keeping him on the defensive, bleeding him with small cuts. The Manitou tried to get inside of sword distance to grapple or slash with an antler, but the Wendigo was too cunning to let that happen.

And that was the difference. The Manitou realized that in this battle, the Wendigo was stronger, faster, and more experienced. It was the better fighter. It could wear him down to failure if he did not find its weakness.

He worked into the Wendigo's attacks, trying to push his parries into counterstrikes. The Wendigo was prepared for this and turned the attacks back on him. As the Manitou lost strength, the Wendigo seemed to gain it. He felt the battle slipping away from him, despair and

THE DIVIDED MAN BOOK TWO

desperation leaching into his future. He forced them down in his mind and countered faster, leaving more of himself exposed to slash at the Wendigo: head, diagonal, side, all parried.

He drew back, forcing a pause in the battle, and dropped into a wheel stance. The Wendigo's eyes glowed as it raised its sword over its head. The black blade began to pulse as the Wendigo pushed strength into it.

The Manitou tried to focus his will into his blue tachi, but he could not find the way or parse the eons of data in his mind to use that ability. He could only focus on his training from this mortal life.

The Wendigo charged so swiftly that human eyes could not have followed, and brought down its sword.

The Manitou slashed diagonally, both strokes landing at the same time. But where the Manitou cut skin and bone, Wendigo's dark blade sliced through one of his antlers and hit him with a force strong enough to break a mountain.

The Manitou sailed through space, bleeding and broken. He hit the ground with unimaginable force, leaving a burning furrow hundreds of yards long. He lay there, dazed, crushed, already beginning to heal, but this time knowing that the battle was at an end. His sword was gone from his hands. He dragged himself to his knees, searching for it with his eyes. His left arm was broken, numb, and not healing. Blood gushed from his sliced antler. He shuddered as the mantle of the Manitou faded from him, and only Luke remained.

The Wendigo strode out of the darkness, a long gash running from its neck down to its navel. Luke could see the rotted flesh knitting back together, glowing worms scurrying along the ground to climb its legs and reinsert themselves into its body.

"The light always does this," the Wendigo said as it stood before him. "Picks a virtuous warrior and sends him into battle with a sword —and no real knowledge of how to use it. It is a wonder you lasted this long. If you would have chosen the dark, there is no telling how great your reign under me would have been."

Without the cacophony of the Manitou god-minds roaring in his head, Luke felt calm and centered. There was no fear. There was no failure. This battle did not seem done. He settled into the void, where his ability to fight had always been best, and sensed, beyond him, on the ground a mile or so behind the Wendigo, his sword.

Luke reached out his working right arm and raised his bleeding head.

"No," said the Wendigo. "There will be no mercy for you."

The Wendigo lifted its black blade one final time.

Luke remembered what Gray Cloud had

told him. He opened his hand and said, "Equilibrio!"

The Wendigo paused, then coughed green blood as Equilibrio ripped a hole through its chest. The blue blade flew back into Luke's hand, and the Wendigo dropped to its knees. *Call it and it will come,* Gray Cloud had said.

Luke struggled to his feet, swaying to keep his balance. "No mercy. This time, you go back to the beginning. "

Equilibrio was light in his hand. It glowed brightly, infusing him with power. The Manitou settled on him once again. His cut antler reappeared, body restoring to strength.

The Manitou slashed once, twice, and the Wendigo's antlers fell to the ground. It's anguished howl shook the universe. Then the Manitou brought the sword around and cut off the Wendigo's head. It bounced across the dirt and lay there, facing him. "You have won nothing," it whispered . . . and died.

The Manitou felt the dark spirit leave the body, then the earth and this plane of existence. It went far, far away into the dark realms, where it would find a new host, and over the millennia, the cycle would begin again. As it left, he saw sparks of darkness across the earth and scattered throughout the realms connected by the Tree: the seeds of evil the Wendigo had strewn, each with the potential to affect the balance. When that happened, he would be called, as this was the work of the Manitou. But not now.

The whirlwind of the Manitou god-mind roared in his head—hundreds of thousands of lifetimes of the Manitou all at once, all with things to tell him. "Stop!" Luke commanded, and the voices went silent. "We are going find a way to work together. There is much to be done."

Integrating everything he knew, all he had access to, was going to take time. And he felt now that his time here on earth was short. Around him, the stars faded with the first light of dawn. The battlefield was just a patch of high desert, desolate and empty of life on the surface. With his new senses, Luke felt the gentle flow of life energy in the small, scrubby plants, the insects, birds, rodents, and lizards that sheltered in them and fed upon them. The mule deer and antelope that roamed here. Coyotes and now wolves gradually migrating down from the north.

One day soon, there would be buffalo and great cats and elephants and other creatures that had escaped from zoos and private ranches, mixed with the new fantastic creatures that had come to this world. Life, everywhere.

He returned to his human form. Luke sheathed Equilibrio and slid the sword into his belt. He walked back to the mountain on the Colville Reservation, and each step he took was miles in length. A road unfurled from the great river of fire in the sky, the Spirit Hoop. It lay in his path, and he took it, climbing above the earth into the Spirit World. The Key of Seven could now be completed. And connected to the Spirit Hoop, he saw what his future was to be.

In a flash, he became an eagle, then a man with the patterns of life glowing in his skin in every color. He took the shape of the Manitou, a man's body with the regal head of an elk. In this form, he descended to the Council Fire, where the pantheon awaited. He stood in the center, and each god came to greet him.

"Welcome to our fire, Man-God," they said. "Welcome to your fire."

"We are united," he said to them. "The Tree of Life will bloom again. Mankind and godkind can connect again, here and in all realms. In this cycle of the balance, man must learn to live with the earth in a harmony that will perpetuate, not decay. This is something in which we can only give guidance and hope for a deeper understanding. The time of transition, of change, has still to pass. Now comes a time for learning, for enlightenment, for balance. Gods of light, plant the seeds of truth, love, and understanding, so the mistakes of the past will not be repeated. Gods of the dark, there will be balance, so choose your interactions wisely, lest I be called. The worlds will not take another such blow. The People have come. Now let them complete the Ghost Dance."

He took a step back and found himself in a small teahouse. The simple structure was built of fragrant cedar. Outside the open windows, cherry blossoms floated from branches into a wide, still pond, each blossom sending ripples of possibility into the world. There were three guests with him, each dressed as he was in a simple white kimono. Luke bowed, and they returned his bow. They sat at a low table. He poured hot water into a fragile teapot and added green tea powder. Using a bamboo whisk, he mixed the tea, pouring four small cups. He offered the tea to his guests, hand to hand, head bowed, with reverence and respect.

They sipped the tea, savoring its clean bitterness, the silence about them, the tranquility and harmony of this sacred space.

"I have wronged you and want to make amends. What is it you wish?" he asked the first guest.

"This was by my hand as well," replied Nicolai Trinkla. "We had dirty jobs, and we let them get personal. For this, I apologize to you both. I had a family once, a wife and two sons. I would be with them again. "

"So it shall be." Luke bowed to Nicolai, and the ghost faded away, a smile on his handsome face.

Trinkla walked up the path to his front door, service bag over his shoulder. His oldest son saw him from the upstairs window and came running through the door.

"Mama! Pietre! Papa is home!"

He swung his son high in the air, the dust and pain and loneliness of the Afghan mission behind him forevermore. There would be no more war. Nicolai Trinkla was home.

"My friend," Luke said to the second guest, "our road together ended poorly. I should have been a better friend. What is it you wish?"

Matthew Pierce smiled, and it was bittersweet. "Is it too much to ask for a second chance?"

"It is the least you deserve. So it shall be. I wish you happiness."

Luke bowed, and Pierce was gone.

In the Scottish Highlands, a woman labored in the final stages of birth.

"Push now," the doula urged, "I can see his head!"

The stone hut was warm and well-lit. Her husband held her upright, breathing with her.

The baby came forth, silent. The doula quickly removed the cowl from his face, and the infant gave his first cries. She wiped him off as the father blessed and then cut the cord. The doula swaddled the boy and brought him to his mother.

Matthew Pierce looked up into the warm, loving eyes of his mother and father. He sensed the community around them, around him, a small village of survivors, growing as more people found them and children were born. They were people who would need a leader one day, a person of character and integrity. He hoped he would be worthy.

The doula joined them, listening to his cries. She touched her finger to his lips and whispered, "Shhhh."

Matthew smiled at the angel, feeling supreme joy as he forgot everything and began anew.

Luke turned to his last guest and bowed. "My love," he said.

Reiko bowed in return. "My love," she answered.

"I am so grateful to be able to be here with you, to share this moment with you. What is your heart's desire?"

She raised her head with a smile bright as sunshine. "I have learned so much in our time apart. You will know my heart's desire when the time is right for you. Come find me. *Arrigato*, my love."

Then she was gone, the teahouse somehow rightly defined by her absence. Luke bowed his head all the way down to the tatami mats of the flooring. "*Arrigato gozaimashita*, my love."

The teahouse faded, and he soared with the wings of an eagle. Below him was the mountain, and at its base, the MOC. He drifted down to his friends.

Heavy mist lay in every hollow. Boulders were strewn across the roadway. It was a miracle that none had crushed the MOC. Tony sat on one boulder that had embedded itself in the middle of the road, kicking it with his heels, staring groggily at the mist-covered mountain.

He could still see it in his mind's eye, the great, towering peak cloaked in cloud and shadow, then the waves of light that had come from beyond the mountain and stunned them all. A sound like the earth had been rung like a bell. The winds had knocked them to the ground. When they could get up again, the vivid blaze of the Wheel of Fire reached across the sky. It was one of the coolest things Tony had ever seen.

Ellie was crying. She thought Luke was dead, killed by the Wendigo. Tony didn't believe it. From the moment they had touched minds, Tony had felt a bond with Luke that he knew the others did not share. He was not sure how to feel about Luke. Try as he might, Tony could not remember much about being in the city, or his parents, or anything before seeing the unicorns. Touching the unicorn had woken him up. They had talked to him the way Samson spoke to him. Sometimes he loved Luke, pretending he was his father. Sometimes Luke scared him. Often Tony thought of him as Luke Dad, desiring a hug or to be carried, or just to play. But there had never been enough time.

Since they had touched minds, Tony could feel where Luke was. If the Wendigo had killed him, Tony knew, he would not be able to feel

Luke now. And he could feel Luke coming closer.

"He's not dead," Tony said flatly.

Ellie sobbed and buried her face in Cal's chest. The big black man held her silently. Mike and Mindy hugged each other, lost in each other's thoughts. Billy simply watched the horizon. Tony thought they all looked dumb.

"Luke isn't dead!" he said again.

"That's wishful thinking, my friend," Billy replied. "Nothing could have survived that. I think the Wendigo took him out. "

Tony shook his head vigorously. "Uh-uh. He's coming. I know."

"How do you know?"

"I feel him. You all should too."

Mike shook his head. "He's gone, man. We have to see Old Joe now. He'll tell us what to do … if there is anything left to do. "

"Ha!" Tony laughed. "You're wrong. "

They fell silent, brooding.

Luke's voice shocked them to their feet. "Tony for the win! Why are you all sitting around? We have things to do!"

There was a clamor as they greeted him with a mix of joy and questions.

"Yes," Luke answered, "it's over. I have won. *We* have won. I am whole."

Tony touched Luke's sword. "You're different. No longer the same. You have both your eyes back!"

Luke ruffled the boy's red hair and then

picked him up in a hug.

"No longer the same. Yet everything I was meant to be. You'll see soon. We must go to the Tree of Life now. "

Tony shut his eyes tight as the hug enveloped him. He whispered, "Dad," and felt the feather touch of Luke in his mind. *"Son."*

Mike shook his head. "We can't move. The road is blocked."

Luke, holding Tony, walked around the MOC and returned to the group.

"I think we can go."

The others looked up and down the road. There was not a boulder to be seen.

"What did you do?" Ellie asked.

Luke touched her face. "Just cleared the way. You'll see. Let's go!"

He drove them directly to the Tree of Life. At the Tree, they held hands, as they had before, again feeling the magic between them. Now that he was whole, the Key of Seven was complete. But that in itself was not enough. As Luke Manitou, he could feel the roots of the great Tree, the dormancy of its spirit, reaching deep into the earth and the universe, into other dimensions. He could see, clearly as if it stretched out before him, the full pattern of it all: the crystalline lattice of their strengths interlocking with the core of the Tree, a symbol still far greater than he could ever have imagined, glimmering faintly in the darkness, waiting for the spark that would bring it to light—a spark only a bridge between worlds could generate, a small, missing segment of the lattice, waiting to be filled by him.

"Wake up," the Manitou whispered . . . and the Tree began to stir.

They heard music, the great Symphony of Life, faintly at first, but growing quickly in power and strength until the earth and sky vibrated. A platinum, blinding light formed in Luke's chest and spread down his arms into the others, from body to body, mind to mind, linking them and their strengths into one being. Their soul lights joined his, and they saw the lattice connecting light and dark, the balance. It was beautiful.

The spark of their union touched the balance, setting it aglow. The living light spread quickly, arcing across the universe-wide construct to the farthest reaches of light and dark, until all of creation shown as brilliantly as them. The balance pulsed in time with the Symphony, the beat of the Ghost Dance, and the Tree of Life came fully awake.

Caught in the moment, they saw what Luke had become and were frightened.

"Be not afraid, his mind spoke into theirs, *for I am still the man you followed through the wilderness, the man you trusted, the man who needed you. I am whole now, able to love and feel. All along, I fought to defeat what I thought was a greater evil. Yet I discovered the enemy was only me, my darkness, as it is in all of you, dark and light,*

making each of us a balanced whole.

They saw him as Luke, then as the eagle, and in the full form of the Manitou. Yet the essence of his spirit stayed the same.

Now, in this moment, see what you have become. See the gifts you will spread to the People of the future.

They saw Ellie, raven-black hair whipping in the wind. She had been a doctor who had overcome hatred to heal. Knowledge poured into her now, of healing herbs and compounds that could be found across the globe, plus the power to ease pain and suffering with the laying of her hands. She would teach the world to heal itself.

Calvin, a scholar, had broken the impassible barriers of prejudice to see all men as they were beneath the skin, by the light of their souls. What came to him was the art of the story, to captivate minds and open them to the wonders of the world, the power to teach men the mistakes of the past . . . and how to avoid them.

To Michael, a musician who had forgiven what he hated most for the sake of harmony, came the score to the Symphony of Life in all its breadth and scope. It was all the music that had ever been . . . and more. The music was its own special magic, with possibilities that made him gasp in wonder. He would teach the world to hear the harmony of life.

To Billy, who had turned his back on one

life to seek a spiritual existence, came the prayers and rituals of mankind, of every religion . . . the return of his spirituality. As a medicine man and a warrior, he had found a philosophy of one love, one life that he would spread to the people of the world.

Mindy had forsaken everything in her life for the love of Michael, while keeping alive her dreams of the sun. With the scientific equipment necessary to build LightForm gone, Mindy received the knowledge to make a simpler, more effective variety of LightForm organically, with minimal equipment. It provided a way to give the people the power of the sun much more quickly and easily than she could have dreamed. Mindy had become the keeper of the sun.

Last was Tony. Although a boy, Tony had been forced to experience more than any child should bear. The smooth, unbroken line of tissue across his palm from the Unicorn's horn had marked him for a destiny beyond his dreams. His ability to communicate with animals set him apart. He would always be one with the People, but on the outside as well, marching to different drums, to different worlds. There was nothing he could receive for the future; he *was* the future.

But the one thing he could have, the one thing he wanted most of all, was his past. It came to him in a rush. His memory returned, of parents and puppies, a warm, loving house and family, skinned knees and bumblebees—all the things the war had taken away. It took the edge off of his feral nature, giving him grounding, a past, making him whole again. It was all he had needed to make him not happy, but at peace and able to accept his future.

Luke's voice whispered in their minds. *You have become so much. Listen. Feel. The Tree is awake.*

The Tree of Life began to shiver as roots and branches long dormant stretched and grew. The balance evened out as the roots moved, blindly touching rock and soil deep beneath the surface of the earth. They found moisture and drew it in, softening the iron-hard wood, warming it with new sap. Around them, the snow began to melt as the Tree warmed, its need for water drawing the icy crystals deep into the soil.

They heard a cry, faint and far away: the wail of a newborn baby. It was discordant, out of sync with the Symphony of Life. The Tree shuddered and stretched, reaching an inch taller toward the sky, to the life-giving light of the sun, and the cry became a shout as the Tree of Life became aware, its consciousness blooming into their minds. In the great newborn branches, they felt a sentience that breached galaxies, an intelligence that humbled them all. They felt the Tree sink its roots deeply, extend its great branches, learning what had happened to the world, to the races of man. The Tree's shout became a wail of anguish, a sad counterpart to the Symphony.

Then the Tree saw into the future, saw yin and yang of unity and faith. The Tree of Life rejoiced, and its voice joined in harmony with the Symphony of Life, which now was perfection in itself.

"See," the Manitou commanded, and they opened their eyes.

On the lowest branches of the Tree, tiny green dots pushed to the surface: buds. The new growth bulged farther and segmented, budding into tiny leaves. Soon the entire Tree was covered with green foliage. The Symphony faded into the background, still there for them to hear, for any to hear, if they only tried.

Luke loosened his hands, and the others separated, returning to themselves. Tony reached out with wonder to touch the great trunk. It was warm and pulsed beneath his hands. The Tree spoke his name with affection, and Tony felt the paths to worlds beyond his understanding—worlds he would one day know.

"We did it," he breathed with wonder.

"Yes," Luke said. "We did it. Now we build a future."

The first of the People came from the village. Joseph followed, supported by Antonio. He touched the warm trunk, greeted the Tree, heard it greet him in return. Tears flowed down his seamed and weathered face.

"Thank you, Luke. Thank you from all of us."

Luke took the old man's hand. "It is I who thank you for your faith, for believing in me when I could not."

The People surrounded them, laughing and crying, praying in a multitude of tongues and religions, caught up in the awakening. In their songs and prayers was a common thread of joy, of love, of harmony with each other and the world. One love. Luke knew that it would not always be this way. Man would continue to fight, war, hate, and die, to push the balance. Other beings in other worlds would also fight the balance, some with light, some with dark. As the Manitou, he would be there to keep the balance.

There was magic in the world now. It was the cornerstone upon which great things would be built. The Six would be here to guide them, and their children and the generations of children who followed, carrying fire to the darkest corners of the world, would bring the people to a new way of life, a promised land.

But not for him.

BEGIN AT THE BEGINNING

The MOC was parked on reservation land on the tall bluff overlooking the Columbia River basin, not far downriver from the Grand Coulee Dam. Ellie and Luke stood a few hundred yards away, hand in hand, taking in the vast, peaceful beauty of this high desert country. Ellie leaned her head against Luke's strong shoulder.

"What are you?" she asked again.

Luke hugged her, laughing. "I am the man you helped bring back to life. I will love you always for that."

"But you're a god too."

Luke shrugged. "I have the divine in me, yes. But so do you; so does everyone, if they just choose to see it. Now I am as you see me, just a man, almost. Are you sure we loaded it with everything?"

Ellie nodded. "All set. What do you plan to do with it?"

Luke turned her to face the MOC. "Watch."

Every firearm the Seven owned was inside the MOC.

"One of the reasons mankind almost extinguished itself was that death had become too impersonal. If lives are to be taken, man must learn to meet death face-to-face again. Firearms have no use in our future. Let man hunt and defend, even make war, if that is what the balance calls for, but with bows and arrows, spears, swords, and knives. Face-to-face."

Luke cupped his palms together. They filled with orange fire. He molded the flames into a ball, raised it to face level, and blew softly. The fireball streaked away towards the MOC. There was an explosion, and the war machine went up in flames.

Burning brightly with fire hot as the sun, the MOC melted into a pile of slag. Luke and Ellie winced when a long series of sharp explosions—bullets—let loose inside the vehicle. When it was a mound of melted steel, Luke breathed a sigh of relief.

"There. I lived by the gun for so long, I never thought I'd see this day."

"So, your solution to end gun violence is for everyone to run around with swords and bows and arrows?"

Luke raised his hands palms up, then dropped them. "It's not *my* solution. To attack and defend are both aspects of light and dark. Every sentient being at the top of their food chain evolved from this, and none of them have left their ability to generate conflict behind. If beings have to fight, doing it face-to-face at least encourages the opportunity to find another way, or leaves them with blood on their hands that they can see and feel and think about. This is the balance, and it is the way. I hope you can see that."

She pondered that as she leaned her head against his shoulder. "So, what happens now?"

"The world moves on, and the old world dies away. Ammunition will go bad. Guns will rust. Disagreements will become more personal, and people will relate more. Not just here, but everywhere. And magic is in the world now. Some magic things must be accomplished by magic means. Your healing powers, for example. We all have to come to terms with it."

"Well, without the MOC, are you going to magic us home?"

Luke leaned forward and hugged her. She wrapped her arms around his neck, and he held her tightly.

"Better than that. We're going to fly."

Still holding her, Luke leapt over the edge of the bluff. Ellie screamed and wrapped her legs around him as she felt herself falling. But the fall leveled out, and she found herself riding the back of a giant eagle. She screamed, then laughed, clinging tightly, gazing in awe at the landscape passing beneath her. And so they flew, for miles across the land, savoring the closeness of each other's company. Luke brought her up high over the land so that she could see the world curving away. The land below them faded as Luke flew even higher.

"Come back in time with me," he whispered in her mind.

Luke put them into a dive. As they sped lower, Ellie saw a city spread out beneath her. In the distance, she could see a glass pyramid. Cars sped past on the highways. Ahead, a helicopter seemed to float in the sky. Luke soared to the helicopter and came so close that she hugged him tighter. As they flashed by, she saw that the pilot was Luke. She saw the startled look on his face, and then they were past, winging off into the sky and higher again.

"There," he chuckled. "I saw this happen years ago. Thank you for helping me close the loop."

As they moved westward over the plains and mountains, she held him, feeling his magnificent strength, until the sun set and they had to return to the village. Luke set them down in a small field and returned to human form. They walked through the village to the Tree of Life.

All around the village, the People greeted him shyly, knowing a god walked in their midst, yet feeling a kinship with the man. Preparations were in full swing for the Ghost Dance. Since the Tree of Life had been reborn, people had been pouring into the village, swelling its ranks twofold in as many days. The Ghost Dance would be the culmination, the turning of the greatest hoop of all. He was to address the People tonight.

The Tree glowed with life. Thousands of decorations and paper lanterns hung from its blossoming branches. Luke sat on a root with his back to the Tree as the sun set and stars filled the sky, happy to be alive, happy to be able to feel, relishing each breath here because he knew they were close to being his last. A presence eased next to him and lay in the grass. In the darkness, he could just make out its shape.

Luke called out, "Samson. Welcome, brother wolf."

"Welcome, brother man," the wolf answered. *"You have finally come full circle. You are man, eagle, and elk."*

"Wolf, I always wondered what your part in this was."

Luke could feel Samson laugh in the darkness, could see a brief flash of very white, sharp teeth.

"In me is the essence of Teacher Oldman. I was to remind you of the wolf you killed as a child, of the lessons you learned on that sad day. How you hated my species! But you overcame that hate. Now there will be a bond between man and wolf. You have paved the way. Tony will be the first . . . in many ways . . . followed by others who will have

the gift of animal speech. My last duty is to spread the word of the rebirth of man to the animals of this continent. In this, Tony will join me, for I will become his teacher and guardian in your place."

"Then you know my path?"

"Yes."

"Is Tony strong enough to follow his?"

"Were you?"

"That was different. I battled an aspect of myself. Tony will not be ready for that, for many years."

"Not so different. You wanted strength, and the balance gave you challenges to make you stronger. It will be the same for him. Tony will be strong enough if the cycle is to continue. It is fate— the Hoop."

Joseph joined them from the darkness. They watched in silence as the old man built a fire in a special pit away from the Tree of Life.

"Will you stay?" Joseph asked Samson.

"Yes," the wolf answered, *"I would not miss this. All the animal brothers must know."*

"This was not part of the vision," Luke mused, "but it is good. I think Black Elk would approve."

The old medicine man gave Luke a pouch. From it, Luke took a jar of crimson pigment. Carefully, Luke painted a new, wider red band around the trunk of the Tree of Life with his fingers. Then, stripping down to a breechcloth, he painted himself red, with Joseph helping him. When they were done, Joseph tied an eagle feather to Luke's short hair.

Luke grinned. "How do I look?"

"Red. Very red. What happens next?"

"The people come. Now."

And they did, bundled against the cold fall night. The blazing fire in the pit helped keep the chill from Luke's nearly naked body. At his request, Joseph had brought some musicians, Michael at their lead, to sit to one side. When all had gathered, Luke stood and raised his arms.

"See this!" he commanded, and immersed them in the vision.

The people saw themselves sitting before the Tree of Life, Luke standing before them. In the vision, Luke spoke to them the words Black Elk had heard. Luke brought them back in time to Wounded Knee, so they could experience the first Ghost Dance and the horror of the ensuing massacre.

He spoke. "What these brave people wanted was to return harmony to the land. But the world, the people in the world, were not yet ready for harmony. Now, we have the power to make things right! It is in all of us. Life belongs to all of us. We belong to it. What a great hoop to share!"

He brought them back to the Tree. "Hear again the words of the vision."

As Luke spoke, his face began to change and soften. Multicolored lights surrounded his

THE DIVIDED MAN BOOK TWO

body, giving him a powerful aura even those with no precognitive ability could sense.

"My life is such that all earthly beings and growing things belong to me. Your father, the Great Spirit, has said this. You too must say this."

As one, the people chanted the words. The aural glow softened and faded like candlelight in the wind. Luke reappeared as the Manitou. The people gasped.

"See the pattern of the Ghost Dance," he called to them. "Bring it into your heart. Walk in the balance. Make it your own. You will dance this dance with the setting of tomorrow's sun."

Luke began to move, giving them the steps of the dance, the captivating, compelling movements. He could feel them comprehend and understand, could feel them assimilate the Ghost Dance.

His attention went next to the musicians sitting beside him, especially Michael.

"Bring this music into your hearts. Make it your own. It is of the Symphony of Life. Take this music."

The musicians' eyes widened as the music came into them. Their hands began to twitch over their instruments, feeling the beat and rhythm.

Michael laughed, already having the music in him, and said, "Yeah, man. We can do it!"

In the crowd of people, Luke felt for the

minds of those with the ability to sew and make clothing. Into their minds he gave a special design, hoops within hoops.

"This is a sacred design. It is part of the first Ghost Dance, part of all our lives as we are now, and part of the future. Sew this design onto shirts for all the people to wear. Let it be a guide for your hands and your hearts."

His voice rolled like thunder across the clearing. "Believe the words I bring to you. Look now into your hearts. Know the truth of your nature!"

For a brief moment, in the space of time between heartbeats, each of the people saw into their souls, saw the balance of light and dark that made every one of them whole and complete and human. They saw their successes and failures, their loves and hates, joys and pains, the duality of human nature. Each was naked before the others, their individual histories revealed for all to see . . . if they could look past the darkness in their own hearts. The truth poured out of the people like a rising flood. In unity lay strength. One love.

Michael began to strum his guitar. The words he sang surprised some briefly, though there should have been no surprise at all. What they were about to achieve had been dreamed of by many over the years. The Manitou smiled . . . and Luke was before them again, simply a man. He remembered the Wailers, times spent on the island of Bimini, chasing blue marlin and listening to reggae by night at the Complete Angler Bar. Happy memories. He joined his voice with the rest:

> *"One love, one heart,*
> *Let's get together and feel all right!"*

Dawn came bright and rosy over the far mountaintops, catching the smoke from fireplaces and the outdoor fires of those who did not yet have houses. Ellie and Luke lay twined in bed underneath a thick goose-down quilt, watching the sunrise. With his Manitou mind, Luke could feel the cold, iron-like hardness of the ground, the slow quickening of life as the sun began to warm the sap in the trees and the creatures of the forest awoke. It brought to mind a morning from his youth, when the ground had been so cold that a dropped log made it ring. The air had been so crisp and clear that the echo could almost be seen. A morning filled with special magic.

Small things, but important things. Luke wondered what Moses had thought about on his last morning of life, when his children were on the first steps of a new beginning, the Promised Land, a doorway through which he knew he could not pass. Tears filled his eyes, and Ellie brushed them away.

"What's wrong, honey?"

Luke held her tightly. "Nothing. I'm just happy to be here, alive, holding you. I feel such joy, such an upwelling that I have to cry. I never thought I could feel this way. A candle that burns this bright can't burn very long, can it?"

"What do you mean? Everything is done. You've brought us here, brought the Tree back to life. This is our time."

He hugged her close, so her head rested above his heart. "When the Manitou passed to me, Gray Cloud said something that I didn't understand, but I do now. I can't stay here. My presence is too much of a temptation. Beings are geared for survival, and when times are good, they are wired to seek an advantage. My presence here would encourage people to try to curry favor and rise in power over their peers. Some of those people would be natural leaders, but some would become tyrants. It is not the balance, and just being here for some time creates the imbalance. I will never be able to spend much time in the presence of sentient beings, of which there are many. My path will be to wander to where I am needed. See."

Maybe Ellie slept and dreamed. She saw the universe through the Manitou's eyes. Not just this world, but all of them, connected by the Tree of Life. She saw darkness rise and the Manitou fight it back before moving on. Her mind equated it to being some sort of divine firefighter, rushing from place to place to put out brushfires before they grew into blazes. It seemed so lonely that tears streamed down her sleeping face.

"This is so cruel," she whispered. "Don't you get to be happy?"

"This is what I was made for." His voice was soft but came from everywhere. "Happiness is a choice I will have to make along the way. I will miss you, but find joy in your path."

Ellie saw herself in a clinic delivering a baby. She saw the child, healthy with her eyes, and sensed the strong aura of the child with her mind. There was a man, her husband. There were children of her own. Tony, growing strong and becoming a man of purpose. The village thriving. Life. Happiness. Her purpose. The sorrow she felt over Luke leaving fading over time, replaced by the joy of her own life—as it should be in the balance.

Luke could feel her lips curl into a smile against his chest. He gently closed their mental connection and lay there for a time, feeling the weight of her, the warmth of her presence, and the beautiful glow of her spirit. What he felt was . . . gratitude. Gratitude that he could feel this way and have this moment. Gratitude for everything he had lost and found again. Gratitude for the sorrows he would face, the battles he would fight. Gratitude even for the loneliness, for without it, he would not be able to appreciate the love and companionship he would find along the way.

Dawn was approaching. He gently slid out of bed, making sure Ellie stayed covered and warm. Luke dressed simply: a pair of cargo pants and a pullover, a pair of sturdy brown leather walking boots, and a leather belt.

There was a small table with a set of chairs in the middle of the dark room. One moment it was empty, and the next, it held a broad, conical hat of a style that had once been called a coolie hat, after the Asian immigrants that had brought it with them to the new land they had called the Golden Mountain. Luke picked it up. It was woven from finely split cedar roots in the Northwest tribes tradition. The hat was lightweight and would protect his head from wind and rain and sun. He kissed Ellie on her cheek before settled the traveling hat on his head.

Before he left the house, he picked up the bundle of swords: one for him, one for Tony. Luke looked back at Ellie, wrapped in happy dreams, as she deserved. He wiped away his tears and left to pursue his destiny.

As he crossed the square, Luke felt eyes on his back. He stopped and turned to see Joseph sitting on his porch. Luke walked over and waited for the old man to speak, but Joseph said nothing. Finally, Luke held up his hand, open palm, in the universal gesture of peace. Joseph returned it.

"Watch out for the boy. He will need your help and guidance. Please."

Joseph nodded. "It shall be done. I know

you, Manitou. I will always know you."

"Thank you, Joseph. Train the Guardians well. I will see you again one day."

Luke turned away, searching for the aura of the boy. He found him at the Tree of Life, curled up between the great roots, with Samson to keep him warm.

To the wolf, he said, "Goodbye, my friend. May your pups always be strong."

Tony stirred as Samson uncurled himself and shook his fur. The wolf licked Luke's hand, paused for a second, then trotted off into the dawn.

Tony looked at Luke warily.

Luke held out his hand. "Come with me, son."

Tony shook his head slowly. "No. I don't want to."

"I'm sorry, but you have no choice in this matter. You are the only one."

"I don't want to. I just want to be a kid, at least for a while. I want to play. I want a mommy and a daddy. I don't want to think about the things I think about now. Can't I just be a regular kid, for a little while?"

Luke cupped the boy's cheek. "Yes, and no. All of us connected to the Tree have different paths in front of us. You are connected to the world in ways others are not. This is a part of you. Growing up is hard, but in the end, you will be truly happy. As the man who loves you and would have loved to be your father, I promise you this."

The boy began to cry, tears filming his strange, vivid green eyes. Luke hugged the wonderful boy, holding him, letting him grieve and build his courage. A while later, he felt Tony slide his small hand into his own.

"Okay. I'm ready."

"You're sure?"

Tony nodded. "Yes. Let's go."

Reaching out to part the air in front of them, Luke opened a doorway to the top of the mountain. They stepped through. Luke left the way open so Tony would be able to return.

Tony walked around the surface, gazing at the land below them. "It's so peaceful here."

"Yes. No one will be able to come here after today, except you. . . and those who follow you down the road of time. This will be your place."

Moving to the center of the mesa, Luke kneeled to face the rising sun. He motioned for Tony to kneel facing him. He placed the two swords between them, the tachi in front of Tony. He bowed, and Tony returned it.

"This sword was given to me by people who loved me. It is very old and has been carried by samurai and other great warriors. It is a weapon of honor. Incredibly sharp and tempered to withstand great damage. Care for it. Treat it with respect. There are people in the village who will help you learn the art and way of the sword. If you reach out and feel the Spirit Hoop, you will find others there who will teach you. One day you will travel the balance. Always keep the tachi with you, and you will be safe. Now pick it up."

Tony lifted the sword with trembling hands. It was almost as tall as he was. Under Luke's guidance, he placed it at his left side. Luke took Equilibrio and slid it under the belt on his own left side. Again they bowed to each other.

"Stand with me," Luke said, and Tony did, watching a strand of fire separate from the Spirit Hoop and drift down to them. The fire widened and solidified into a road, long and winding, a way to distant and melancholy places.

A spark awakened in Tony's mind. He could see down the road, see some of the Manitou's future, feel this goodbye. It filled him with loss.

Sobbing, he asked Luke, "What is it you wish?"

Luke knelt and embraced Tony in a big hug. "I wish for you a happy life, where you will be loved and feel love. This isn't a final goodbye. I will see you again someday."

He kissed Tony on the top of his head and stood. "This road is yours to follow, when you are ready. All you have to do is reach for it."

They heard a warbling flute call, and two bursts of rainbow light zipped past their feet. They stopped on the road, and Tony saw two small creatures, hunchbacked and covered in short fur. They held small sacks, and each clutched a reed flute in the other hand. In their eyes, Tony saw bright gleams of intelligence and mischief.

"What are they?" He bent down, and they hopped over to him, giving him a critical once-over. They let him touch them, briefly. Their fur was soft. One of them made a sound on its flute, much like blowing a raspberry, and they were gone, bursts of rainbow light along the road.

"Those are Kokopelli. They are kind of like the messengers of the Spirit World. If they like you, they can help you. If they don't, you might find a lot of your things missing. Don't ever hurt them—ever."

Luke stepped onto the road and began to walk. His steps took him a long way. When he stopped and turned, he could still see Tony in the distance. He raised his arm, and the boy waved back. Luke turned, and the past was soon lost in the distance. As he journeyed, the land changed, becoming mountains and then painted lands, then humid jungle and grassy plains. Other roads crossed his, and he saw travelers much like him, some human in form, and some so different as to defy description.

As he traveled, he spoke to the past Manitous. All the voices wanted to be heard, to share their wisdom. He picked one to act as the central presence, to filter the vast experiences of all and be his adviser. "What shall I call you?" he asked the presence.

"Call me Koda," the presence replied. "It is the Dakota word for 'friend.'"

"Thank you. Now, how does this all work?"

They began to talk, Koda sharing the histories of the Manitou and how he interacted with the universe. Luke learned enough to know that this learning would never stop. No Manitou before Luke had ever thought to organize the past lives. They approved, for it would make Luke stronger on the path to keeping the balance.

Eventually, the ground beneath his feet became a long, dusty road stretching across tilled fields of ginseng and vineyards bordered by cedar and cypress. The land rose in waves to distant snow-covered peaks that reached the roof of this world.

At the end of the road was a low wooden farmhouse with a flowing Japanese roof. The house was simple and elegant, made and cared for with love. A great tree grew behind the house, tall and flowing like a bonsai. He felt the spirit of the tree and felt it reach out to him. The Tree of Life would call him when he was needed, and he would always be close to answer the call.

He approached the front step and stopped, happy and sad at the same time, missing the boy and Ellie, the People, yet expectant for what awaited him here.

The wooden door slid open, and Reiko stepped out, dressed simply like him. She held a naginata, and at the top, the short sword-like blade was the same blue-patterned steel as Equilibrio. She bowed to Luke. He returned the bow and came up the steps, caught her in an embrace, and kissed her long and deep.

"I'm home," he whispered.

"Yes. You are home. We are home," she answered.

She took his hand and led him inside, the next thousand years of their existence bright before them.

Tony stood watching the road long after Luke was gone. He wrestled with the whirlwind of his thoughts and feelings. He felt lost, sad, angry. The power he had inside him pushed at his control, ready to lash out and break something. He pushed back, sobbing.

When he wiped his eyes, he saw something approaching from the horizon: the great wings of a dragon, blue and gold catching the sun. The dragon saw him and came his way, landing a short distance from him. As it landed, it condensed into a swirling white cloud. Out of it stepped a girl.

Her hair was long and dark. She was his age, maybe a year older or younger, with Asian features. Her eyes were as violet as his were green. She wore blue silk pants and a blue *gi* top trimmed with gold. She looked around for a moment, then walked up to him.

"Hi," she said brightly. "My name is Kim. You look like you need a friend!"

She was smiling, and just that by itself lifted some of the weight from his heart.

"Yeah. I'm Tony. "

She held out her hand, and he took it. They walked, not on the road, but on a path of their own making. And it was good.

DANCING THE
GHOST DANCE

The boy was pale-skinned, with red hair and vivid green eyes. At first glance, he was frail, but if you looked again, you saw strength and felt the aura of one many years older. A hide shirt, slightly too large, covered him. On it was a design that glowed with magical power. The ghost shirt was belted, and within the belt was an old but well-cared-for Japanese tachi sword. In his hands were a bow and arrows cased in the hide of a white buffalo. Across his face, from cheek to cheek and over the bridge of his nose, had been painted a red band to match that around the Tree of Life. All the People had red bands on their faces today, and eagle feathers in their hair.

Behind him was Ellie, a hand on his shoulder. Billy, Calvin, and Mindy stood behind her. Mike was with the other musicians, at their lead, waiting for a sign from the boy. Tony did not have to look behind him to see the last of the people come into line. He could feel them. At his lead, they would begin the Ghost Dance, moving in a great spiral inward toward the Tree of Life, and then back out and in again, around and around, a living prayer, a pathway that would lead to a unity of all life. It had been such a journey.

Wolves, majestic elk, and every species of animal lined the clearing, roles of predator and prey put aside, drawn by the same one love that had drawn the People together. Beyond them, flickering between this world and the other, were spirits of those long gone and those more spirit than man, waiting, poised on the cusp of the moment, for him to clear the way.

Everything, man and animal, had waited long enough. Time to bring them across the threshold into the Promised Land, into the future. Tony nodded to Mike. The musicians began to play a pervasive beat that moved them all. Tony bowed his head, concentrating on the pattern in his mind: hoops within hoops.

The Spirit Hoop in the sky spun faster, shooting out tendrils of flame. Lines of people appeared from the flames, dancing and chanting in time to the music as they neared the ground. Leading them was a Native American boy just a little taller than him. He was wearing a beautiful handmade Ghost Dance shirt. It was made from deer hide bleached white as snow, then dyed in patterns of the many colors of the sunset, with a double row of blue trade beads down the front. White stars were sprayed across the front and back, and a large golden eagle spread from shoulder to shoulder on the chest.

The gathered people watched in awe as thousands descended from the sky. Their voices joined together, hopeful and full of joy, full of promise. There was a balance in the universe that had been upset, and now was the time to help bring it back. This was the first step.

Tony smiled at the Native American boy. He smiled back and took Tony's hand. He showed Tony the dance steps, and Tony tried them. It was good. Without looking at the rest of the world, knowing the time was now, he placed one foot in front of the other and began to dance.

AFTERWORD

Dear reader, no one writes a book on their own, and *The Divided Man* novels are no exception. So many people have helped me over the decades in every way, from teaching me about Native American culture and myths, to editing and proofreading, to listening to the many iterations this story has gone through—and even a hot cup of coffee from a tired but cheerful waitress, in a diner in the middle of nowhere in the Dakotas, late in the night.

In writing *The Divided Man* novels, I traveled the route Luke and his party take to reach the Colville Confederated Tribes reservation. At the time, I did not realize how the reservation would have an impact on my future life.

Some moments of my journey stand out. Walking through the Pipestone National Monument and finding an older Native American man making a pipe with traditional tools, just sitting out there on a nice late summer day. We spoke for a time, and he showed me how he was forming the pipe with stone and bone tools. His kindness became both Teacher Oldman and Stone Smith from Book One.

Sitting in my car at the parking lot of the Wounded Knee Massacre Monument and feeling the sad forgotten-ness of the place, even though I knew, I just knew, that there were ghosts here who needed to move on. This feeling has always stayed with me. I felt it again when I visited the forlorn small monument dedicated to Chief Joseph outside Nespelem, Washington.

Visiting a friend from college in Durango, Colorado. Her brother had been killed in an avalanche the previous winter, and she still grieved. We hiked up a mountain and sat in a meadow on a log. I listened while she talked about her brother and his life. She leaned against me and cried. Parts of her story became both Ellie and Mindy.

Chasing a very large chinook salmon over wet, slippery rocks on the Wilson River in Oregon on very light spinning tackle. I lost that one.

Eating spit-cooked salmon and corn on the cob at a roadside feed hosted by a local Oregon tribe. It was delicious.

Reaching the place on the Colville Reservation where Luke meets the Manitou, throwing my hands in the air, and yelling until my voice echoed. It was cold, I was tired of my journey, and it was time to go home.

Decades later during my military service with the Washington State Guard, I received my wildland firefighting training via the Colville Confederated Tribes. I live five hours from that part of Washington state and visit often.

What this adventure has taught me is that life is a hoop. Everything comes back around at some point and offers a chance to think about what you did and how you can be better. I have finished this turn of the hoop, and it is on to the next of the novels of the Ghost Dance. Thanks for sharing this journey with me.

If you like what you have just read, I would greatly appreciate it if you left a review on Amazon. Thank you for your time and see you on the hoop.

Made in the USA
Columbia, SC
23 June 2023

18804152R00176